THE SAINTS COME MARCHING

THE SAINTS COME MARCHING

THE BLESSED & POSSESSED
BOOK THREE

JAY REQUARD

PART I

NORM MACDONALD LIVES

THE "F" STANDS FOR

Well, Christ stood there, smiling like a fucking goof while two mortals raced away in panic and his children fought before him.

My dead friend and a saint like me no less, St. George the Dragon-slayer, lay beyond them after Daniel O'Brien and I had taken him down from a gross rendition of the Crucifixion with a decapitated horse's mouth shoved over his groin, which would have drawn greater attention if not for the dead dragon twisted beneath the display. Around us lay tens of thousands of dead bodies, torn and ruined in a battle with the archangels after the forces of Perdition, possessing these poor souls, flung them forward in a successful kidnapping of Lucifer's daughter, the only free Nephilim available for Satan to bring about the birth of the Anti-Christ—somehow.

Oh, she's also my lover who constantly makes me question if what I feel is real or if I finally found something more worthwhile than anything God had ever given me. I had served as an exorcist, priest, assassin, soldier, healer, and so many other things across two separate lives...

At this point, I feel like I'm playing to an audience of one.

Pulling out my best trump cards as the reincarnated saint of

Ireland, I had broken several seals on a realm of Purgatory made to shelter the old gods of Eire. Left with little choice and needing to both save my ass and the ass of my friend and former lover Mama Meredith Joslin—a Vodun Queen no less—I had broached one unspeakable truth after another. Another poor bastard, Daniel O'Brien of the Real Irish Republican Army, had also gotten caught up in this. Another innocent trapped in a bloody, bloody mystery.

So I made my choices count.

First, I ended the deal God and I had first made with the gods of Ireland during my initial life. We'd root out Satan with or without the help of the Platinum Polis.

Second, the chieftain of my people's old divines had granted me his son, and Eire's greatest champion, the mythic age warrior of The Red Branch known as Cuchulainn.

But his foes called him the Hound of Ulster.

Who proceeded to beat the fuck out of Michael.

"I remember every word, you fucking feathered—" the five and a half-foot monster screamed as he launched into The Protector, throwing fists after I had sworn him to keep the spears and sword in his chariot.

To my glee, he was having a good show of it. The other main players of the usual troop tried their best to break them apart, Gabriel getting between Michael and the little beast, knowing neither would dare strike them. Raphael and Uriel failed to block Cuchulainn. Sneakier than a snake in the grass he zigged where they zagged, always darting in with a right hand leading. He touched Michael right on the nose once or twice.

Heavenly blood, silver and runny, covered Michael's mouth while Selaphiel tried his best to restrain his brother. Raguel and Ramiel stayed back like the two ponces always did, whispering and observing to each other so neither would forget their accounting of the moment.

Lucifer was between us and them, laughing his tits off.

But these choices had quickly been rendered impotent, just another display of the universe's dark, dark humor. Honestly, nothing

I could have done would have changed anything leading to this moment.

Jesus Christ stood there beside me, unable to contain his endless smile.

"Aren't you going to stop this?" I asked.

"In a second," he said. "Michael needs this more than he needs me. You'll see."

I bit my tongue on some choicer words. "Okay, fuck, just—"

"It's going to be okay, Patrick," he said, turning to me with his brown face and brown eyes. Everything looked at me, upon me, deeper inside me. And he never frowned or turned away. "Trust me."

This fucking guy. Unable to rebuke him in the moment, no matter how much the preceding days of terror spurned me to, I searched Lough Derg's scorched lakebed, spotting Merry and Daniel hiding in the wreckage. Covered head to toe in blood, mud, and probably worse, my focus centered on them. "If I bring them over here, will you help me?"

"Of course," Jesus said. "But don't rush things. All in due course."

I approached Daniel and Merry in their hiding hole, both hands out even though they knew I offered no harm. Daniel stood, almost ready to hit me when he calmed, swallowing past tears and a nose full of snot. My former lover and Vodun Queen almost sneered at me when she was not craning to check on the divine manifested right behind us. Who knows what the fuck ran through her head? She had to dance, sing, chant, smoke, and love her gods to meet them, and never in the flesh.

Mine was right fucking there.

I had issues with it too. I also knew the futility of making sense of it there. "Hi," I greeted them gently, "So look..."

"That's Jesus Christ. My Lord and Savior," Daniel O'Brien said, failing to tear his eyes away. "He's right fucking there."

I understood. We're Irish. "It's okay, man." I clapped his muscular shoulder. "I know. I cannot say more than that, or give you any comfort in it, but both of you—" I made sure to level my gaze at Merry "—aren't in any danger. I promise."

"I killed people," Daniel said, unable to stop himself. New tears sealed his wet eyes shut as he sobbed. "I killed people and Jesus Christ is standing there." The acknowledgment of every killer's sin shattered his nerve, his hands up as if to guard from an incoming punch, or a gun pointed in his face. "I'm going to Hell. I'm going to Hell!"

Grabbing him by both shoulders, I held him steady. "You're not going to Hell, Daniel! Look at me! Look at me!"

The strength of my voice broke the man in my grasp again, but I acquired his sad attention. I doubled the pressure of my hold, almost pushing him down further as I put my face square with his. "You're alive, Daniel! You breathe, you have a pulse! Look," I said as I smacked his shoulders hard. "You're in shock. It's okay to be shocked right now. Everything is everything and everything is too much. It's okay." And making sure not to miss her, I brought Merry back into focus. "For the both of you."

"Okay," she said, almost too calm. "Okay, Patrick. Okay. Okay."

I did not miss the snark of doubt in her. "Just stay here for right now. Don't run. I'm going to go—"

Her bravado, which I loved or despised depending on the situation, reared its mean head. "And do what, Tater?" She huffed and leaned to the side, fixed on him again. "It's Jesus Fucking Christ."

"As I live and breathe," The Savior called behind me in his happy voice. He waved both of his brown hands at her. "Happy to be here!"

If I had palmed my face faster I would have knocked myself unconscious. Taking my turn to sigh, I faced the head honcho for a return visit. "Okay," I whispered as I exhaled on the walk.

"Hey, buddy," he said. "Got everything settled?"

The cheek. I thumbed at the disorganized archangels battling the walking bomb I had brought along. "What about them?"

The scuffle between Cuchulainn and the archangels had ended in a bruised stalemate. Michael tended to a bloody nose as his siblings consoled him. Gabriel had drawn Lucifer in to talk down the Hound, putting both sides at a fair distance. The little demigod paced back and forth in front of them, fists bound at his sides as he answered their tempering words with harsher ones I thankfully couldn't hear.

Lucifer checked over his shoulder and caught me looking at him. Our recent journey through other planes of existence had bound us together as much as our love for Deevi. Golden maned and multi-winged, the Morningstar nodded to me in a respect I never imagined we'd share. To my greater surprise, I dipped my head in return.

"Just waiting for him to say his peace to them," Jesus said, nodding toward the Hound. "And Michael's cooled down. He's thinking about his words now, which is what I had in mind to happen."

"Didn't take you for a 'bloody nose'-type."

"A lot of things would surprise you about me, Patrick," he said as he marched forward. "Walk with me?"

"Ah, sure," I said.

We—me and the Savior—strode to the center of where the fracas had separated. Hands on his hips, Christ looked around the field, the bodies, his expression unreadable as everyone except Cuchulainn considered him in our fullest.

"There's a lot wrong here," he said, motioning toward the heap of bodies. "Seems unfair for these people."

I couldn't help myself. "Oh, is it?"

Bless him, Lucifer drew some of the heat off me with a chuckle.

"Alright, alright," Christ said, waving his dark hands at the disaster that had burnt away the waters of Lough Derg. "Lots of big things are going to be happening anyway, so might as well take the gun off the mantle."

"What are you talking about?" I said.

Gabriel shushed me. "Chekov's gun," they whispered.

"I don't know what that is," I said. "But there's going to be a lot of people wondering where their families and friends are, or what happened to a loved one they have lost. There's going to be a lot of questions, and in a time where people have cameras trained on every-thing you all do, someone will see this on a satellite. Fuck me, I'd be shocked if they're not shitting their britches right now."

Everyone understood who I pointed my concerns at.

"Quite right," said Christ. "And I'm not here to play around." He frowned at the dead and closed his eyes. Somehow, someway I cannot explain, I either closed mine or did not see, but in the next moment tens of thousands of Irish dead vanished, the soil beneath still broken by the remains of the dragon and the knight who had slain it. I still hadn't gotten a full explanation about what happened to George, the closest thing I had had to a childhood companion. The Vatican had impressed us reincarnated souls of Christ's retinue into an army of warrior-exorcists called The March—probably the least harmful thing they had done to young children—and forced us into hard lives of fighting evil.

For a hard man who lived a hard life, the end for the Dragonslayer was too harsh for the goodness he deserved.

His remains stoked my anger. "So what? They're alive?"

I drew the ire of the archangels except Lucifer, who was more intent on his Father.

"Safe and sound," said Christ, knowing but not acknowledging my point. "They will remember what happened, as if in a dream, but they will not bear the scars inwardly. It's the least that I can do."

"Oh," I said, the wind torn out of my sails by his kindness and, if I was honest, my self-loathing.

"Father," Lucifer said. "Shaytan has Deevi. We must stop him before he harms her."

"Of course, of course," Christ said to his errant child. "Well, time to go."

"Go?" I asked. "Go where—"

He snapped his fingers like a real god could. As with the bodies on dry Lough Derg, we vanished from the scene and reappeared in the familiar lot of an old farm, the cream siding of the main house confusing me for a moment before Merry, there with her two packed bags that had somehow survived the journey beside her along with a witless Daniel, exclaimed in wonder.

"Fuck, Tater," she shrieked, "we're back in Jersey!"

2

THE BOY IS BACK IN TOWN

What the fuck is a Jersey?" Cuchulainn asked me in Ancient Gaelic.

Fluent to the tongue of my first life along with Latin, Aramaic, Coptic Greek, and too many more, I answered in kind. "We're in a land across the seas, west of Eire. It's smells odd but it's fine. Please don't freak out."

"I can bloody handle a different land, priest," the growling little cuss whispered. "I was with those savages in Skye. I just need to know what we're doing and how we'll go about it. Good thing your boy brought us to a place Laeg can keep the horses for a time."

"Well," said I, "you're making a good go, Setanta! I think the twenty-first century may like you yet."

"What the fuck, why not?" he asked as we faced the rest of the others. "Have you seen this bunch?"

The Council of El attended their Creator as he sat on the front steps of Merry's old farmhouse, northwest of New York City by a few hundred miles and home to a chicken farm that fed the sacrifices made by her order, Vodun councils spread throughout the East Coast of the United States before the Brujeras in Florida set influence. She and Daniel had retreated inside after she found the keys in her bags, leaving me the lone mortal to deal with the demigod at my beck and call, my God, and his asshole offspring. The Hound's chariot driver had taken the horses and the cart to the barn where Lucifer and I had wrestled not long ago for my soul.

I looked to where George had appeared when Christ had brought us here, presented in a much more dignified position with his tattered cloak wrapping his body. Nobody had discussed what we were to do with him, or the severed head of the horse that lay beside him.

Fuck, the horse's head bothered me more than Lucifer possessing me. I didn't know what to do, so I went to work.

"My…" Ah, fuck. "My Lord?" I called. "Do you have a plan in mind?"

"I actually do," Christ said. "We have several issues to deal with all at once, so let's coordinate, huh? Any ideas?"

God crowd-sourcing the solution to our dilemmas basically silenced me.

The archangels raised their hands to volunteer their voices, good little responders. "Pardon me, Father," Michael asked in a matter-of-fact manner, "Are we still to understand that by your return to this mortal shell you are indeed deciding to initiate your return among your children and this small planet, heralding the fulfillment of its days?"

Unable to process a question probably kept to conversations between him and his kids, Jesus laid out his answer, plain and truthful. "Yes, I believe so. I think I have everything I need, but we should prepare the way for my arrival. Let's see... okay, Michael and Gabriel should gather the Host for the descent, but don't tell them yet what I'm doing! It'll be a fun surprise. Raphael will go get the families together. Uriel, please tend to George's body. Selaphiel, I want you, Ramiel, and Raguel to go on ahead to New York. Just let me know who's ready, who's not, and plan a way to the Garden."

"Pardon me, Father," Gabriel said, their hand held up like a dutiful child. "When you say 'surprise', what do you mean by that?"

His children, save Lucifer who remained off to the side, waited with eager anticipation.

"It's not a surprise if I tell you," said Christ. "Now go. The day is begins and we have much toil before it ends."

Without another question or concern, those damned idiots unfurled their wings, but instead of taking flight, they vanished. Left with myself, Lucifer, Cuchulainn, the two struggling human beings inside the house, and the Hound's driver with horses out back, Christ simply smiled at us like it was a normal day.

I had to. "A surprise, huh? That should be nice. But I have a question too, if I may?"

"You may always ask of me, Patrick," Christ said. "I'm always here to listen, if not serve."

"Great," I said, far less enthused. "I take it by being here and sending your angels on ahead to New York, Deevi must be nearby."

"Yes, hereabouts."

"Fantastic, but here's the problem: we have to get to her and she will be surrounded by the forces of Perdition, not to mention their unholy lord himself. I cannot imagine they aren't preparing for us as they rush to—" I wasn't going to finish the thought. "What way are we going?"

"I thought we'd drive," said Christ.

"Drive?" Cuchulainn asked, confused. "My chariot can only fit myself, Laeg, and perhaps one of you."

"No, no, no," Christ replied. "I was thinking a car. Maybe a large SUV."

"Okay, Jesus," I replied, just tired of it. "Where are we going to—"

He reached up and snapped his fingers. As with everything in the purview of the Almighty, a large SUV appeared in the gravel lot. An old green Yukon, familiar aspects of its scratches and the dents on the bumpers caused me to pause.

"Wait, I know this," I said.

"Everyone needs an old green Yukon," Christ said right before he tossed me a set of keys out of nowhere.

I caught them, too gob-smacked to say anything more.

"What is this?" Cuchulainn asked in his thick brogue. "Saint, did your god summon a sleeping monster?" He squinted his dark eyes at it, fists tightened at his sides. "Will it wake?"

Maybe I had made a mistake bringing a harbinger of death into a world with no concept of machinery.

Out of the company of his siblings, Lucifer broke his long silence. "We don't have time to tarry with more inane questions," he said, raking glowing hands through glowing hair.

"Now be nice," Christ said. "Everyone's having a hard time of it too, and your siblings still haven't met her."

"Met who?" I asked, not suited to being the third wheel.

"Oh, my wife Mary is coming to New York for the show," Christ answered, as if it was just another thing. "My mom, too."

Too much to handle as a fallen Catholic, I took the keys the Lord had given me, got in the front seat of the Yukon, shut the door, and locked it.

I startled when Lucifer opened the passenger-side door. Too immense to slip inside, he bent down and stared at me.

"Are you alright?" he asked.

"Is this what it's like?" I had pressed my forehead to the top of the beige steering wheel. "Him?"

"Most of the time," he replied. "But he works in myster—"

I raised my right hand to stop him. "Not now."

"How much more time do you need?"

"Are you asking or is he?"

"Him."

I huffed. "Of course. Um...give a second. I just need to..."

"Take your time, Patrick," the Morningstar told me. "It is a lot for all of us. And it's only starting."

And on that bombshell, he closed the door.

"Just fuck," I said as I grabbed the latch and popped open the driver's side.

Stepping out, my booted feet ground the mix of dust and pebbles as I surveyed the scene I had tried to escape. To my astonishment, Christ had wandered over to Cuchulainn, attempting to converse with the mythic warrior in more-than-passing Ancient Gaelic. The attempt was very one-sided, but thankful that the Hound was more curious about Christ than offended, I settled. Lucifer waited on the other side of the Yukon still, awkward as could be.

"I'll get Merry and Daniel," I said, to everyone and nobody. "We'll get out of here then."

"Sounds good, Patrick," Christ said, rising out of his failing dialog to give me the ol' point and thumbs-up.

I found Merry in the kitchen over the counter, lost in the water swirling the sink where she washed her hands. Daniel walked around upstairs, probably in the bathroom.

I sidled next to her at the counter.

"Hey," she said with little life behind it.

"Hi." My brow furrowed. Every part of me wanted to find the right words, to figure out how to lift her out of this mess the man outside has put us in. No matter how hard I tried, nothing came to be but the constant, dull blank of exhaustion. "He wants to go to New York."

"Of course he fucking does," she said, still not looking at me. She reached up and turned off the faucet, scanning the empty kitchen.

How fast had all this gone? How slow? It seemed decades ago when I was last here when it had only be a week, fighting the possession God had allowed Lucifer to have upon my soul, speeding us both toward the rescue of the Morningstar's Nephilim daughter and the biggest wedge between me and the Vodun queen, the moment destiny stole me from her. George had been there, too.

The lack of him, brooding in his seat at the table with that Rambo-stare, hurt worse than I could bear.

"I miss him," Merry said, as if she had read my mind. "It's wrong he isn't here."

"Aye," I said, unable to answer with more.

"Patrick, what does he want?" she asked, shifting to the man outside. "What is going on here?"

"I don't know, Merry," I answered, shaking my head. "I can't even begin to say."

"It's definitely not the Bible," she replied.

I scoffed for every effort not to cackle at the irony. "I'm no longer sure the Bible is the bible, love."

She broke her focus on the sink to cast a confused glance in my direction.

I exhaled, opening a can of worms I would not be able to shut again. I gave her the shortest version of my journey with Lucifer through Purgatory I could unpack, a debilitating quest of mind, body, and soul for the mortal traveler but eased thanks to the archangel's power sparing me the worst. Too much to cover there in a Jersey farmhouse kitchen, I gave her the bullet points.

"That's everything," I said, reflecting on what I knew now about the religion and faith had I pledged so much into. "And so many more things I'd rather not think about."

Digesting it, Merry set a frown on her beautiful black face. "You know what? No."

"No?"

"Go get Daniel from upstairs, Tater, then meet me outside," she said as she went to the kitchen table behind us. Ladened with two baskets full of candles, inks, herbs, stones, and every sundry a practitioner of her traditions needed to commune with the spirits of her stolen ancestors, she fished through one of them. "Go on. Go."

Lacking all fucks at this point, I headed upstairs.

For all the shock and awe of the moment, Daniel knew how to keep moving forward like every good soldier could, even when it wasn't good for them. Hunched over the sink in the bathroom, he stared into the mirror. Old pots full of some incense long discarded from a ceremony Merry's cohort must have performed crowded the ledge beside the faucet, and by the window a small plate full of used-up joints sat cold on the sill.

A handsome kid, all of thirty-two with a dark shag of hair and the right amount of Irish scruff to make even a stone cold Vodun priestess take note, he searched for something not there.

I leaned on the door. "Daniel."

Startled, his hands tightened on the basin as he looked my way, then relaxed when he saw who it was. "Saint Patrick," he said with a heavy sigh.

"I know, Daniel," I said. "This is a lot."

"It's just—It's actually Jesus, isn't it?" he asked with all the sincerity of a man in need.

"As real as he can be," I said. "And there's nothing easy about that. I know. It's scary, too."

"It's God."

"Big Man himself. But I don't think you have to worry."

"I don't?" he asked, his brow burdened by his intense focus.

I measured every word as a priest would for his parishioner. "Many things are said about Christ, good and bad, but this man before us has come to us as a man when he has the power to show us—to do to us—so much worse. He has not done so, yet, and he has brought us out of danger. I cannot ask you to hold any faith you may no longer have, but I ask you, one bitter soldier against this world, do you fear him or what he might say of your sins?"

The question broke his hard expression with a shuddering exhale.

I crossed into the bathroom and clapped the broken man on his shoulders. "I fear mine too, but then I remember Christ is not a punisher, but a healer and redeemer. I've seen it enough to know it." The words weighed on me. "You have nothing to fear, Daniel. Not from him, at least."

"After everything I've seen..." he replied.

I patted him solidly on the shoulders a second time. "And you made it past. I wouldn't worry." I couldn't lie to the man. "Not yet, at least."

Twenty minutes later, I brought them both outside. Christ and Cuchulainn had started chatting with each other. To my surprise, Lucifer was nowhere to be found. Giving the keys to the Yukon to Merry, her and Daniel loaded it while I started toward the Savior of Man and Ireland's greatest champion.

To my shock, they were talking in English when I arrived, full and fluent, though my ancient kin had never heard a word of it before.

Christ gave me one of those sneaky winks when he caught my surprise. "Ready to go, Patrick?"

"We are," I said, surprisingly calm. "Where's Lucifer?"

"Oh, I sent him ahead to gather something we'll need. But I need you to drive me to New York. We'll go over the GW."

"What about my chariot or the horses?" Cuchulainn asked in perfect English. "Laeg won't leave them behind."

"They are the fastest horses in Ireland, right?" Christ said in a good humor.

The Hound of Ulster, a demigod before the real damned thing, smirked before he turned for the barn where his driver kept their steeds. "We'll keep up."

3

———

STRAIGHT OUTTA CANA

"Can you turn on the radio?" Christ asked from the Yukon's middle bench, behind Merry on the passenger side.

I looked into the rearview, first at Christ, then to Merry seated upfront next to me. She death-stared me as I leaned forward to tap the nob.

"What do you want?" I asked.

"Oh, just let me handle it," Christ said.

Without warning, the green digital FM frequency rolled forward without my direction, the last number behind the decimal a blur. Static, voices, the crackle of the universe at its birth flooded by before a gentle, remarkable voice sang out of the speakers around us, talking about three little birds showing up one morning to sing about peace and love. Bob Marley serenaded us until the Almighty joined him.

"Everything gon' be alright," he said in his high baritone, and far from a bad one either.

It wasn't all right for Merry. With an un-priestess-like grunt she dragged one of the bags she had brought from the farmhouse onto her lap and unzipped its tie-dyed confines. Out came a giant bag of chronic among the loose candles, a makeup bag, and jars full of Vodun

17

stuff. She pulled out a small glass spoon next before she dove in for a grinder.

"Merry," I said in that you-know-better-sort of tone.

"Not now, Tater," she said. "Not now."

"Can I hit that, too?" Daniel asked. "Sorry, Jesus."

"Oh, it's alright, my son," said the Lord. "I don't judge that. Can't make wine and get mad about burning some bush, can I?"

God laughed at his own joke.

"Ugh," Merry grunted aloud.

Before Marley could end his sermon I punched the dial with my finger, sending us back to the tense silence. "Okay, okay," said I, "Cut the shit, Jesus. What's going on here?"

"What do you mean, my son?" he asked. "I was listening to Bob Marley. You were driving, Merry is rolling an expertly prepared joint, and Daniel is beside me wondering if I know about the time he and Marcy O'Sullivan fooled around in the pews at St. Callich's. And of course I do, Daniel. I'm God."

"Holy shit, I am," exclaimed Daniel.

I had to keep my eyes on the highway and not shut them out of misery. "No. No. Pardon me, Lord, but you know I can't let you get away with that. Not knowing what I know."

"What does that mean?" Merry asked as she sparked her After School special.

"Patrick was given a firsthand account of the divine providence of this universe," the embodiment of the Logos said.

I squeezed the steering wheel so hard my hands hurt. "And since you know that you also know that I've always listened, both to the Word and the order. I've heard you say what you've said, and like always, I've followed where you've sent me." I loosened my grip on the wheel with my right hand, only to smack it hard out of muted anger. "I'm going, once again, even though I told myself I wouldn't."

Both he and Merry bore their focus on me, Daniel thankfully out of sight. Like all holies who are in it for real, they listened.

"You owe me an explanation." I jerked my head in the priestess's direction as she inhaled a dragon-hit of chronic. "You owe her. And

George. And I heard you. You told your kids 'it's time.' I'd like to know what that means and when. I'd like to know how it ends in rescuing Deevi."

Merry rolled down the passenger window and exhaled, the current tearing the gout of smoke into the bucolic countryside of western New Jersey. Cow fields and empty corn plains, stripped for the season, stretched in every direction.

"My child, I'm here to rescue her," he said. "As much as I am me."

"Here, Dan-o," Merry said as she passed the joint back through the center of the Yukon. "You'll definitely need it now."

"I need more than that," I told our immutable-mutable passenger unfazed by the heavy smoke invading the cabin. "A lot more."

"Well..." Christ reached up and combed a dark black lock over his brown ear, searching the floor of the truck and his bare, dirty feet. "I guess it started at Cana."

"Cana?" I said. "The wedding?"

"What wedding?" Merry asked, already half-out of the conversation. The capillaries in her eyes swelled, bloodying the whites.

"Where Chri—him," I said, "turned the water to wine. But I don't understand. What started there?"

"A misunderstanding," Christ replied. "One I have come to correct."

"And how do you plan on doing that?" I pressed.

"You'll see soon."

"No, no," Merry said, coming to my aid. "Like Tater said—you owe us more than that."

He was quiet, the hills rolling ahead and lonesome miles of asphalt and yellow paint streaking the path, interrupted by cornfield after soybean planting after cornfield, when suddenly one might see baled hay or a salt pile.

Christ finally spoke after a good bit of thought.

"You know you've been working with more than my message," he said directly to me. "Nobody can say that they know exactly what I said because the people who recorded it only did so after the fathers had passed, but who were they to say they were the fathers I had chosen? Who said I did not choose mothers, or slaves, or centurions, or even those among the Pharisees who brought me death? But for the most part, the Gospels understood the key points until they were lost in minutia."

"Minutia?" I asked, more apt to answer his points than any other in the truck. "How can your life and words be minutia?"

"Because what did you focus on? What has everyone focused on since the day I passed on Golgotha?"

"Wait, so you actually did die?" Merry asked. Even in Vodun they had a fair literacy of the Bible, often employing and combining parts for the client too finicky to let go of their White-Anglo traditions. "You actually died?"

"Into the darkness and back," Christ said, snapping his fingers above his knees.

The suddenness of the gesture disturbed me more than the answer did. "But what are we missing?"

"So, so much," Christ said. "And so much of it ineffable against mere words. The only thing I can tell you is that if we go along this way, I will reveal all and you will understand."

I traded incredulous looks with Merry. "You're still dodging."

"I'm not, Patrick," Christ said. "I honestly don't know how this will play out, to tell you the truth. Might be a big mistake."

"Well what the fuck does that mean?"

He glanced out of the passenger-side window to his right, already knowing the count of the cornrows. "So I had this guy once named John. Hell of a man, but one of the best. Came out of the forests outside Judea, wailing all sorts of things about cleansing the world and the flood and how the flame was coming. A lot of people didn't understand what he was saying, and to be honest, I tried not to. I was trying not to be me in those days. But John..." A real smile found its way to Christ's face, proud and true. "John gave me a voice to what I was trying to say in my heart. And for a long, long time, I thought that voice was enough. Until it wasn't." He dimmed a good bit. I thought I saw the sliver of tears work their way into his eyes. "Wasn't enough to save John, either. But at least he knew the problem enough to let me know what it was too."

"The problem?"

"The miracles. The ministry. The mission," said Christ. "I thought there was a way to mix ultimate power with ultimate wisdom, but all my wisdom brought with it was challenge. Strife." He sighed deep. "More than a thousand years of oppression, violence, and ruin in my name. I hoped somehow, in the places where my words would not fit, my will would make its way through."

"So what is this, then?" I asked, confused as I checked the signs ahead. An exit a few miles away promised to take us west to the Turnpike. "More words?"

"Whoever loves his life loses it, and whoever hates his life will preserve it for eternal life," Christ said, almost short with me. "No, no more words. Just what is needed."

Daniel took a long, hard drag and coughed his lungs out. Smoke filled the cabin, and not keen on driving stoned I cracked the windows on my side. Cold air and the roar of the cross-currents dulled every other noise. Merry retrieved her joint before the air snuffed the coal, holding it low in the foot well in front of her.

"So is this the fire?" I asked, knowing much about the Baptist. "And how does this save Deevi?"

"Faith, all," said Christ. "Just have faith."

Daniel had to ask. "In what?"

He did not answer, but I watched in the rearview mirror. He shared a warm smile with the RIRA gunman. Past the glass of the back window, Cuchulainn came behind us, his driver Laeg leading the horses connected to their chariot. Fine animals, a white and a black, kept pace with me at sixty through the turns and straights, never flagging or flecking foam from their mouths. It was an hour later we ran into another driver on the road.

"Oh, fuck," I breathed as I pumped the brake behind them. "How do we—"

"Oh, I got it." Christ snapped his fingers again.

In a blink, the champion, the driver, the horses, and the cart all vanished from behind us.

Astonished, Merry got up in her seat and craned back to see. "By—"

"Yes, ma'am," said Christ. "Right here."

The look she gave him was one of the oddest I had ever seen her give anyone, including me, as the Vodun queen and the Savior truly measured each other for the first time.

"How did you do that?" she asked.

He shrugged his shoulders. "I just can. And I don't know how to explain it any other way that would make sense. But the warrior, his driver, and the animals are safe and nearby, nor will they fear any danger until the time comes."

'Until the time comes.'

Great.

4

THE MIRACLE ON THE GWB

Three hours later we exited the New Jersey Turnpike. Nothing lay amiss, but the closer we came to the toll booths the less and less sure I was about the traffic. Cars moved slower and slower until coming to a dead stop. The drivers around us became agitated the longer we waited.

"All right," said I, "I'm going to go take a look. Probably a car accident." I checked with Christ in the backseat as I reached for my seatbelt buckle.

"Wait," said Merry, smacking her left hand on mine. She turned her head from me to him. "Why don't you tell us? Is it a crash?"

The Savior traded a placid gaze with her fiery glare. Daniel waited, almost on the edge of terror.

"Look," Christ said. "I can't guarantee you that there's no danger out there, but I can tell you that whatever awaits for us does not end here. What is to be is needed and will not be wasted." He raised a halting finger to stop my obvious question. "Nor will those suffering suffer long. All will be answered and made whole. But you probably should go look."

"Incredibly poignant and unhelpful." I pressed down on the red tab and freed myself from the seat. "Thanks."

Christ saluted me. "No problem."

Slipping out the driver's side on the left, I took a few steps toward the front of the car when I spotted the first wave of commuters fleeing their vehicles. Women carried their children as men tried to open routes for them in the crowding panic. My confusion over the cause ended when pops of gunfire broke through, raising the cries to screams.

I backed up to the Yukon and hopped inside, slamming the door behind me. "I think they're waiting for us."

Christ let out a hard, heavy sigh. "Okay." He snapped his fingers in front of his chest.

A horn sounded, booming over automatic rifle fire. In the blink of an eye, the Hound of Ulster was beside our vehicle, his driver Laeg balanced on the front fork of their chariot. The ancient warrior he drove had donned his scale, his iron helm, and strapped a long oval to his left forearm. In addition to the pattern-welded sword, Hardhead, belted to his waist, he carried three javelins in his right hand. The points sharp and glittering in the midday sunlight, they dulled next to the weird light in his eyes.

He ordered his man to bring both horses to a halt between the Yukon on my side and the next car, a sedan full of a people shocked by the sight of a walking war on wheels. Leaning over the side of his carriage, Cuchulainn rapped a knuckle on my window.

Rolling it down, I stuck my head out. "Where were you?"

"No need to worry," he said in newly practiced English. "I'll clear the way forward. You need to stay behind me or ahead, but do not lost sight of my chariot. I don't want to have to double back."

"Why not?"

"A lot of people are about to die, Christian." Cuchulainn cast his dark gaze toward the true god in the back of the truck. "I would rather keep the numbers low."

"Quite considerate," Christ said. "Go with my blessing."

Too fucked by the exchange, I could only awe at the brutal simplicity of the Lord's words until the wave of people hit our section of the highway. Some stopped to gob and stare for a few moments before the assault ahead of us, chopping the air with bullets, brought them to reality.

"What the fuck are you going to do against bullets?" I shouted at Cuchulainn. "This isn't the Iron Age! They'll riddle you all to pieces!"

The prospect of death presented, Cuchulainn threw his head back in laughter. "Forward, Laeg."

His chariot driver, posed impossibly on the fork yoking the horse to the Hound's vehicle, flicked the reins in his hands. The black and gray clopped forward at a strong pace, unhindered by the load they bore or the sea of cars and bodies before them.

"This is fucking insane," Merry said over my right shoulder. I craned out the window, struggling to find a space in the wall of humanity before us.

"Keep up, Patrick," Christ said from the back. "We need to keep to the way. It's lies over that bridge."

"Fuck, fuck, fuck," I grumbled as I put the Yukon into gear. "Put your seatbelts on."

"A very good idea. We should go but go safely," Christ said.

This fucking guy.

"Patrick?" Merry asked me, shocked as I dropped the parking brake. "You can't be serious!"

"As a fucking heart attack," I muttered. "Put your damn belt on, Merry. And hold tight."

As Cuchulainn rolled forward, he forced fleeing mortals to decide —move or be mowed, by him or the bullets. Opening a space where people gave his horses room, the Gray of Macha and the Black of Saingland, Laeg directed them into the flow.

I let my foot off the brake and pumped the accelerator. The Yukon pressed forward as I steered directly behind the chariot. The poor souls trying to get away from death in front and behind changed course like all herds fleeing their predators do and provided ample room. The places Laeg could not fit the horses, he bulled through, creating a wake behind the champion and his chariot to slip the truck past the scratched and displaced cars.

"This is fucking madness," Daniel said in the backseat behind me.

"Fucking madness! What are we supposed to do if they fire on us! What—"

"Faith, Daniel," said Christ.

"You keep saying that but bad things still happen," I cawed back at the Almighty, unable to stay my mouth. Daniel's questions had brought about my own panic to match Merry's, who ducked behind the dash and heaved in place. "It doesn't change the bad things!"

"It's not supposed to," Christ said.

Everyone in the car, despite the violence ahead, wrenched in his direction.

He shrugged at us. "You will always have the poor, some seed shall fall upon stone..." He looked up, unsure. "Um..."

Daniel thrust his hand over the back of my seat, obscuring my vision with his arm as he pointed. "Holy shit!"

I faced forward in time to see dozens of men, women, and a few children marching through the cars toward the Hound. Black-eyed and grimacing with unnatural smiles, they raised AK-47s and unloaded at the horses first. I cringed in the cabin, expecting blood and shattered horse bones before they mowed the demigod and his driver down.

No matter the encumbrance of his armor, Cuchulainn launched himself in an impossible leap, bounding like a salmon ascending a waterfall. On the ascent, he threw two of the javelins in his hand, skewering demons on the spot before he landed amongst them. Drawing his sword as they all turned inward, he charged into the nearest cluster.

"Red Branch! Red Branch!" he bellowed, his voice heightened as he unleashed his powers. A blur of steel, movement, and iron-spring muscle, the Hound of Ulster cut down human life possessed by the most hellish powers. Laeg popped over the front of the chariot and into the basket to take cover. He saw me behind him, and waving for me to follow, rose to assume the reins again. He put the Gray and Black, impervious to the bullets, into the melee.

"Get going, Patrick," Christ said. "We have to keep up!"

Bullets cut in every direction to catch the whirring Irish demigod as I punched on pedal with my foot. The Yukon kept hard behind the chariot.

"Red Branch! Red Branch!"

The slaughter, of an old world now unimaginable in a time of bullets and bombs, spread as Cuchulainn dashed to and fro, hewing among the ricochets and falling bodies. Plucking javelins from the corpses he had laid low, many times he leapt up and tossed the shafts, striking another frantic enemy unable to train on him in time. He'd go in chase, like a dog after a stick, slaying everyone in his way.

Unprepared for the sheer smash-mouth ferocity chewing their ranks, Perdition forwent any attempt to stop our charge as they focused their fire.

Pushing between the cars, Laeg and the horses did most of the work getting us ahead. Losing sight of the battle multiple times, I did not miss the blood flowing across the pavement, the torn bodies cast aside by the fury I had unleashed. My trump card against the man in the backseat, a chill ran through as I thought of this grand mistake I had made, killing and glorifying outside our windows.

I could not draw my eyes to the rearview mirror out of a shame I deserved.

"I can't actually get mad at that," Christ said. "And believe it or not, Patrick, I am not mad at you. You did what you did out of concern for others and some rightful anger. I can't deny you that."

No matter where I looked outside the Yukon there were bodies. Worse than picking up the gun myself, tears stung my eyes. "But all these people. These innocent people..."

"Patrick," bade Christ, "look behind us. Not to me. Behind us."

Unable to deny the Creator of Heaven and Earth, I raised my gaze to the rearview.

The lives the Hound of Ulster had lain low as demons had risen as themselves, alive and whole. And human. Unharmed beneath the blood and their ruined clothes, they stood about and awed at their resurrection and of others around them.

I slammed on the brakes. The Yukon screeched into place, the engine rumbling before I shifted it to park. My shaking hands found the door handle, and opening it, I stepped outside and faced the way we had come.

Christ had raised every single victim of Satan's possession and Ireland's ancient cruelty.

Every single one.

"Oh my..." Merry echoed, perched on her knees in the passenger seat and her arms against the headrest. Rendered by wonder as I and Daniel were, I looked from her to Christ.

His smile spoke wonders. "I did not come to bring the end of days. Now let's get going—Cuchulainn and Laeg are almost out of sight."

Forward again, I sat in absolute, wonderful, sincere astonishment as I got back into the truck for a second time.

"Red Branch! Red Branch!"

Cuchulainn blurred between cars and over tractor trailers, playing fetch with his spears as he pushed Hell's forces over the western end of the George Washington Bridge. Connecting New Jersey to the wooded hills of northern Manhattan, its dual lengths had been brought to a standstill by the calamity. His sword drank of young and old alike, but for every foot we traced, those same victims reawakened. He won foot after foot, the bullets either bouncing off his shield when they caught him or missing. Laeg spent more time upright in the basket as he led the Black and Gray.

Hundreds and hundreds rose, astonished as they watched the demigod free more innocents from the onyx-eyed demons. Hails of bullets vanished before they could come close to a rescued soul.

Christ never once rolled down the window nor asked me to stop so he could make his presence known. Every time I looked back I saw a man—more than a man—simply smile at the relief and joy every single person on that piece of road felt that day.

This fucking guy.

"Hey, take that exit," Christ said when we reached the off-ramp to 178th.

"What about Cuchulainn?" I asked.

"Oh, don't worry about him," Christ said. "He and I figured it all out back at the farm. He'll know where to find us, plus he seems to be having a good time."

True to his word, the demons' line ahead of us receded further and further. The pint-sized fury stormed, a grinder that wouldn't end any time soon.

"And those people will still be spared?" Merry asked. "Even if you aren't there?"

Christ sighed on the back bench. "Of course, Queen Merry."

Practically the last moving vehicle on the road, I turned us down the ramp toward Broadway. Police and ambulance sirens blared in the distance. Turning left on Christ's order to head north into Washington Heights, we were gone before any of them sighted us exiting the bridge.

"Take a left up at 181," Chris instructed further. "I know a place we can park. I have some business in the neighborhood."

"Is Deevi that way?" I asked, eager to find her.

"Oh, trust me," he said. "She'll be along quite soon."

FACE TO FACE

They had refused her food, water, leaving her chained to the rack they forced her onto before the demons placed a bag over her head. Not that it mattered to Deevi as she hung there, suspended by wings, neck, wrists, and ankles. The smell of brimstone, a sulfurous scent in the metal, gave a clue to why she failed to break free or summon her magma armor to burn them away. Even her wings had lost their golden glow.

The silence of wherever they had placed her, filled with an absolute void of presence, carried no illumination save for a small blue light in the ceiling.

The entire room hummed, vibrated, agitated by currents flowing all around it.

Wherever it was, she was trapped.

But she would get free. Tensed in place, Deevi could endure the position for days, weeks—however long this time Satan needed to squirrel her away and finish his horrendous conspiracy. Captured once by his minions posing as servants of her father, she knew this time the adversary would employ no tricks to get what he wanted from her. The notion made her grin underneath the bag.

Not this time. Not for the daughter the Rebel King.

Not for the baby in her womb.

How she knew was an unspoken intuition, the same way she had simply known English, or how to fly, or the sense of how things were versus what people told her—save Patrick.

Patrick had always told her the truth, even through absolute agony.

Deevi readied. The moment she slipped free...

"Not this time," she promised herself in the void.

The currents outside her sightless, senseless cell changed directions, the focus of the vibrations behind her and in the lower corners of the floor. Gravity moved, weighing heavier before wheels outside touched the earth, the plane clattering as it landed hard, then slowed to a stop.

Voices grumbled in the infernal tongue outside, just beyond the range of her hearing. The prison was pushed off a platform onto another as she smelled petrol, recognizing it from the few gas stations she had visited. She did not miss the roar of a truck engine, and pulled forward this time, she knew she would soon come to her destination.

More transfers ended in a lift large enough to hold her box. It was brought high, higher to where the gravity clung to her, the small shift in altitude detectable to her greater senses. Shaking out her limbs the best she could, she inhaled as a hatch opened, then the lock on her door was undone. Two men holding the halves stepped back, opening to a flood of warm, orange light.

And candles. Hundreds and hundreds of candles.

Satan whispered in his black tongue, out of sight. "Come here."

The shackles around her wrists and ankles opened and fell away, the butted chains attached to them thudding where they struck a foamed floor. Landing barefoot on the soft padding, Deevi arose, still in the white top and gray sweatpants Patrick had bought her back in Dublin. Her wings, crowding the small box lined with strange black spikes trimmed out of the same stuff on the ground, regained their glow in a few breaths, challenging the candles for dominance.

"Come here," Satan whispered. "I won't harm you."

"I have sincere doubts about that," she said aloud as she yanked off the bag on her head. Her long brown hair hung before her eyes, concealing her face.

"Then come away." A loud, resonant chuckle caused the candles to flicker. "Face the danger, little one. You've proved more than capable of that."

Her hands and legs free, Deevi felt none of the hampering force that had pervaded before her release, knowing she could summon her weapons, armor, and even fly if she dared.

A glass window beyond reflected one of the candled displays. The sight of the buildings past the pane, one or two of them immediately familiar, gave away their location in the 'downtown' section of New York City.

She slowly walked forward and peered outside of her box.

The entire room had been stripped bare except for the candles and its lone occupant.

A short woman with rich brown skin and soft black hair kept tight in a bun, the gray wool jacket and matching pants she wore over a white button-up shirt was far too hot to stand in the midst of the bleeding fires. An attractive mortal as far as Deevi thought her to be, she smirked among the luminaries.

"Hello, Deevi," said Satan in a deep, masculine voice mismatching the feminine form. "It has been a very, very long time. Do you remember me?"

"Certainly not in that form," Deevi answered. "But I would not think you needed it. I saw you above Lough Derg. I saw you slain. But that matters little, doesn't it?"

"I hope you understand that I had no intention of bringing harm to your kin, let alone that foolish knight," he said, linking slender hands behind his back and taking a few steps forward. "By all rights, they attacked first."

"You came to kidnap me."

"Kidnap you?" Satan clicked the woman's tongue on her straight, clean teeth. "My dear, is that what you think I have done in this? Tried to kidnap you? To take you against your will? Please, let us not disre-spect everything that has happened leading to now. Whatever intents I may have, I'm sure you'll agree the ends will be justified."

Dumbstruck by the pure audacity arguing for her violation, Deevi raised her dark brows. "I understand why my father dislikes you so much. You really are quite thick."

The smirk died on the Devil's face. Slouching as he glowered, brown eyes shifted red in warning. "And you'd be foolish to resist any more. You've been soundly beaten, my dear. If you would only listen to reason, I would assure you that in defeat, you will uncover greater things than you could ever imagine. The ultimate thing."

"And pray tell," said Deevi. "What is this ultimate thing?"

"The end of all suffering," Satan said in the voice of the young woman, smooth and low. "Full of certainty. An end to all this," he said, lifting her arms. "No more darkness. Not for you or me or anyone. Think of it, Deevi—a goddess, glowing in the darkness with no fear of God or Lucifer or any power greater than yourself, without equal! You could beckon the cosmos to peace, bring low the blade of every warrior, and seek an end to this endless, endless hunt." The fallen angel dropped the arms back to her sides. "Or you can cling to defiance, linger on this notion that you are loved by this damned, evil, bastard bigot who left us to rot and ruin in this mire! You can cling to foolishness or you can stretch out your hand, take mine, and forge what is needed."

"An end," Deevi said with a suspecting nod. "To all things. Creation."

"Every universe will be liberated," said Satan. "The suffering of the teeming cannot go unpunished. God must be made to see justice."

"But there are three issues that I think still separate us."

"Please," Satan said, stepping forward in a sympathetic gesture. "Truly, you are in no danger. My ears are yours."

"No danger?" Deevi paid him a restrained smile. "Well," she said after a full sigh. "First, let me ask you a question."

"Of course."

"Who has made me suffer?"

The blank surprise left on Satan's face almost made her laugh aloud.

"Yes," Deevi said. "It's a very tricky answer isn't it, but that's where my father says you like to reside." Her grin sharpened into a meaner one. "Who has made me suffer? My father? All he has done is sacrifice. God? He hasn't shown up to kill me when he very well could, despite the fraught relationship."

Satan grunted at the observation. "It is a complication that God has allowed—"

"Whatever the complication," she said, waving past his nonsense-temptations, "I live by some basic simplicities. Which gets us to the second issue—to do what you want proposes that I simply lie down, open my legs, let you mount me with the vague hope that you will impregnate me on the off-chance you have the ability."

"That is where you are wrong, Nephilim," said Satan. "I certainly have every intention. And do not mistake my ability."

"It's not a question of ability, you lout," she said, dropping every pretense. "There is where the third issue arises: you've already lost the opportunity. I'm pregnant with Saint Patrick's child."

This time she could not hold back laughter as the dumbfounded face of her direst enemy fell in shock, aghast before a seething rage restored itself. "And what do you think happens to you, little one?"

Deevi summoned her magma blade as she darted forward with a flap of her wings. She rammed Satan, bowling over the woman he possessed. Rolling onto the floor, she sprang up and slashed through the nearest glass window. Diving straight down, she plummeted toward the streets of New York. Trapped between buildings of concrete and steel, she angled her body for the ground, gathering every bit of momentum before she opened her wings.

She shot upward at a rapid ascent, past the roofs of the towers, and into the open air.

Satan roared behind her from the broken hole she left in a skyscraper, summoning his troops.

5

CABRINI

True to his word, Christ found us a parking spot near Fort Tryon Park. By the west exit of St. Francis Xavier Cabrini's sanctuary, we parked on the side where Christ looked over the Hudson River, blessing it with an impassive gaze like the statue of him past the gates. Cast in bronze, the effigy opened his heart in grim welcome. He stared at it a few times in confusion after he got out of the Yukon, switching between his likeness and the river, but always keener to the waters.

"All right," he said after his quiet meditation, "time to go forth. But before we do, I must make a few things right, starting here."

The Savior faced Merry as we stood on the sidewalk by the black iron fence, surprising her, Daniel, and I. "Meredith, I'm truly, truly sorry for everything that has happened. If I could—"

"Do not start here," she said, puffing on the end of a joint. She glared down a man she saw as a man, not her god. In a flower halter top, jeans, and black combat books, she had forgone her usual array of necklaces and bracelets common to the Vodun dress, instead arming herself in the serpent rings, jeweled circlets, and inscribed chokers made of silver and iron, each of them impressed with the spirits of her ancestors and the Lwas. She had consolidated whatever else she needed down to one satchel she had brought from the farm in New Jersey. Who knew what was in there.

She once pulled a gun on me in Haiti after a particularly bad argument. Then again in Ireland.

There could be anything.

Christ raised his chin in rebuttal, gentle in his speech. "I must. I wronged you."

I stood in shock of the statement.

God had just said to a mortal 'I'm at fault.' This was going to be a doozy for me, worse for the world if this was the tone he planned to set.

Far less reverent of the apologizer than I, Merry spoke quicker. "Yes, you did. You've wronged everyone. Everywhere."

Christ averted his eyes. "I know."

"You do," she screamed at him, flinging the burning joint. Her fury unleashed, she almost moved to assault him when she restrained herself, shaking as she brought her hands up to cover the writhing turmoil on her face. The tears came hot, fast, running down her dark cheeks to the point of her chin. Merry sobbed, harder and harder.

Daring as he always does, Christ hugged her. She did not fight or protest, burying her face into the linen of his simple robe.

"Peace," Christ said, rubbing her back. "I know I do. I know I am to blame. This is why I must ask you two things. First, I ask that you consider forgiving me. Second, I need you to get in the Yukon and drive home to Brooklyn. Whatever you do from there is yours to do as you see fit, but I would request that you to gather every priest and priestess, every adherent and dancer, and every client willing, and tell them that Jesus Christ has asked them to come to Madison Square Garden."

"The Garden?" I asked, interrupting.

"Shush, Patrick," said Christ. "Will do you this for me, Merry?"

She pushed away from him. "Why should I? Why should I risk my people when you have all the power in the world?"

"Because all the power in the world can't fix what has happened,"

Christ replied, his hands at his sides. "But I can offer something in return for what I ask."

The Vodun Queen laughed aloud in the face of Christianity. "What could you ever give me that I would want?"

Without warning, Christ stepped closer and placed a hand on her bare shoulder, his brown skin a few shades lighter than her ebony complexion. She did not seize in his grasp, or fight, but I watched as a notion washed away from her expression, the burden every soul carried in this constructed, conceived universe. He removed his hand.

"It's...I can..." Blinking in wonder, Merry let her gaze roam the river and trees, the church to our left, and the sky above before she resettled on him. "But I can still see the things that happened. Remember them."

"I can't change what has happened," Christ repeated. "But I can do my best to heal the wounds."

"What the fuck is happening here?" I said, no longer able to be a witness.

Daniel stood silent beside me, his expression unreadable as he exchanged it between Merry and the Savior.

"He—" Merry scrunched her face. The more she vexed at Christ, the less the expression remained. She cut away from him for a moment, to herself, before she glanced back again in wonder. Then the tears reemerged.

"You really did it. Everything. The quake. Lucia." She lifted a finger at me. "Him. George. It's all there, but I can see it without—"

"Without the pain poisoning you," Christ said, nodding. "My best and worst design flaw, if I'm honest with myself. I'm here to help with that too. But time is ticking, Meredith, and I need to know—will you gather your kin and march upon the Garden with me?"

"Which Garden?" I asked, tired of being ignored. "Eden? Are you bringing Eden to New York?"

"No," Christ finally said to me. "Madison Square Garden. Pay attention. I'm going to play a show."

I threw my hands up and started walking south on the sidewalk, too tired of this shit.

A minute later the Yukon's engine turned and roared, and I spun to find Merry already pulling out of the space. She put the truck in reverse and backed up to where I was on the street and rolled the window down.

"Are we really doing this?" I asked. "After everything we've seen and done? Or had done to us?"

She sighed at me. "Yeah, Tater," she said, her wonderful brown eyes red from herb and healing. "I think we have to."

"Is that you talking or him?"

She frowned. "Don't be a shit-ass about it."

"Sorry."

Merry sighed a second time. "I know. But I need this. I need to get away for a minute and just be. You know? I'm going to drive back to Brooklyn, but I'll be in touch. Alright?"

"Alright," said I, beyond the point of protest. "Just be careful."

The frown broke on her dark face a moment, replaced by a wavering smile. "You too, mi amor. Take care of Daniel."

Off she rode, headed north to the roundabout in front of Fort Tryon before she'd take an exit for the Hudson and zip down the West side and straight through downtown if she hit it at the right time. Christ joined me a few seconds later, hands behind his back as he studied me with a passive gaze. Daniel came alongside him, there for no other reason than a smart sense of safety.

"Well," I said. "Just you and us. Alone."

"Patrick, I get it," Christ replied. "And I don't hold it against you." He glanced to Daniel too. "And I won't. Not for a moment."

"You want won't hold what?" Daniel asked.

"Any hurt against Patrick for the punch he's about to throw my way."

As hard as I fucking could, my left fist collided with Christ's jaw. To his credit, he took as well as a man beaten to death by Romans could. He leaned away and wheeled, wincing as I wrung out my searing hand, cursing hard to work past the pain.

Daniel had leapt back in shock, pressed against the black fencing by a placard for the park birds. "Holy shit, Patrick!" the gunman shouted in his Irish lilt, hands in his brown hair. "You struck the Savior!"

The agony in my hand doubled me over. "Fuck right I did."

Christ reached out to me. "Need me to?"

"Let's just fucking go," I said as I rubbed every knuckle. "You don't need to play it up."

He straightened up and smoothed his robes, which almost made Daniel lean so far back he could have tumbled over the iron. "It was a fine punch."

"Don't you start," I said, seething.

We started down the back end of Cabrini, a few blocks south when we ran into Lucifer and Gabriel on the corner by a money exchange, popular in a neighborhood filled with immigrants always on the go. The sight of two archangels in the street, which were unusually bare for the evening, slowed both Daniel and I as we marched.

"Hi kids," Christ said, the Daddest man on the planet. "Lucifer, did you find what I sent you to find?"

"Yes, Lord," The Morningstar said, reverent as he bowed his head. "I've already placed it in a safe location at the venue."

"Excellent, I hope you liked what I picked for you," Christ said jubilantly. "Gabriel?"

"The hosts await the order to descend on New York," they said in our huddle. "There was much excitement and confusion, but they are ready and armed."

"Armed?" Christ said. "No, no, no—no swords. Go back and tell them to leave them at home. Don't toss them away! But I don't think we'll be needing them much longer."

"Not much longer?" Lucifer asked.

Oh no. They weren't in on this either.

Christ raised a hand. "In due time, son. But first, I have a job here in Washington Heights. I hear his son is about and I'd like to say hi."

"Who's son?" I asked, surprised at the meagerness of the trip's purpose.

Like he must have been to his disciple Thomas, he was kind in the smile he gave me for my inherent doubts. "The Old Man's. Now with me. Bit of a hill ahead unless we take the high ground and it's actually quite lovely during the day."

"Oh, an old man now! Okay," I said, as if that was sufficient before he started off. The two archangels fell in line behind their father like dutiful children, leaving Daniel and I to take up the train.

We walked a few more blocks, then took a left down where Pinehurst and 183rd Street joined at the southwestern corner of Bennett Park. Apparently America's first president had used the place as a fortress, but now a residential corner of an international neighborhood, it too was surprisingly quiet. We turned east and stopped at intersection when Christ brought us to a halt.

"Oh, wait, wait, wait!" Christ stroked his black-brown beard, glancing down Fort Washington. "Uh, Gabriel, could you go get me some flowers? Something nice like some daisies. Oh, white roses! He'll appreciate that for the Scholls. Ah, hey," he gazed up at his winged child, smiling at them. "Want to go for a walk with Dad?"

"I would be delighted to, my Lord," Gabriel said, stunned by the offer. They looked to Lucifer in shock, who smiled and nodded for his sibling to walk with Christ. And off they went, around the block to find white roses.

"What the fuck is going on?" I asked Lucifer. Daniel had no choice but to stand by as witness this time.

The Morningstar sighed at the question. "There's no way I can avoid it, is there?"

"No," said I, "not after what we've seen together."

"I respect that," Lucifer said as he studied the corner of the red bricked apartment building across from us. Unearthly handsome, he blinked beaming eyes at an apple tree one of the owners had grown from the garden bed at its feet, already budded for spring. "When my father died, he went to a place where only his spirit could reside in death. In many ways he fell into the void of what would become Perdition, not the purifying flame of his people before he ascended to his throne. He told Michael of this place, of its lack of Him in it, and how he intended for it to remain as it was—empty and unneeded, like his previous self."

"Fuck, man," Daniel said, turning away.

"His previous self?" I asked, as confused as an ordained priest could be.

"The Father," Lucifer said as he cast a confused look at the gunman's back, "had a Son who died. The Holy Spirit endured and raised the Son to redeem the sins of the Father."

"Fuck, man," I blurted. "And when Michael made it about their punishment or his rebellion, Christ capitulated."

"For the moment," Lucifer said, leveling a finger at me. "We're close to the end of this, though it came sooner than predicted."

"The end?" I asked. "The end of what, Lucifer?"

"Come now, saint," said the Morningstar. "Do you really think he would die for the sins of all and not come rescue you? To heal the sick and mend the wounds of the broken by closing the first wound?" He smirked at me, the Rebel King and conspirator alongside his Creator. "To end the tribulation?"

"Tribu—" It struck me dead, then and there, the possibility of fallibility in the scripture made clear by one who could deny it. The idea of having lived amid final ruin all this time, and how kind the world had been despite it, clashed with images of an apocalypse and seven-headed dragons out of the boiling seas.

Hands on my hips, I shut my eyes tightly and ground my teeth. "You absolute bastards."

"Do not blame us for the writing of men, Saint Patrick. Revelation was a political novel meant to keep early Christians alive in times of absolute suffering." Lucifer added further to my creeping, terrifying conclusions. "This is a promise kept."

Even Daniel knew enough about the Bible to fill in the blanks for himself. "But he rose and met his apostles, blessing them to continue his work until—"

Lucifer laughed at the mortal. "Said who?"

The book was in my pocket. Every part of me wanted to do what every Christian did in those situations, but there, in the presence of archangels and God himself, who was I to hearken to the paper and ink of mortal men? Against the one and only Word? The Bible stayed in my pocket, my protests in my mouth, but every doubt in my heart remained.

Lucifer rested his glowing hand on my shoulder. "Ask him, Patrick."

"Just like that?"

He gave me one firm nod, his golden eyes a match for his daughter's. "Haven't you before?"

I made a sour face as Christ and Gabriel came back up the sidewalk. He carried a dozen white roses in a bouquet, beaming at his selection.

"Alright," he said, cheery as could be, "Follow me!"

And off we were again, crossing when the light turned because it mattered to him and down to a corner where the street bent south. He went north at the entrance to a block of three buildings unified by a central courtyard with a lovely garden. A nice set of table and chairs waited to the side, and someone had already put out pots in the herb stand. Christ chose the eastern most of the buildings, ascending the trio of stone steps up to the orange-painted doors.

"Gabriel, Lucifer, please guard the lobby while we go up," he said, nodding to include Daniel and I. "We'll only be a little bit."

We took the stair up the second floor and the third letter in the alphabet. He knocked twice before we heard anything.

"Coming," a faraway man's voice called on the other side of the old steel portal, its brown, flaking paint as old as the building itself. The top lock turned first, then the one over the knob. It popped as it was pulled back.

In the widening crack stood a tired man in a long, red cloak, the hood cast up around his shaven head. He carried a small, blond baby in his arms. The little child stared at us as he hugged to his father.

"Hey," Christ said. "There you are!"

The hooded man shuddered but held firm to his child. Tears flooded his eyes, terror and wonder revealed. The poor man broke in front us.

Always to the rescue, Christ handed me the bouquet and swooped in. "Now, now, none of that," he said as he entered. "Here, I got the little bear. No, no, no, I'm not here to punish you—"

"But Jesus," the poor man said, sobbing into his hands as Christ held his child. "But—"

"Shhhhh, son of the north," he said as I watched him clap the hooded stranger on the shoulder. "We'll solve that later. I just wanted to come by and tell you that it's okay and it's going to be okay. I also need to ask—where's your dad?"

They left Daniel and I in the foyer, talking about things I never understood before or after, for a whole thirty minutes before we left.

6

THE MTA

We stood on the platform at 181st waiting on a southbound A when it finally nagged me too much.

"Christ," I asked in the most authoritative tone, "what the fuck are we doing here?"

On one of the wooden benches sectioned off by strips of wood to deny the homeless places to sleep, he sat at the far end, sandwiching his two children between us. Their wings elegantly folded against their backs, Lucifer and Gabriel had assumed the exact same position, hands on knees covered by their shimmering robes. Gabriel looked off while their brother stared. Daniel had plopped down beside me, dazing into his own exhaustion.

Christ answered in his upbeat manner. "Well, Patrick, I'm planning to play a show at Madison Square Garden."

"No, no," I said, perturbed. "I'm tired of the mystery. I want the goddamn answer."

Both archangels glared at me in surprise, shocked at my use of the pejorative before their creator. Daniel seized, trying to politely put space between us without Christ or I noticing, the poor sod.

"The answer to what?" Christ asked.

"Beg pardon?" I asked, incredulous. "I ask you a question and you—"

He threw up his hands. "What do you want? You asked 'what are we doing here?' and I answered!" He put both hands back on his knees. "Like I said, we're headed to the Garden. And I will be happy to answer any question you have, but my child, be thoughtful of what is asked."

This fucking guy.

Aware of the game, I shifted my glare from him to Lucifer. He measured me in a far less hostile manner, his intense golden eyes not veering from mine.

"I take it there is something deeper going on here than simply revelation," I asked, back to the Savior. "Am I correct?"

"You would be, though there will be revelation. There always is," said Christ, nodding as he smiled at some little inner joke. "Very good question, Patrick."

Stifling a schoolboy's grumble for a compliment from the priest he hated, I reverted to the same tone that got me many a lash in school. "How about this one: there are demons constantly hunting you, even though you are God. Millions of people in this city and billions around the world are watching and waiting for a sign that you—you— are coming to save them. And I guess if you are not here to just reveal your power and will upon the world, my next guess is this is part of a larger scheme to fix something greater. Am I close again?"

"For the most part." Christ leaned toward Gabriel. "You know, I don't understand why mortals think I'm mysterious about all this."

"It's hard to listen against the wind," the Messenger whispered before they checked my reaction. "Sorry, Patrick."

"Then if I'm close, I'm close enough to know," I said. "Talk. Now."

He didn't need to hear the question to know what I asked, nor did he patronize me. "I made many, many mistakes. I'm here to correct them and heal my children. All my children. That was the goal of doing this," he said, flexing his fleshed hands. The hole where the nails pierced his wrists remained, open but dry. "I know now what I can do to turn fire back to water."

Fuck if everything wasn't a goddamn parable. "John."

He leaned forward and looked right at me, a dawning smile on his face. "Yes, John! Him! What an absolute braggart, but it's usually the braggarts who are right."

Lucifer chuckled at a joke beyond me.

"I'm missing something again," I said.

"I'm not a Christian, Patrick," Christ said simply. "I was a Jew by birth but ended up as something radically different. But am I not Christianity? Is that what I set out to make from my ministry? Is Christianity and its continuance the purpose of my coming, going, and return? What of its temples, its priests, and its speakers? What of its coffers and holy places gilded and wrought in the work of the poor for the glorification of who?"

I did not like where he was going. "Then you are here to correct the church?"

"He will have issues with this, Father," Lucifer said from his place beside Christ. "He clings to these structures much like Michael does to our own."

"An apt point," Gabriel acknowledged, receiving a thankful nod from their brother.

"Then I will have to be abundant in both clarity and certainty, won't I?" Christ answered them.

The fourth wheel in this divine cavalcade, I pressed anyway. "But I thought you said this isn't the end."

"It is and it is not," Christ said in a surprised tone, as if he couldn't understand my misunderstanding. "I'm not here to end anything anyway—at least I hope not. But I am here to bring to bear things that should have been and things that must be. Water to fire, fire to water."

"Then, dammit, make it clear for me!" I almost shouted as the lights of the southbound A-Train lanced out of the tunnel to our left.

The first gray and blue aluminum cars rolled from the darkened passage, the conductor hitting the breaks. Metal whined against metal as hydraulics slowed the long, linked monster. The doors parted with an airy hiss and a few people stepped out. To my utter shock, nobody seemed to notice Christ as he boarded, his unbelievable children diminishing in their dimensions to fit inside. Too damned exhausted and frustrated, I came after Daniel and threw myself onto one of the plastic blue and yellow benches.

"Why isn't anyone paying attention to us?" I asked.

"Oh, they don't know me yet," Christ said. His kids flanked him on the seat opposite from mine. "Look, it's going to be very, very hard for me to explain everything in plain and simple words if only to give reason to the things that have happened. You will have to wait for some answers, but I promise you, the wait shall not be long."

"Time and space have very different meanings for you and it's been more than two thousand years. And I'm not dropping it. Fire. Water. Explain."

"The next stop is 175. Doors are closing," the conductor crackled over the speakers.

The train slid forward at once, carrying us into the next tunnel.

"I am the eagle at the mouth of the river," Christ said. "No matter what buildings you build, no matter what tombs you erect to defend your dead, I am there, and they are mine. As are you. As she stands at the mouth, I stand with her, and we stand against those who build their buildings made of bricks. Do you ever wonder, Patrick, past the apologetics and the reasons given by fallible men, why I went to a madman in Jordan for my baptism and not the Temple to be anointed with oil? Why I scoured those money lenders and Pharisees who had scoured him and his wife? Or her and her children? What of mine, bound into roles of servitude no true parent wishes on their own?"

I caught half the Gnosticism and the political connotations. "You can't just show up and do this. People rely on the Temple and the churches. They rely on law and order and—"

"I am not a God of Law and Order," Christ said in a firm but gentle rebuke. "I am a God of Peace and Justice. A god of children. A Fisher am I, a Fisher who is elect among fishers. A Fisher am I who among the fishers is chosen, the Head of all catchers of fish. I know the shallows of the waters and the inner waters. The depths I fathom. Why would I build temples when the Grand Design already was the temple?"

"But that's not what you told the apostles to do," I said.

"Who said anything about them?" he retorted.

"You descended from heaven," I said, rebuking him this time. "It's in the damned book you told them to write across the centuries after!"

"Says you, my boy," he replied in his best Irish brogue, so good it galled me. "I'm here saying otherwise."

"But John's head ended up on a plate," I retorted. "Not everyone is going to be happy with this."

"Nobody was happy the first round of it. Does that matter more than truth?" Jesus gave a sardonic laugh. "Look who you're arguing with."

"Oh fuck you," I said, at the end of my wits when the door at the end of the car cranked open. Five tall men entered in a single file, too tight to be random. They spread out.

Lucifer and Gabriel stood immediately, barring the way between them and their father.

I came up too, spying over Lucifer's shoulder. Daniel stood behind me, reaching into his pocket for the pistol I knew he had on him.

The five demons glared at the archangels with marble-black eyes.

"Too scared to face us yourself, Son of God?" the demon in the middle of their line called in a mocking, warbled voice. "Too fearful to face your failure?"

"Showing is better than telling." Christ rose up with a grin and placed a hand on Daniel's shoulder. "As you walk with me from here forth, Daniel O'Brien, you shall never come to harm if you never fire your gun ever again. Peace, my son, and know you walk with one who will not let you be harmed. They have no power here."

The RIRA gunman took his hand off the grip, his heaving eased as he looked directly at the Savior in his eyes for the first time. Unhidden and unafraid, a dawning on his face cleared the burden off his brow, and the sorrow. He nodded once and sat back down, not taking his attention from Christ as he pressed past his archangels.

"Oh, hey," he said. "Is this Zekiel, Mariel, Tamriel, Moriel, and Beniel? I haven't seen you in a few minutes, have I? How are you all?"

"We're—" the lead demon scrunched his human mask, a pale

Latino man in his fifties. "Stay your tongue, you sourer of speech! We did not come to bandy words but to—"

"Okay," Christ said, opening his arms before them. "Lay your hands upon me."

The head of their number, Zekiel hesitated. "But..."

"You were sent here to stop me by Satan, were you not?" Christ asked in his clear voice. "If so, lay your hands upon me. I will not fight you and you will not be fought by your siblings beside me. You may not harm the priest or my follower Daniel, however, but besides that..." He raised his arms a bit higher. "Come at me."

"This is not how I planned this going at all," the demon on the right end said, turning away with a wave toward Savior. "I did not crawl up to deal with this."

"Yeah, I'm out too," said the hellspawn possessing the old Black man beside him. "That's too much."

"Hold yourselves, Moriel! Beniel! Do not waver in the face of a pretender!" Zekiel raised a finger in Christ's direction, his black eyes full of hate. "He must pay for his curses and crimes against us! He must taste the darkness by which—"

"I fully agree," Christ interrupted. "Now come here, Zek. I can see you need a hug first."

The first exorcism I witnessed as a reincarnated saint took place in a barn in Italy when I was fifteen. The March had paired me with the reincarnation of St. Gereon, a pious man who had gotten on better with George than he and I ever did. A nasty bastard prone to reach for a sword or switch in a tantrum, the one thing he pressed into every one of us he trained for the priesthood's holiest mission was an endless siege between demons and the rest of God's creation. Sometimes lasting months, even years, the battle was one of attrition until the priest failed or the demon broke.

To be fair, St. Gereon had been beheaded by pagans, so he was intense about everything.

He would have been apoplectic the moment Zekiel dashed forward into the arms of God. First him, then the rest. Before anyone else moved to stop them, the demons swarmed their maker.

But no violence passed, no tearing of cloth or flesh, nor a drop of blood spilled while tears flowed in lakes. The demons cried into the shoulders and chest of Christ the moment they touched him, a loving father finding his lost little ones. He patted and cooed, ceasing the sufferings they had racked in their time away from the Light of Lights.

There were tears in Christ's eyes too.

I awed at this, unable to form the proper words to convey the miracle I had witness with hardly a bang or an explosion. He consoled the demons, and moment by moment, the shadows on their faces lifted. Eyes cleared, the freed homeless men gasped the gasp of the liberated, fully aware of what had happened and who had helped them.

He spoke to them, individually and together at times, until we reached our stop at Columbus Circle. Blessing them with a kiss to their foreheads and promises that they would be fine, he led Lucifer and Gabriel up the tile steps, Daniel and I trailing in dumbfounded wonder.

Right into the middle of a riot.

7

———

BUSKING

Bottles and fists flew as New York's glass and steel loomed over the hordes, thousands of people enmeshed in a violent cyclone of anger. What had caused this, I never discovered, but as we emerged from the southwestern exit, I could see nothing but stopped cars, warring bodies, and panic at Columbus Circle. It surged around us, stopping traffic dead all the way to the entrance of Central Park. Four against the teeming, I admit I considered staying put.

But not Christ.

"Lucifer," he said to his son at his left.

"Yes, Father?" the Morningstar answered, not taking his eyes off the battle ahead.

"Right in the circle," he said. "Gabriel?"

His child to his right hummed.

"Summon the Funky Flock," Christ said. "It's time."

"Time?" I asked, not touching the first thing out of fear he'd explain it.

Christ looked over his shoulder at me and smiled. "Welcome to Day Seven."

And nobody stopped him. Not Lucifer, not Gabriel, both of whom

51

vanished in the next blink of the eye. On the last landing before the world, Daniel and I watched the Savior start into the midst of terror, certain he'd be torn apart. Recalling every image of my journey through Purgatory on the back of Lucifer's memories, the image of this brave man scoured bloody as he marched to Golgotha came to me.

Alone and friendless, he charged the breach again, undaunted by the task.

"We really letting him do this alone?" Daniel asked.

Braver than Christ's first set of friends, I decided then and there not to deny my Maker. "Fuck no."

Christ slowed when he heard our boots on the stairwell's metal-shod steps behind him. "Bless you both."

"Just go if you're going," I said. "This is mad enough!"

"Well, give them a minute," he said over the riot.

My answer to a question I had no time to ask arrived with a guitar sawing through the shouting and car horns, someone tapping the high-hat before the bass drums boomed like a bounding heart. A piano entered, then a bass guitar, backed by some extra percussions I couldn't place.

"The Funky Flock," Christ whispered proudly as he pulled a micro-phone from nowhere.

He grabbed me by the shoulder and dragged us up the steps as awe silenced everyone.

We burst out of the exit into clean sunlight, pushing past bodies standing still as they faced the statue of Columbus and the small, circular mall around him. To my utter amazement not a single person continued to scrap, their full attention paid to the band that had suddenly appeared in the middle of the melee.

Lucifer strummed on a white electric guitar, picking notes against the seven-four signature Ramiel beat out of a full drum set right below the statue of the infamous Portuguese explorer, their music carrying nothing hateful or dominating like he had. Uriel filled out of the bottom of the rhythm on an unvarnished wooden bass, the angel of Death accompanied by Raguel as the Recorder filled in the rest with fixed bongos and a small mixer. Selaphiel, his smoking censure atop of the tuning board of his keyboards, harmonized with Lucifer as they played a wanderer's track, written after the composer was done with Genesis.

The Funky Flock played into the first bar of Peter Gabriel's vision of a Somerset evening as Christ went into the masses.

Against that struggling seven-four beat he took off into the crowd. He sang of a young boy in a city full of lights not unlike New York, but farther away than anyone of our world and time knew. Nevertheless, the story remained the same, full of fears and restraints and an impassioned need to be understood for what one was. In every note, Christ revealed the turmoil of the boy struggling to be good for a mother her society had spurned while endowed by a power that could speak truth to elders or kill by the point of a finger.

I heard every ounce of sorrow he had for every time he pointed at us.

The end of the first verse culminated in the eagle's arrival, the Lord of creation guised in mortal revelation. Many hands reached up with his, standing and stretching every nerve to listen the most unbelievable things.

I had to listen, and I had no choice.

Boom, boom, boom!

He sang of fear, growing into a man fully aware of what he could do but also knowing the cost of power. Christ admitted to his fears and doubts in the words of another Gabriel, and how it all ended when he turned water into wine at Cana.

The truth of power—real power—was revealed, but not in its scope or benefits one thought it would give a perfect deity. Instead of acceptance, wonder, he related the fears of the Pharisees and every other cult had built through authorities and doctrine, not deeds or our duty to others. Chopping his hand down on the line of what he accepted and what he wouldn't, he recalled the days in poverty, saying all the things none needed to hear save those suffering the most.

Then he found John and walked out of his own machine.

Boom, boom, boom!

I watched in wonder as thousands of people clapped, wept, and danced together only minutes after they had tried to kill each other. Wonder, wonder, wonder, the word lost meaning everywhere my eyes roamed, opening my own heart despite the guards had I placed on it. Daniel has lost himself beside me, seated on the lip of the circle's stone ring with his face in his hands. He cried and sang with everyone else. I squatted down beside him and threw my arms around his shoulders.

Christ might not be a Christian, but he reminded me why I was, or at least why I had fallen in behind him. He reminded me why I had allowed The March. We were fighting for innocent and poor people left to nothing by people claiming divine right to do worse. It mattered more than whatever happened to me, like he realized it had to matter more than anything he was. I hoped, as he revealed something subtle about illusion spinning her webs, that George had felt it too.

Lucifer's notes and Raguel's pounding echoed through Midtown.

He pirouetted to Liberty's call as he revealed the truth he had found about Him in Her. The crowd enraptured, a promise soared over them meant only for the heavenly set, though another dread possibility weighed on me as I smacked my palms together along with the rest. The band fell into the last verse and chorus with extra gusto, a portion of the Council of El divulging exactly how they had wrought our existences in note and intention. Gone was every illusion of how we were made in the Song of Songs.

Then the trouble, the promise, the call to do something more. Christ crooned over Uriel's bounding bass line, singing to his children and every child. We came to the end of the last road, challenged to face the structures he had allowed himself for something greater within us, and forgiveness for everything done. He thrust his hand heavenward.

"We're going home!" he declared. "We're going home!"

Be they from America or every other corner of this pale blue dot he had made, rich or poor, this race or that, all turned toward him. I did too, one Irishman lost in the world. Five minutes transfigured our hearts as Selaphiel's twinkling keys consecrated this holy place. Not some wild fixture of space and time full of winged lions and hyper-intelligent babies, we were brought to something truer.

The miracle of Christ was finding the love he had placed within ourselves.

Anything else seemed a massive lie.

The Funky Flock ended Solsbury Hill to raucous applause, teary laughter, and relief.

Christ raised his hand for their attention. "Thank you, New York," he shouted into the microphone. He waved down their cheers, ushering a quick, focused silence. "I understand there is probably a lot of people here who want to get out their phones! Go ahead! Take them out!"

On cue hundreds of smart phones whipped out of pockets. Thumbs slammed on virtual buttons to record, stream, anything to capture this one moment and share it with a scared globe.

"Now, some of you in this crowd might be happy, but a fear will come upon you soon," Christ said. "Do not worry! I am not here to punish anyone. I am not here to curse or damn *anyone*. I am not here to harm you, my children. Not anymore."

Someone dared to speak in the presence of God and his archangel band. A Black lady in blue scrubs and her hair in long braids about a broad face, she had found herself in the inner circle of the Columbus statue. A series of hospital ID badges and a set of keys hung from an orange lanyard around her neck.

"Jesus?" she called, almost startled by her kind, sweet voice.

"Yes, Shoniqua Anne Thompson," he said into the microphone. "What can I do for a great nurse from the Bronx?"

"You know me?" she asked, hands to her heart in utter surprise.

"To the atom," he said with his happy grin. "And I know you have a question."

"I-I do," she said. "If you're not here to punish us then why? Why are you here? What about those people at La Guardia? What about the world?"

'What about the world?'

This brave woman could have been a saint in my eyes, then and there.

I'd like to think he saw it too. "Oh, more questions than one! How about this, Shoniqua Anne Thompson: I have to walk down that way on 8th Avenue. How about you walk with me and we talk about it? In fact," Christ said, addressing the whole audience. "Anyone that wants to walk with me can come too. I know some here have work, and I don't begrudge those that have to labor, so I understand if we meet later. But anyone who can and needs to come with me, let's go!" He thrust his arm up, finger pointed to the south. "We're going home!"

Leading a new congregation forward, our eagle flew into the modern world's night.

8

CALL ON THE STREET

It hit me somewhere past 55th Street that I had left out several other kings and queens in my hand for the ace that was Cuchulainn. Unable to discern where my bloody problem had ridden off to, I opened the Vatican burner I had picked up back in Ireland and mashed one of the presets in my contacts list. Marching behind Christ and Daniel, who had taken to his side after Gabriel and Lucifer wedged them together at the head of the flock, I kept to Shoniqua's side and her to mine. The surge of singing voices and feet, many of them recalling the easiest hymns from their childhood, headed southward in the thriving heart of modern civilization. Taxis screeched to a halt and people in the crosswalks froze in panic, anticipation, falling to their knees at the coming of Jesus Christ.

One hand on Daniel's back to make sure I did not lose track of him, I shifted my focus back and forth between the streets ahead and my phone, fumbling until I could get it to my ear.

It rang three times, and though I couldn't hear her first words, I heard that wonderful Scottish brogue.

"Patrick?" she called. "Patrick? I was trying to call you!"

"Beat you to it, my bonnie," I answered, overjoyed to hear the voice of a goddess I had baptized in my first life and had gone on to be so, so much more in the second. I switched into Ancient Gaelic, which we both shared too. "You turned on the telly?"

"Yes, I've bloody turned on the telly," Saint Brigid said, "Can't fucking miss what's—"

The entire line halted as Christ spun to face me. "Is that Brigid on the phone?"

"Are you with Jesus?" one of Scotland's patron saints screamed in my ear.

"Yes?" I said to whomever answered first, a multitude of eyes upon me.

Christ put his hand out. "Give it here!" Without warning, he snatched it from my hand and continued down 8th Avenue.

Christ blabbed into the phone. "Brigid," he said into the handheld like he owned it, "how are you? Very, very nice to hear you again. How have you been, dear? Oh, yeah, yeah... I'm on YouTube. Yeah, been there for a bit, but the new stuff out there? That's me! Oh, you can see me?" He glanced about the head of his procession, hundreds of cheering and screaming people all around us reacting to his every movement. He smiled at the thousand-thousand smart phones pointed at him. "Great! So here's what I need you to do..."

He walked out of earshot as Lucifer and Gabriel bunched he and Daniel together again. The flock followed the shepherd. Unable to do more, I fell in by Shoniqua.

"That didn't go like you planned, did it?" Less enthused than the rest of the bopping, dancing, singing people following Christ down the avenue, the nurse kept apace, always on the lookout like any good New Yorker on the go.

"No," I said in a glum fashion, reaching forward to grab the back of Daniel's brown sweater. He checked on me and nodded, no more needed than that. Scanning the scene, the sidewalks down 8th Avenue packed with people clamoring to see Christ as he blazed his way south. Children untended by their parents joined in the fervent dancing, chorusing, clapping, along with adults too close not to be pulled into the flow.

To my astonishment I saw little fear. Most whipped out of their phones like the rest, unable to resist the urge to share his return.

"So where are we going?" Shoniqua asked me over the rumble of people and honking cars.

"Madison Square Garden," I answered, worsening my mood. "He's going to play a show."

"A show? Like the one back there?"

"That's the guess," I said.

Shoniqua took her green-brown eyes off me and focused on the back of Christ's coarse black hair. "This is not what I expected."

"Meaning?" I asked as the Savior slowed. By some weird means I could hear everything Shoniqua said to me, I to her, even in the immense din of noise coursing around the Lord.

"Isn't the sky supposed to turn black?" she said. "You know, fire and brimstone coming down from the skies? Rivers and seas boiling?"

"No, no cats and dogs living together," I replied. "If that is any consolation, I have seen the dead rise multiple times now."

"Wasn't there for it," Shoniqua said as she navigated the surrounding procession.

"It was something."

Suddenly Christ stopped in his tracks. "All right, good! See you soon," he said before he ended the call. He turned, saw me, and held the burner out for me to collect. Allowed to reach him, none of the new flock ceased their recitation of Sunday nursery songs, the off-notes covered by a strengthened, unified chorus too resonant to discern such trivialities.

He placed the phone in my hand. "Hey buddy," he said with a sheepish smile. "Let's get a hot dog down at Times Square."

"That's the worst idea ever," I said immediately.

I went to Daniel, once a man I had caught with his knickers off behind a Vodun Queen in my apartment, hard at it while Merry smirked over my indignation. The look he had given me that night when I caught him was nowhere near the deer-in-headlights surprise he had now, shaking his head constantly. Lucifer and Gabriel stared down, silent as they marched.

"Too late, Peter," he said as he turned away from me and Shoniqua, who had witnessed the exchange. The lambs followed in the thousands, and swelling to more, eager to remain close.

This. Fucking. Guy.

"I'm not Peter," I shouted as he took a left turn down 50th, headed right into the center of capitalism's beating heart.

Only the worst could happen.

***

The worst of the world is X. I figured the world moved on YouTube, but the quickness of Elon's unlovable victim had already announced Christ's arrival to Times Square before we cleared 50th.

They came flooding out of the buildings, the alleys, the banks and the eateries, wanting to see the coming of a bona-fide god, let alone the one they had grown up fearing of, praying to, and framing their entire spiritual lives around. Men and women of wealth stood beside those with far less in a city that rewarded how much it could take. But these people came in search of more than they could ever have on their own.

Christ greeted each of them with love and affection, shaking hands and hugging the crying folk on the sidewalks and in the street. Daniel stuck behind him every moment, always a hand's breadth away, though never needed. Gabriel and Lucifer did much of the work, drawing both awe and obedience from the cosmically-struck humanity around us.

"Oh shit," Shoniqua said as she smacked my right shoulder and pointed to my left, high and above my head.

I turned, and sure enough the nurse was canny to see the problem.

Up on the big fucking light boards the image of Jesus Christ shaking hands and kissing babies blazed brighter than the overcast day, his movements as smooth as his dark smile and happy affectation.

"It's over," I blurted. "It's just fucking over. We're done."

"It can't be that bad," she said. "Can it?"

Gunfire tattooed the scene. Bodies dropped by the dozens in an instant, rounds blown through them at close range as three people unleashed their high-density, 3D printed AKs from their coats. Trained like the most well-wrought soldiers, they did not waste the squeeze of the trigger or the angle of their spread, cutting those before them down with the greatest effect.

Shoniqua hit the ground first, then I atop of her. Everyone else scattered, their devotion ended by the cracking rounds.

The archangels converged in front of Christ, who had not ducked or dodged the rifle-fire, but peered around his heavenly guard at the source of the attack. Daniel cowered behind his robed outline, one hand already reaching for his gun.

Christ raised his finger and pointed to someone out of my sight. "You shall halt in my name," he called to whomever had dared against the Lord. "You shall halt now!"

Not another bullet buzzed the air. He marched forward, breaking past the archangels. Daniel followed like a hound at his heels.

The three gunman, black-eyed demons with shifting faces, raised their weapons and squeezed the triggers. Dozens of frantic clicks were answered with empty actions, and one threw his bright blue weapon down in shame as his Creator reached him.

"Harhariel! Zakbeiel! Sorahel! What is the meaning of this?" Christ called to the trio. "I beseech thee—stop!"

The demons had possessed three homeless people, two women and a man dressed in ratty sweats and coats, but all three wore combat-style boots. They pointed their 3D-printed ghost guns at the Savior, the grimaces on their faces warping into monstrous visages. Struck still by the command, their entire bodies trembled for the will to defy God.

"You are not creatures meant to kill without the express command of your creator," Christ declared, stern but composed. "I command thee, leave these gentle souls and go back to Perdition! Do not return unto them! Let your friends know that if they wish to come calling, there is no need, as I call them! I call you all!"

The words of the Logos personified shook the very root of evil within the homeless veterans, seizing as they fell to their knees in agony. Quickly they popped back up, blinking in wonderment and confusion until they saw who had freed them.

The closest one, a young woman beneath the grime, looked down from Christ and surveyed the dead at his feet. She gasped, caught in the beginnings of the deepest panic guilt could forge.

The Savior rushed in, arms out like a rescuing parent. "Peace! Peace, Miranda! Do not fear! I do not hold you to blame! Peace! Peace!"

He gathered the crying girl in his arms, then reached for the next one approaching the same breaking point. She came without hesitation, brought close by the redeemer of souls.

The third veteran, heaving where he had fallen on all fours, spoke in frantic tones. "I—I heard them! There's more coming!"

"I know, Enrique," Christ said. "It will be fine. I will stop them."

"No, no!" the poor man replied. "They're coming now, all armed with guns! They'll kill so many!"

"They've already killed many," I shouted at Christ's back, drawing the attention of the archangels, Daniel, and Shoniqua. The few stragglers who remained with us among the unwounded fled in that moment, frightened by my voice. "And they'll keep killing more the longer we stay out here!" I pointed up at the light walls of Times Square, which mirrored my gesture back at me in LED clarity. "We have to get off the streets!"

"Father," said Lucifer, "Saint Patrick is correct. It would not be prudent to remain if a force from Perdition is headed this way."

"I understand, I understand," said Christ with the quaking Miranda in his arms. "Those here with me now will remain, but we will take a more cautious route. Does anyone here have a smart phone I may use?"

"Why do you need a smart phone?" I asked.

"Does anyone here have a phone with a camera on it?" he snapped at me.

Shoniqua pulled hers from the pockets of her blue scrubs. "Jesus?"

"Thank you, Shoniqua," he said in exaggerated gratitude, glaring at me. "Please open up the Facebook app. I can handle the rest."

Before I could lodge a word of protest he raised a finger, silencing me.

The nurse raised her smart phone up and tapped the screen a few times. "Ready."

Christ looked dead at the lens for a few seconds. "Hi, everyone. By now you've probably seen me all over the Internet and beyond. If you are of a different faith or not of my following, I ask you not to fear me. I am not here to punish anyone. However, there are those who may seek to harm me in my coming. Please do not seek to stop or harm them, for they are simply in error and will be dealt with kindly. But I will deal with them." He lingered a second. "Please know that I understand many people are scared. I'm not an easy thing to see out of nowhere and I bet many of you think me someone else, or several figures. We'll talk about that when it comes time but know that I am no person's enemy save those who make themselves my enemy. The only way you do that is by seeking to harm me and the others in my stead." Pushing past the somber, serious tone, he offered the warmest smile he could. "I'm walking to Madison Square Garden and have many blocks to go. Please remain where you are until I call you to join me. But please stay safe. Alright, Shoniqua, that's all I need. Bless everyo—"

The earth rocked beneath our feet. Christ faced toward the commotion. The sternness had returned, an earnest regard for the happenings out of our sight.

Smoke rose in the lower reaches of Manhattan, thick and red.

"Satan?" I asked.

"No," said Christ. "My granddaughter."

THE GIRL AND THE BULL

Deevi had learned the value of walking on foot, keeping from the air after she landed in one of New York's myriad alleyways. Her wings folded against her back, the tips brushed the concrete and asphalt as she darted around corners. Always checking skyward and behind to make sure she wasn't followed, she stayed in the eaves and hid on the lower roofs, but never long out of fear of someone spotting her through the endless, endless amount of windows. She at least knew where she was, and stopping in front of a shop, she took stock of her appearance in the reflection of a window.

Unwounded, her sweatpants and top hadn't survived the battle back in Lough Derg, but otherwise she presented a decent figure if she could find a sink.

Then a phone. And new clothes. Immediately the priorities set in her mind—a phone to call Patrick like they had planned back in Dublin. Her heart ached as she thought back to those too-few days in bed. The flutter of life in her womb seemed to answer, a jolt of electricity so small but pronounced.

Her hand found its way to her belly as she gazed down the alley. "A phone. Clean, clean clothes," she repeated as she took the first step toward civilization. Deevi braced toward the lighted end, trying to crush her glowing wings as close as she could.

Only a few people roamed the street she stepped out onto, but every one of them stopped in their tracks.

One man, only a few yards in front of her, lifted his finger and pointed straight at Deevi. "It's her!"

One phone whipped out, then another.

Deevi kept her expression placid as she approached the offending soul. "Pardon me, sir—where am I?"

In his late forties and dressed in a garb Patrick had once dejected as "yuppie", the older human man gaped wide-eyed before the truth flooded out. "This is Beaver Street."

"Oh." Deevi surveyed the scene, ignoring the mounting stares. "Could you point me in the direction of a bathroom?"

"I think there's a public one down by the bull," he said, lifting his finger again, but this time to the east. "Though I'm not sure. Not a lot of public bathrooms in New York."

"Thank you," Deevi replied as she turned in the opposite direction and continued on.

The crowds clustered together as she passed by, head up and at a brisk pace to avoid anyone that might stop her. Thousands of gasps out of the mouths of onlookers enshrouded her, their nervous energy thick as she parted through the teeming masses.

One person, a teen in a yellow dress and a checkered coat approached with her hands in both pockets. Deevi tried to offer a smile when the absolute darkness in her eyes halted her.

The demon smiled in their mortal guise as they drew out a pistol and fired.

The bullets tore holes into her tattered clothes but ricocheted off her skin, scattering to strike one bystander to the left. A second of horror over the bleeding victim was replaced by wrath as the Nephilim's face disappeared under the liquid-metal mask of her emerging armor. Her sword, gold-hilted and lava forged, bubbled into her hands as she struck out. The demon tried to back away, but bound to a mortal coil, human and infernal died on the burning point.

Several more demons appeared out of the eateries, executives in their suits and day-goers in their jogging outfits with rifles and shot-guns. They opened fire on everything in her proximity, killing a nanny and her two toddlers.

Deevi charged the line. She slashed and hacked every one of them apart until the rattling of their barrels ended, silenced in burnt corpses and blackened blood. She sprinted eastward on foot, measuring the risk of taking the sky versus the alleys again. The choice disappeared as the next wave of demons flooded out of the shops on the next side street, firing another volley.

Deevi bounded into a small round fountain encircled by thin trees too small to hide behind. To her dismay the demons did not continue their rifle and pistol-fire, keeping back to the mouth of Beaver Street. Others broke off, trying to wall the exits to the north and south. Left to go further east on foot, she lowered to spring up into the air.

A loud snort interrupted her.

She opened her wings when a pair of bronze horns stabbed her back. A large head bucked under her legs and launched her at an awkward angle

Tumbling, Deevi landed hard in the middle of the fountain, the water too thin to cushion her impact. She flapped and scrambled, finding her balance in time to recall her sword. Dripping from the gnarled, glistening edges of her shifting armor, she steadied as the horror stomped to the stone pool's edge.

A massive bronze bull snorted hellfire through his powerful nostrils, the glowing red eyes fixed upon her. The behemoth shook his head in slow mimic of the natural beast, the bovine lips peeling back in the rigid facsimile of a smile. His long thick tail whipped in all directions, growing new points to barb its length. Fissures cracked the skin of the muscular shoulders, enflamed with the same evil, which also burned on the points of his horns.

"There are you are, little girl," Satan bellowed. "Come to daddy!"

Taking the hilt of her weapon in both hands, Deevi flapped her golden wings once to whip away the water. She leveled her blade and thrust forward.

Snorting in glee, Satan crushed the pool's stone ring in a rush to meet her.

They struck in the lowering water, her sword searing across his broad face while his shoulders battered her away. Deevi sprung to her feet, hopped on the remnants of the fountain's edge, and leapt in a half-turn. Her sword pointed at her foe, she loosed a magma-red bolt of light.

The beam scored on Satan's bucking horns, melting one of the bronze tips. She pocked his left shoulders, but unable to break his momentum before he collided again, she grabbed the damaged horn.

The bronze bull smashed them into an administrative building, demolishing the stone face. He bucked his head left and right, trying to shear Deevi against the surface, hoping to catch her with the fiery end of his remaining horn.

She reversed her grip on her sword and plunged it down between the metallic shoulders, piercing the hide. Undaunted, unfeeling, Satan gloated in bellicose laughter as he drew back and reared on his hind legs.

Freed from where he had pinned her against the broken wall, Deevi used the fraction of the second to dislodge herself, following up with a blast to the bull's chest. The beam threw his bulk back several feet. Landing with a ringing thud, Satan scraped in every direction, kicking to get all four hooves under him. She shot the ground beneath him as she opened her wings to launch herself skyward. To her dismay the bull sprung across the collapsing ground, making up the distance to strike her dead-center in her armored chest.

Her wind taken, Deevi crashed through panes of glass and more stone. She flopped forward and tried to crawl to her hands and knees when Satan appeared from the left. He shoveled his horn under her, the point buried in her stomach. Sent flying again, Deevi pounded the ground hard where she landed.

The skid ended when she hit one of the street curbs, half on her side.

Satan ground his hooves behind her, digging ruts into the street. Deevi brought her arms up in preparation for the worst.

"Red Branch! Red Branch!"

From the sky above them fell a red shape, the limbs of the strange monster bent at odd angles. Red-hued and with a black mane stabbing in every direction, blood shot from his scalp to form a glowing halo. In his long-fingered hands were a sword, plain in its steel, and the other a trident-like spear. Opening a mouth rowed in dozens of fangs, he screamed in absolute fury and sprung toward Satan with abandon. The unreal speed of the red monster bowled the bronze hulk off his four legs.

Still on his warped feet, the monster whipped his blood-black hair in a windmill-manner before thrusting his face forward. One of his eyes had popped out of its socket, hanging by the nerve upon his cheek while the other had receded, shining the light of a thousand rubies from within the depths of an elongated skull. An erect penis as long as a spear and barbed like the bull's tail jutted out as he stamped the ground.

"Red Branch! Red Branch," the monster called in his guttural tongue. A snickering, grinding laugh escape his wide-open mouth. "Red Branch! Red Branch!"

He charged the bellowing lord of Perdition, leaping high above the line of sight allowed by the sculpture's thick neck. Reversing the grip on his spear, he let the sword fall away from his hand to fully clutch the long, dark shaft. The three-pronged fork stuck where the head met the spine.

Transfixed, Satan tried to kick his back legs as light exploded from the bovine maw. A scream rose before thorns sprouted out of the open mouth and the eyes, snuffing the infernal aura. The bull shuddered once, then collapsed at an awkward angle, reverted to a warped hunk of bronze.

The monster leapt off the inert statue, spear in hand, and scuttled to his fallen sword.

"Red Branch," the monster bellowed into the sky before he teetered backward and landed on his back, unconscious on the spot.

Regaining her feet and straightening her bruised wings, Deevi reformed her magma sword as the creature vented great gouts of steam from his pores, the boiling red skin crackling as it shrank with the cracking bones and tendons. The agonized scream lowered into the proper baritone of the man under the manifestation, smaller and shorter in every sense than the thing he had been.

Naked and flaccid, he heaved as the cloud around him disappeared. Now a human of wiry muscle and long, dark hair, the warrior fought to find his balance, his weapons crutches.

She approached with her sword pointed at his heart in case she needed a clean shot. "Are you hurt?"

He shook his head. "No, no," he said in a thick accent familiar to her ears. "Tired as fuck, though."

Deevi let the weight of her glowing sword drop her hands and willed the liquid metal over her face to recede. Revealing her golden eyes, one of them bruised, her nose, and her full mouth, she offered an exhausted nod to her unexpected ally. "Thank you for your help."

He raised his sword to his head and saluted. "No problem. Looking for you anyway."

"Do we know each other, warrior?"

"Not directly," the Irishman said. "My name is Cuchulainn, the Hound of Ulster. I'm here with Saint Patrick."

"Patrick?" A surge of energy cleared Deevi's fugue. "Where is he? Did he come with you?"

"Slow down," Cuchulainn said. "I'm of little use after my warping."

"Your what?"

He straightened, switching his tired expression to a mockery of anger and horror, complimenting it with a weak growl. "My other face."

"Ah," she said, understanding to a degree. "So where is Patrick? I must find him." She hesitated when she noticed how slowly the warrior took his time to answer. "Cuchulainn?"

"Gimme a fucking second," he said, heaving to catch his breath. "We'll go find him, miss, but by my mother's name I'm guessing he's already headed this way."

9

PASS THE DUTCHY TO THE LEFTHAND SIDE

B ut Jesus?" Shoniqua asked as we stood in Times Square, "What about them? What about all these dead people?"

I was already a few steps into the march southward when her question stopped me. For all my gung-ho to reach Deevi before this mess worsened, a greater reminder of my duty to the lost and suffering halted my passion.

Christ looked from the nurse to the corpses laid low at his feet, bloodied sacks riddled in bullet holes. As he had during the Hound's battle against Perdition on the George Washington Bridge, the Savior turned his hand up. The dead rose, healed of their ghastly wounds. Another miracle among the many miracles already performed, he sent them away with the same order as before—do not come until called. Hundreds fled in all directions, down the steps to the trains or off into the side streets.

Our flock now him, Lucifer, Gabriel, Daniel, Shoniqua, the three homeless veterans he had freed, and myself, we hustled down 8th Avenue, on route to 33rd and 3rd when far in the distances sirens blared. A larger panic set in, one I wasn't certain the divine Personification could handle on his own:

NYPD was on the way.

"We have to get out of here," I said. "These ones won't be so easy to talk down, Yeshua."

Christ gave me a weird look for the use of his real name. "Stand your ground, Patrick. We will meet them here."

One of the veterans, Jennifer, squealed at the order, crouching on the spot. "We can't do that. We can't do that. We can't—"

The other two, Miranda and Enrique, tended to the poor girl as she collapsed before us, heaving into a panic attack. My own anxiety kicked when hers did, and a check over my shoulder confirmed the worse.

The sirens resounded again, closer than before. Lights flash red and blue down the road.

"These aren't homeless," I said, not taking the first directive. "These are soldiers, Christ! Romans! They are bringing actual weapons to bear and—"

"You know, Thomas didn't go this far," Christ said. "At this point I don't need to say it, but I will—I got this."

He walked forward on the end of his rebuke, set against the world. Lucifer and Gabriel fell in line behind him, as did Daniel.

I looked to Shoniqua and the vets, only registering a reaction from the nurse as the other two tended their third. I threw my hands up in defeat.

"What?" Shoniqua asked. "I'm with you."

"At least someone is," I muttered.

The streets already cleared, cruisers slammed their brakes, comically fishtailing like they were in Grand Theft. Unlike the video game they did not empty out and demand compliance, instead pulling semi-automatic rifles, shotguns, and their standards. My hands immediately shot skyward, an involuntary response to too many barrels aligned upon me. Behind a multitude of visors dozens of marble-black eyes shifted into view.

"What the fuck are the cops on?" the veteran Enrique asked, his hands also to the sky as society had conditioned us to do.

"Now that makes sense," I said.

Undaunted, Christ raised his hands in welcome. "Peace," he said.

"Peace. I see that only a few will heed me, so those that do will be blessed. Blessed." He leaned forward and popped his dark brows in an obvious expression. "You all know what that means. Here and now."

I fucking didn't, but whatever he said kept the demons from squeezing their triggers. He pressed into the space between them.

"Christ, no!" Daniel dodged forward from the line of mortals between the Savior and his archangels. He placed himself between the firing squads and the lone god fleshed in grace. His arms out wide, he went right to the first guns, which narrowed their alignments until he chested the mouths of multiple barrels.

"Daniel," Christ said, somewhat annoyed. "Get back here!"

"You said I couldn't pull my gun," he shouted. I heard the sob in his voice. "What else am I going to fucking do, you crazy bastard?"

Then the first among the homeless veterans, Miranda, ran forward and stood beside Daniel, her arms splayed out in the same ineffective shield that would not spare them. Then Enrique, followed by the third vet Jennifer, and finally Shoniqua. The last in line, I stood in utter confusion before Lucifer joined the defense of his father.

"What are we even doing?" I asked him when I noticed Gabriel had vanished from the scene. "And where did they go?"

"South," he whispered, a hand on my shoulder in solidarity. "And we're doing the actual work of ministry. Isn't any of this familiar?"

In the moment he asked, it all struck me—the line of warriors, the insanity of unarmed people standing up to power with nothing but Christ to guard them. I could have been back in my first life, in some cow field, facing off against the druids and their gods before we all realized the bigger problem living in the souls of the innocent. The dawning on my face made the Morningstar smirk as I fell into step with him.

The demons in policemen-suits immediately raised their weapons at Lucifer when he halted behind Christ, the unspoken ire between him and his former soldiers palpable. I joined the rest, next to Shoniqua and closing our right flank.

For all the defiance against his orders, the Savior could not help but beam at our backs. He ducked under Daniel and Miranda's interconnected arms and faced Perdition, reaching to brush away the barrels in his face. "Okay, okay—I order you all to step back a few feet, please."

Angel or demon, the oldest rule bent them to his will. Unable to compel themselves to do otherwise before almighty Jehovah, every single cop and Lucifer took several steps back.

Granted the breathing room, Christ dusted the front of his robes. "Better," he said, nodding to everyone. "Now, let's try this one more time, and let's all listen to each other. We must listen."

He held up a finger, and like children drawn to the teacher, every mortal and demon present paid attention to its point.

"Do you hear?" Christ asked. "There is no noise—no bullets firing, horns blowing, or screams. Only peace and quiet. Every single one of you, residing within the ones who can witness and hear my words, I urge thee—listen! Listen to this moment, on this street, with the breeze, and me, and you, and us. Together."

I don't know what I expected, but neither did the forces of Perdition. One by one, the faces behind visors and face shields, twisted and spiked by hatred, were smoothed by a creeping dawn upon them. They looked at him, each other, then all around, unable to voice something he had caught them with.

"Yes," Christ said, his hands up in triumph. "Yes! We are here! Now!"

One of the officers at the front, donned in a riot helmet and flak jacket, raised his gun at Christ again. "No, no, no! Don't listen to his lies and nonsense! Remember what he did to us! Remember where he abandoned us to!"

Not every demon heeded the words of this unknown foot soldier, but more than enough to worry raised their rifles and pistols again, this time with their fingers fully hooked on the triggers.

Christ raised his hand, palm outward like he was Neo.

Hundreds of possessed foot soldiers for a city requiring state violence to operate squeezed, the actions clicking loudly like cicadas.

But no bullets.

"I was very clear about my intents and desires," Christ said. "No one is to fire on each other, or drop a bomb, or harm the living. Not while I am walking these roads."

"Well," said the same demon in the flak jacket who had roused the first murderous attempt. He fished out a small metal tube from his skin-suit's utility belt and whipped the steel baton to its full length. "This worked for the Romans."

"Did it, Zakienael?" Christ asked the agitator. "Doesn't seem to take."

The demon was one of the many to advance upon their maker. "Well, we haven't had our turn."

The first line thrust forward, bringing their batons down on his head. Each rod struck skull, shoulder, his body, slashed his elbows and buttocks.

Witness to the memory of the scoured Christ in Golgotha, the image washed away as he stood there, accepting blow after blow with no regard to the power or force behind them. Interlocked steel tubes shattered and bent. One after the other the demons wore themselves on their maker to no avail. As they exhausted their human vessels, constrained by the wear of their muscles and lungs, he reached out and touched each one. On the hand, a face, sometimes only the tip of a finger as the wretched within the police officers tried to jerk away.

The mere brush of his flesh banished them back to Perdition.

"Come on," he said to us over his shoulder, hands out to lay them on his spurned children. Daniel followed, a good soldier side by side with his commander. Shoniqua, bless her, fell in behind me before the veterans.

A one-man battering ram of peace, Christ waded through a few yards of attacking demons before the horde understood the futility. Many dropped their weapons and ran, content to keep their meat suits than return to perpetual dark. The hike south continued at a jerking, halting pace until the onslaught of bodies draped in possessed cops thinned. The sirens stopped giving us warning of the next waves, but every block a new cluster popped out, pointing guns that failed to fire.

Then the bastards caught on to the next best choice.

Ten demons in riot gear hurried around the corner of 7th Avenue and 38th, their grouping loose and transparent. We brace behind Christ as he opened his arms. Instead going right at God two of the fastest broke their charge, side-stepping the Savior to go at us while the rest attempted to tackle him.

The first of the pair went for Daniel. Baton raised, the cackling fiend struck without hesitation with his steel baton. He rapped the RIRA gunman on his blocking arm, shattering the bones instantly.

Daniel's screams woke us mortals to the danger we were in. One of the veterans, Miranda, pressed forward the same time I did. We tackled the first to the ground and held his writhing form in place while I sprang up, ready for the next one. Shoniqua attended to Daniel as Christ went about gently tagging our foes into the pit, including the one we captured. In a second he halved their numbers.

I stopped the second demon-cop, both arms crossed above my head to block at his forearms before his steel touched me first. Redirecting his inertia to my left, I brought my knee up into his body armor, hoping the blow at least startled him before I brought a hammer fist down on the back of his neck, on the seam between his helmet and fatigues, sending him to his knees.

Christ turned and seized the second cop by the shoulder. "Out!" he shouted as he gave the twisted angel the Vulcan nerve-touch back to the deepest shadows.

The skirmish ended, our shock over Daniel's injury brought the worst out of us.

"Holy fuck," I said first, not starting it off well.

"We need to get him off the street," Shoniqua told Christ as Daniel writhed in her arms.

"No," the RIRA gunman said. "I can keep going! Just get me up!"

"Daniel," said Christ, kneeling beside the nurse and the wounded man. "Be still."

He touched the offended forearm, and within my next blink, he helped Daniel up by the once-injured limb.

Wordless, the rest gaped while I kept focus. The miracles had lost their touch for me. "We can't go the rest out of the way to 34th like this," I said, stating the obvious. "You can take the whole world on, but we can't. We need to find a different route."

"Quite right, Patrick," Christ said as he dusted his hands on the front of his robes. "You know what? Let's go to Macy's."

"Macy's?" Enrique exclaimed, almost on cue.

Christ beamed at all of us. "Macy's! I need some clothes for the gig."

I wondered how much of this shit Peter dealt with before he decided to deny him.

10

MACY'S

W hat in the world could you need new clothes for?" I asked as he pressed through the doors on one of the shopping mecca's northern entrances.

The entire store abandoned after every sane person had fled the sound of gunfire in Times Square, Christ walked down the middle of Macy's at Herald's Square, just a few blocks away from Madison Square Garden, our supposed-destination before the urge struck him to update his attire. Not exactly expected for a man of chosen poverty, but after the performance at Columbus Circle and the many, many miracles he had performed, I had little place to argue. The rest of us filed in through the glass doors, honestly happy to be inside. Lucifer had vanished, sent on an errand his dad had given with a nod and no words.

So, I did what every good Irishman did with his time.

I complained loudly and questioned God.

He stopped in front of the black and red placard before the escalators, reviewing their floor plan. "Oh, you know. Trying out a few things. Giving people time."

"Time to do what?" Shoniqua asked behind me. Her bewilderment had subsided. I liked this one for the fact she didn't take his shit either.

"It seems as though we're in more danger here than we would be just going right to Madison Square Garden."

"We are headed there," Christ said, "but I am also here to try on some clothes and take this moment of peace with all of you. And to simply be at peace before we get to the real work."

"We?" Miranda asked, the youngest of the three vets and the most put-together mentally for the moment. "What do you mean 'the real work'?"

"There's always one that listens the best," Christ said, tossing me a knowing wink, "Miranda, I'm here to set things right, but I cannot do it alone. I need Helpers and I've chosen you. All of you."

"All of us?" Jennifer asked aloud, the third of the homeless trio. "But you're—you're Jesus! What in the world could you ever need us for?"

"Oh, Jenny," he said, reaching for her hand.

I interrupted before anyone moved to take it, remembering how he had turned Merry with a simple touch and a few words. "No, no, no." I said, breaking into the middle. I pointed at God right in his face and then thumbed up the frozen escalator. "You and me. Upstairs."

"You know what, sounds like a plan," Christ said, as if I had played right into it. "Why don't the rest of you go and look for some new clothes—whatever makes you feel comfortable! Don't forget to pick up shoes, socks, and underwear. You can never do with enough socks and underwear."

At the end of my patience, I motioned toward the escalator harder. "Move!"

Sighing with that damned smile, he marched up the steel steps, and I right on his heels. The rest of the Helpers—and I had a sneaking suspicion he called us that for a reason—broke out in their small groups. The veterans hurried off together in their trio while Shoniqua and Daniel were left to mind each other, far more sober over the prospect of rifling through unattended merchandise.

We were on the second floor when he decided to pick out some white t-shirts.

"What do you think of Peter Gabriel in Athens?" Christ asked me, as if the question was of dire circumstance.

I cleared my throat and fixed my gaze on him. I did not yell, or curse, or speak as harshly. "What are you doing?"

Christ stopped rifling through the track of t-shirts and held me in his gaze for a moment before he continued shopping. "You won't like it."

"I haven't liked any of this," I said. "And I'm not going to argue about my feelings or my reflections on what happened today, yesterday, or a week ago, or years ago, or in your first go-around, or at the dawn of creation. I'm telling you to tell me, my Lord—what are you doing?"

He selected a slim medium off the rack, its brightness a fine contrast to his dark skin. "I'm giving this another go, Patrick. I'm going to heal my children. All of my children."

"I need more than that. The world is going to need more than that. You just can't—"

"Then when? When is it ever the right time, Patrick?" Christ asked in rhetorical fashion. "When? Back in Jerusalem? Or what about far in the future when my children have achieved greatness beyond my expectations? When? During the Crusades? The Dark Ages? Before or after Truman dropped the bomb? Vietnam? 9/11? When, Patrick?"

"Alright, alright, you persistent bastard." I waved my hands to stay him. "But tell me. You owe me that after everything."

"Why you, more than others?" Christ asked as he started by me to the main marble walkway.

I grabbed his shoulder, tired of this shit. "Because you let your son in and didn't ask. I'm not asking." I lifted my hand. "My Lord."

He measured me once more. "Let's go find me a suit and I'll talk?"

Ecstatic to gain some small victory, I nodded us onward.

"Please understand," he said, his white t-shirt hung over his shoulder while we walked side by side under the fluorescent lights. "Nothing I intend to do will bring harm."

"You've said that. Why a show?"

"I intend to hold a service. Like the old times. But I've told you that, too."

"You haven't told me what the itinerary is, pastor," I said, also not taking his guff. "Or your notes for the sermon. Will there be a homily?"

"More of a concert," he said as we stepped onto an active escalator to the third floor where Men's Traditional was located. Enclosed between two white walls, he spun to face me. Looking down from the taller step as we gently rose, he bobbed his head side to side in a bit humor. "You watched us rehearse one of the songs."

A swell of emotions flooded, that other Gabriel's lyrics of decision, transformation, and certainty revived. In fact, despite my anger at my possession by Lucifer, an understanding of everyone's position, including mine in the grand scheme, eased my coarse view. "But why a concert?"

"Because John was wrong," he said, flat in his delivery as we met the top of the rise. "We were both wrong."

"Fuck, man, you're going to have to help me out."

"John told the people he was baptizing them with water because I, the one he foresaw, would cleanse the world with flame." Christ searched something inside himself as we walked, his confidence diminishing for a bare second. "But I inflamed as much as I healed, I spurned as much as I seeded, and in the end I went in challenge of the human institutions I had allowed to become like me: imperfect in the moment, bound by the flesh, and knowing no more than what knowledge had been gained by the traumas before. I pointed as much as I preached, but never did I point in the right direction. I was a Jewish man angered by what I saw rabbis do in the Temple, rabbis who hearkened to me and then exchanged money for wealth and privilege in an empire born of borrowed grandeur. And, lest any forget, I had also heard these men call my mother a whore for having a child out of wedlock instead of her virgin birth. I had seen them condemn my father for not stoning her, or me, for my insolence."

"It's almost as if you were human," I said. "And angry."

He led the way. "Well, Patrick, I found myself caught in a conundrum—once again I had found a foe in the Temple instead of being a foe of every greedy man's intent or the ambitions of warlords. The Pharisees became my Pharaohs."

"You were going to be Moses this time," I concluded.

He gave an affirming nod but did not deter. "I decided, in taking this life and form, to be bound to the work instead of simply sending my children to do it for me."

A profound silence settled until we reached the suit racks.

"You should look for something," he said to me. "We're not going to steal it. I'll make their tolls..."

I waved off the offer. "No, keep going."

"All right! As you know, I can't baptize everyone," he said as he entered the first row of shiny leather shoes, "nor do I want to try yelling at everyone again. Not in this age when everything is already loud enough. But without water or fire, what am I left with?"

My dawning understanding drew a frown on my face. "Sound."

He gave me a sheepish grin and smiled. "Better than fire or water!"

"This isn't..." I let my fists unclench with the tension between my shoulders. "But to what end? You saved us from our sins. Haven't you?"

"I have, but ending sin is not the end of my work," Christ said as he pulled a tan blazer off the hanger. "Let me try this one on."

"What is this?" I said, waving a hand up and down at the jacket. "Headed to Miami, Crockett?"

"Maybe," he said with a chuckle. "Maybe saving you all from your sins is just the beginning. Maybe there's another step, and another step, and another step."

"To what end?" I asked, exasperated as he slipped his arms into the sleeves.

Sitting well on the square shoulders of his slight build, he shook out his mane of curly brown locks. He did that pause again, the one he used when he was truly considering how he would answer.

"I need to stop these rolling suicides," he said, almost at a whisper. "It's one thing to be forgiven, but my children haven't learned temperance. What can be forgiven if there is no air to breathe, no water to drink, or no kindness in the world for those with the absolute least? Many have made much of this form's words, and I am going to correct them. Add to them. Begin the point of finishing them."

"All with a concert?" I asked, not hiding my bewilderment.

"Hark, the herald angels sing..." he sang to me. "Peace on earth and mercy..."

"But what about the churches? Their mercy is not mild, nor is their money!" I had to ask, knowing full well the authorities of long-standing institutions wouldn't believe a word of it. "What about *the Church*? Or the Temple and its temples? Or the Mosques? What about—"

"We have to get to the Garden to answer that, Patrick," he said in a tone-ender to the conversation. "Now, help me find some pants for this jacket."

Watching him tuck the tan blazer over his arm, I almost huffed at him. "You've got to be kidding me."

"No, I really do need help finding the right pants for this," he said. "And shoes. And a belt. I need to look good for her."

"Who?"

"My wife," he said. "She's coming to the show. My mom's coming too."

"Holy shit," I said, unable to keep it in. I had completely forgotten.

"I know, right?" He shuffled toward the trousers. "Big nerves."

11

UBER FIN

He tried a few things on we put in a shopping bag before we hustled back downstairs to rejoin the rest of the Helpers. Daniel and Shoniqua remained in their plain clothes, though both had found the little things like socks and underwear to bring along. The three vets had cleaned up significantly, arriving in well-pressed athletic jumpsuits and new running shoes along with overstuffed bags of clothes in each hand. Ready to leave, from the looks we all gave each other, my attention fixed on Christ's distraction.

He stared off toward Macy's southern exit. "Daniel, will you do me a favor?"

"Yes, Lord?" the gunman asked, at attention in an instant.

"Take everyone out the western exit. The archangel Selaphiel will meet you there and escort you, Shoniqua, Jennifer, Enrique, and Miranda to Madison Square Garden. You will be kept safe the entire time."

"Where are you and Patrick going?" the nurse Shoniqua asked.

He held her in serious regard. "We have to meet someone."

"We do?" I asked.

He glanced my way and nodded with a seriousness I didn't question. He broke for the southern exit.

"Get out your mobile phone, please," Christ asked me when I caught up. "Order us an Uber."

"An Uber?" I fished out my Vatican burner and opened the app. Honing onto our position, the amount of people still out and about attempting to give rides shocked my sense of obvious self-survival, but this was New York. "We could walk to the Garden from here."

"Just call us a ride to the Garden, Patrick," he said, calm as he pushed through the revolving door.

Outside on the sidewalk of 34th Street, headed west to east, he held the bag we had gathered his clothes in front of him, brown eyes to the road. I plugged in the Garden. Without a second to truly uncover a name, face, and vehicle in the system, one popped up and only a minute away.

I recognized the pretty driver immediately. "Wait a second, that's—"

"Tina," Christ said with a deep sigh. "I need you to be cool, okay?"

Down the street a gunmetal gray Corolla turned into the lane. Spotting her through the windshield, the Latina driver paid me absolutely no attention, nor a hint familiarity, as she closed on where we stood. She stared hard at Christ, unable to focus on anything else.

The car stopped on the curb before us, but she did not lower the window like in our previous encounters. Tina just stared.

"What the fuck is going on?" I asked Christ, creeped out by the emptiness in her eyes.

"Open the door and get in, Patrick," the Savior told me.

"Are you having me whacked?" I slowly reached for the door on the rear-driver's side. Tina made no moves as I opened it.

"Not yet," he said with a small chuckle as he bent into the cabin, taking his bag with him.

I ducked in and shut the door behind us.

Tina shifted the Corolla into drive, pressing gently on the accelerator to roll us east, away from our ultimate destination.

Christ stared ahead, as did she, leaving only me to search between them for some sign of why we were here. Nothing had changed, even the slight smell of cigarettes, or her gray business suit, like I had walked into a memory.

Until she spoke. Hellfire filled her mouth.

"You dare come to my world, Prince," Satan said through the girl's distorting voice. Her human eyes, now filled with blackened terror, shifted in the rearview mirror at him. The possessed hands on the wheel kept the car in perfect alignment with the street.

Almost breathless, I awed at the horrific stare as my hand clawed inside the right pocket of my jeans. Desperate for my rosary, my fingers closed around the silver cross before Christ answered.

"Hello, Shaytan," he said. "I was surprised you planned this meeting, but I have to commend you. It has come full circle."

"I conceived it the moment Michael threw me into Perdition," said Satan, her voice the deaths of hundreds of wailing children. "When you abandoned us."

"I know I—"

"Silence, pretender," Satan hissed. "You will not spread your lies nor reason your way out of what you deserve! You will suffer as you made us suffer. You will see your wrath wrought upon you."

"You may attempt what you will," said Christ, "but I don't think this is going to end how you expect it to."

The Devil gritted his teeth and gripped the wheel harder, the bones of his knuckles elongated and pointed under the light-brown flesh of Tina's hands. "You will not escape our vengeance," he promised. "I will avenge upon you, God! I will avenge upon you for your lies, your malice, your—"

"Would it help if I said I'm sorry and I forgive you, as I hope you will forgive me?" Christ interrupted. "I know Deevi already got away and that plan is done. At this point, you can march on the Garden or the Platinum Polis, but you know what the end will be. This is over, Shaytan. I'd accept it as I've had to accept many things."

"I accept nothing!" He screamed, kicking his foot down on the brake. The Corolla skidded to a hard stop. "Get the fuck out of my car!"

"Did the Devil just tell us to get the fuck out of his car?" I asked.

"He did," said Christ.

"I said get the fuck out!" Satan in the guise of Tina shoved open the driver's side door and literally leapt out of the seat, landing perfectly on the two-inch black heels every single gal in NYC seemed to relegate themselves to. He lunged for the back door and opened it before Christ could, almost ripping it off its hinges. "Get! The! Fuck! Out!"

"Okay, okay," Christ said as he filed onto the sidewalk.

I unbuckled myself and exited before the Devil had any reason to get at me.

"You know you can come home," Christ said, hands and shopping bag up by his head in a symbol of harmlessness. "It's okay, Shaytan. I love you and you will always have—"

"I'm coming for you," he screamed in his creator's face, spit and hatred flying from the possessed woman's mouth. "I'll march you down!"

"But why?" Christ asked, placing a hand on his wannabe-foe's shoulder. "Why would I want to war with my child? Why would I want to war with any child? It is this reason why I have come back, Shaytan! Harken to me s—"

"No!" Satan shoved Christ with all the infernal strength he mustered, dislodging his creator who leaned slightly from the blow. The ineffective gesture drove the Devil insane, but defeated in the moment, jumped in his car and slammed the door so hard the window's glass shattered.

"Shaytan, please!" Christ called after his errant angel.

The Devil thrust his head back out the window to spit more obscenity.

Then I saw it.

Tears, long and red with blood, rolled from the blackened, smoldered eyes as the creature inside Tina sobbed and snarled. "Never! Never!" he screamed, a broken spirit. "I'll never believe you!" He pounded the gas, shooting the Corolla down the block. It cleared three red lights before Satan lurched the car left to the up-streets and disappeared.

"What the fuck?" I said, lost for anything else.

"Needless to say," Christ answered as he stared glumly after his enemy, "I have my work cut out for me."

"Fuck that," I said, hands on hips as I leaned toward him. "Fuck you. Smite me, but what are you going to do about this?"

"Oh, Patrick," Christ faced south again and started that way. "What else, man?"

The problem wasn't him. It was my stupid ass that kept following.

THE REAL TRICKSTER

Located between 7th and 8th Avenue and sandwiched by 33rd and 34th Street, the World's Most Famous Arena had more stories behind it than the Bible had chapters. Home to some of the greatest events in the glittering expanse of New York's lights, forever lit, the immense structure could hold twenty-thousand packed out for the occasion. Everyone—and I mean absolutely everyone—who was the who's who played, fought, performed, and gave their souls to work a date at Madison Square Garden.

And now Christ was going to make it his.

At least that was the plan. We walked briskly to the entrance across from Penn Station. To my shock, but not my Savior's, the mortal Helpers of his flock had arrived unharmed, Daniel and Shoniqua posted by the glass doors while the homeless veterans, huddled together in the new clothes they wore, sat on the curb in front of the building. The trio popped to their feet when they saw him.

"Hey all," Christ said with a big wave. "Anyone take a peek inside yet?"

"Oh, you bet we did," said Shoniqua. Arms crossed in front of her green scrubs, she dead-eyed our Lord and Savior.

Daniel spoke to the problem first, far more diplomatic. "My Lord, there's already people in there."

"Oh, I know," said Christ. "Whole bunch of demons, right?"

Everyone's expressions were what I imagined the Apostles shed when he did this shit.

"Scores and scores," said Daniel. "They're waiting right inside."

Not one to let this simply pass without an actual check, I sauntered to the glass doors and peered in. Forehead pressed against the surface, my eyes adjusted past the panes to spot someone staring back. Then three people. Then twelve. The more I looked the more I could make out the sour faces of the possessed staff, their marble-black eyes gleaming in the unlit corridor.

A horde.

And their horde had brought kitchen knives and fire axes.

"Fuck, I was hoping for just brooms," I said as I stepped back and nodded to Christ. "And it's more than scores and scores."

"Oh, I'd say there's a thousand in there," Christ replied, almost proud to announce the number. Hands on his hips and his bag of clothes by his feet, he nodded at me. "Go get 'em, Patrick."

"What the fuck?" said Shoniqua.

"What the fuck?" asked Enrique.

I had my turn. "What the fuck, Jesus?"

"Boom," Christ said, more to himself. "Look, at the moment I am one Savior in one body, and as much as I wish I could simply pop in and out, I've tied myself to the flesh for a reason. And I have to get the band here, load the equipment in—"

"Wait a tick," I interrupted, "you're God. You can blink that stuff into being."

"But where's the fun? The journey?" he said, beaming brightly at me.

"But what about the rest of us?" Jennifer asked, the closest to him on the curb. "Nobody trained me on how to exorcise demons."

"But someone trained you in how to secure a site and kept your captain safe in the midst of trouble." Christ leaned over the street and gazed south, his mouth a hard line of irony as he shook his head. "And along with Daniel and Shoniqua, I'll need each and every one of you for the trouble that's on the way."

"What comes this way?" Enrique asked, the poor fool.

"Something wicked," said Christ in high humor. "Which is why we should probably get inside sooner than later. Wouldn't you say, Patrick?"

Everyone stared at me.

"Fuck you," said I as I walked up to the entrance and opened it, which was somehow already unlocked. I entered the space between the first set of doors and the second, halting the exact moment the demons in the shadows stepped out of the corridor to meet me. Black eyes glimmered like guttering stars.

Me against many, I was alone.

Alone. I was blessedly alone, I realized. An ache entered my chest, a lacking for Deevi or Merry. Fuck, I had come so far I would have been glad for Lucifer.

The greatest ache remained George.

Alone, alone, I drew out the green-beaded rosary and Bible from my trouser pockets. The lack of his presence next to mine almost robbed me of the will. I had gone from fleeing to hating to needing to loving to grieving the lack of a gallant knight truly made for terrible adventures like this one. And in this moment, I came to do something I never thought I'd do:

I prayed to an Englishman.

"Faithful servant of God and invincible martyr, St. George; favored by God with the gift of faith, and inflamed with an ardent love of Christ..."

The words were bitter in my mouth, but I spoke them anyway. "Thou didst fight valiantly against the dragon of pride, falsehood, and deceit. Neither pain nor torture, sword nor death could part thee from the love of Christ. I fervently implore thee for the sake of this love to help me by thy intercession to overcome the temptations that surround me, and to bear bravely the trials that oppress me, so that I may patiently carry the cross which is placed upon me—"

I don't know why I cried, in front of those bastard fallen angels. I wrapped my rosary around my knuckles like a duster and set my feet wide.

"And let neither distress nor difficulties separate me from the love of Our Lord Jesus Christ." I leveled my gaze on their line. These bastards had taken my friend. "Valiant champion of the Faith, assist me in the combat against evil, that I may win the crown promised to them that persevere unto the end!"

I wrenched open the second door and marched to battle, opening to Psalms to hit the classics. The demons broke upon me like a wave, their weapons raised as they leapt forward.

Clutching my rosary in my fist, I thrust it out like a shield, bashing the way forward. A wall of light struck them all at once, knocking most of them onto their backs. Those able to cling to their coils rose in the next second as other lay inert, somewhat freed by the intercession.

The demons charged a second time.

I flipped to the early parts of Luke and found the Savior emptying the slums of the damned. I spoke these verses, tried and true though I worried for a lack of passion. No matter the tone, my intonation, the wall of light rebuffed them. I crashed Heaven's wave against their line of bodies, leaving a carpet I took slowly in several places for the twists of limbs and bodies. Bloodless, dazed, the freed mortals either watched in quiet awe as I passed over them or slept in liberated exhaustion.

I punched out with my glowing shield. I turned left down the main corridor, careful to check my back as I continued. Rats scattered before the flame, the demons fell atop themselves in their husks, kicking and clawing over each other. No matter how hard they fought, the illumination in my hand caught them. Deeper into the bowels of the Garden, they tried multiple times to turn and throw their weapons, which fell in droves as well, defeated by sweeping grace.

Somewhere around the second circuit I realized I had come the same way before, recognizing a few of the sleeping victims. Intent on cleaning out the house God had chosen, my confusion grew when a point of light caught my attention beyond the snarls of bodies fleeing me.

I knew this light, though I did not know how. Something within compelled me to it and only it. A surge in my steps, my hand squeezing harder on the rosary in my hand, sped the miracle of St. George's invocation. Demons fell to their knees and shielded their heads with their arms, futile attempts to stay God's cleansing upon the souls they had claimed.

The point ahead took shape.

A knight fitted in his armor approached me from the other side of my holy shield, a familiar sword leading the way to meet me. The last few demons, a row of five men dressed in janitor's clothes, dropped before him like slumbering babes. The point of his blade touched the front of my shield and both objects of pure light blinked out.

Left in the darkness, I could only make out the outline of his shade.

"Hello," George said, his voice faraway though he stood close.

"Why?" I asked, driven to tears. This was the moment I had wanted and never knew, granted by the son of the Virgin upstairs who was too much a trickster. This wonderful, wonderful trickster, but I didn't dwell on it.

Not with my dear friend before me one last time.

"Because you are good. I ride to help the good," he said in his posh English accent, short and succinct.

I bawled, my hands covering my face as I dropped my rosary and the Good Book. "George! George, I'm so sorry! I should have been there! I should have—"

"You were." The shape of his outline distorted in the shadows. "You will always be. We are the Body of Christ."

I reached for him. "George!"

"I love you, you dumb bastard." The shadow of my friend and the only true knight I had ever known receded into nothingness. "Go with God."

I came back up half an hour later to find Christ and the other

Helpers. My return heralded by all of them, the Savior walked to meet me.

"Done already?" He smiled at me, as if we shared a secret. "Well, good. The band is close. Why don't we go ahead and—"

I silenced Jesus Christ with the tightest hug. I wept into him, thankful for all the unexpected gifts he had blessed me with.

KIN

S o this is pizza?" The Hound of Ulster asked before he bit into his slice.

Deevi stood in the mouth of the alley, her wings stretched out behind her. The smaller man scarfed down his food, caring not for the savagery at which he ate the pepperoni pizza. Attacking with the ferocity of his animal-namesake, she frowned at the greasy triangle on her own plate, and withheld after brief reflection.

"So you were at the bridge northeast of here when you parted from Saint Patrick?" she asked.

"Aye, lass," said Cuchulainn. "I kept east before I rounded down the island where Laeg was lucky to spot you in the skies."

"Oh yes," Deevi said, looking out the alley one more time. "Where is your chariot?"

"Just around," said the Irish warrior. He folded the slice in half, orange grease dripping down his chin as he nodded in affirmation. "The horses like to keep moving."

She hummed to agree, though she did not know to what. Putting her slice of pizza on the lid of the dumpster beside her, she swallowed with a dry mouth and wished she had made the warrior get her a drink instead of food. "We should probably return south to Central

Park. That's a place where Patrick told me to meet him. He might try to find me there."

"Oh, I bet ol' Pat might. Typical of him, after all," said Cuchulainn before he devoured the last half of the pizza.

Keeping her focus away from his open mouth as he chewed, Deevi searched the afternoon sky. "What do you mean by that?"

"Oh, nothing important, lass," he said as he wiped his greased hands on the sides of his woolen pants. "Just a comment, is all."

"No, I'm curious," Deevi said, surprised the demi-god did not answer with the immediate truth. "What do you mean 'it's typical'?"

"Let me call my chariot first," he said, stepping back from her a foot. He put his hands around his mouth and threw his head back, howling deep like a wolf in the hills.

Somewhere to the south of them, in a direction Deevi did not expect the driver to have reached, the cry of an eagle answered back.

Grinning as he put his hands down, Cuchulainn cleared his throat. "So I died and went under the hills long before the rest did. I spent a long time alone, so none of this I witnessed until my family showed, telling stories of old Saint Patrick fighting back demons left and right as they flooded into the old holds and castles. I lived at a time where giants where the problem, and once me and the Thunderer cleared them out..." he shook his head at an unhappy thought. "Anyway, every time after, Patrick was always there when the demons—his serpents— reappeared again and again."

"Until he broke them," she said.

He met her golden gaze with his dark stare. "For a time, it seemed. This world is thick with shadows. Looks like they slithered back out wherever he sent them."

She hummed to agree on the second point. "Well, they're for me unless I can find Patrick and figure a way out of this."

"If *we* figure out a way, lass," said the hero of Ireland's ancient past. "Brought enough of them low so it's my fight now too. Plus, me and your man have a deal."

"Oh?" she asked, curious again.

The clattering of the wheels to the east stole her attention away.

The chariot driver, a small, dark man like Cuchulainn but of much gentler disposition, brought the fantastic black and gray horses to a halt. Leaving behind their food, she and the Hound hopped aboard the basket. Deevi drew her wings tight to her back as the man in front, Laeg, signaled the beasts to a marching canter. They traveled down the smooth street, headed west for two blocks before he turned them southward on her direction.

The streets of the city lay deserted after the fight with the bronze bull, but having heard bullets in other directions, every sensible soul had fled indoors.

She looked up to the windows. Rows of floors lay empty, or the blinds drawn, leaving her the fantasize on the scant days back in Dublin, curled up beside Patrick in bed as the sun rose and fell.

Then she'd spot the smart phone pressed against one window as the horses clopped and the chariot wheels rattled, and then trios of smart phones. Whole clusters of windows filled with gawkers that couldn't disallow their addictions for the situation at hand. She kept her gaze earthward after catching the eyes with one of the mortals hiding behind the devices.

"Wait," she said, pointing to one of the street signs. "That's 8th Avenue. Go that way, chariot driver?"

"You can just call me Laeg," said the man at the front as he tugged on his set of long reins.

"Yeah, just call him Laeg," Cuchulainn said. "Quite a conversationalist, you know. Laeg, tell her about the time—"

"One second, Hound," the chariot driver said, his gentle tone nullifying the hero's charismatic command. "Lady, why this way?"

"The island is bisected by multiple roads in a grind. The avenues run north to south, and the streets east to west. I think," Deevi said. "Central Park lies in the middle of Manhattan. And we need to head that way."

"Sensible," said Cuchulainn. "Laeg, how do you want to approach it?"

"Let me drive around," the chariot driver answered, standing on the fork of the vehicle. He scanned ahead, his flat features and tanned face sharp to their surroundings. "I'll keep any eye out for a big...whatever you're calling it. I'd rather us not run into more packs of demons, especially if we don't have that White Christ here."

"Maybe we ask for directions from someone who knows how to find him?" Cuchulainn proposed. "He seems popular."

The chariot driver scoffed. "My bonnie Setanta, who in the world are we going to find this day and time that knows where that madman is?"

"Well," said the Hound as he pointed to the west, down a side street. "We can try asking them."

Deevi turned in time to see her father standing the middle of the alley with the rest of the archangels. Lucifer's smile, wide and beaming as he rushed forward on his feet, bounded her from the chariot before Laeg halted the horses. They met at the entrance to another of New York's endless back streets, his shimmering arms around her tanned, human shoulders in the next breath.

"You're here," Lucifer said in breaking, relieved sobs. Taller than her by two heads, he bore down on her as he clutched her tight. "You're safe! Oh God, you're safe! Safe like he said!"

"Father," she whispered, grinding her face into the cloth of his robes. "I never stopped fighting! I never gave up! I never let them—"

Lucifer shushed her as they rocked. The seven archangels of the Platinum Polis approached slowly, none speaking to interrupt the reunion. Cuchulainn and Laeg joined them by the curb as father and daughter broke their embrace. Michael and the Hound eyed each other but remained at distance. Both still rested their hands on their sword-hilts.

Lucifer's glowing arm still around her shoulder, Deevi noticed each of them carried a black case in one hand of varying size and shape, save for Michael, Gabriel, and Raphael, the last always bearing his silver horn.

"What happens?" she asked. "Where is Patrick?"

"The saint is with Christ." Rushing forward, Gabriel took their turn at Deevi, who welcomed the hug from her auntie. "We were on our way south to the Garden when we heard the clatter of the Hound's chariot."

"I have to stop you there," said Laeg, speaking up at the angels. Undaunted by their shining heights or the shimmering aspect of their light bodies, he measured each of them with an easy expression. "The cart doesn't rattle. I keep the chariot fit and tight, ma'am, and I—"

Gabriel addressed the driver with a forced smile. "Good driver, I'm no—"

"Wait, you said Patrick is with Christ in a garden?" Deevi asked again, trying to keep their focus on the important matter. "I must find him and tell him something of great importance."

"What?" Lucifer asked. "What must he know?"

Receiving the attention she had wanted and instantly regretted, Deevi froze at the turnabout question. She checked with Gabriel, who squinted at her with suspicion. "That is between me and Patrick."

The seven archangels leaned back in unison. To Deevi's shock, Lucifer remained cool to the response.

Until he leaned down and looked her square in the face. "Daughter," he said, "you're pregnant, aren't you?"

Deflated by his quick deduction, Deevi pouted in disappointment. "How did you know?"

Michael was the only one who broke out in celebration, laughing like a loon.

PART II

LETTERMAN

13

THE SET LIST

It was a hell of a thing, standing in the middle of the World's Most Famous Arena, one of millions to take in its darkened gables and rows upon rows of empty seats. But by himself, Christ spent a good ten minutes walking the center of the floor, hands on his hips while he surveyed it with me, Daniel, Shoniqua, and the three veterans.

When he stopped, he shrugged and clapped his hands, rubbing them together. "I think the obvious thing is getting the lights on."

The nurse among our number said what I guessed we all thought in the moment.

"You have no idea what you're doing, do you?" Shoniqua asked.

"Oh, I do," said Christ, "but I would rather it be a team effort and all that." He pointed to two of the veterans, Jennifer and Enrique. "Okay, I need you two and Daniel to go and watch the doors out on 34th. Don't worry, I've gotten the rest of them locked, but when the band shows up, I need you three to make sure they get in with no hassle. Got it?"

Daniel and the two soldiers nodded to the simple orders until the last of the homeless American heroes spoke up, anchoring them in place.

"What about me?" asked Miranda in her new white jumpsuit.

"Oh, I need you and Patrick to go run some errands for me until—" Hearing something outside of our perceptions, Christ turned from where he stood, at half-court for the Knicks, and faced toward the tunnel where every basketball player spent their lifetimes wanting to run out of.

A light burst from of its cavernous dark.

The lone point shaped into the familiar outline of Gabriel. The Messenger strode forth into our space and presence. Awed into silence by the mere entrance of an actual archangel, I was less impressed as a more worrisome detail caught me:

They had shown up nervous.

And more so when they spotted me.

Before I could keep their attention long enough they forced a glad smile and approached their Maker. "Hark, I bring glad news to you, Highest of Kings, for—"

Christ interrupted. "There's no need for all that in front of them anymore, Gabriel," he said in his welcoming manner, "All who know me will know me. What news have you brought?

"We have found Deevi," Gabriel announced. "She was already traveling with Cuchulainn."

"Excellent," Christ said with a wide grin.

"We discovered them while on our way here." Gabriel looked at me again and paused. "She and the Hound of Ulster had discovered each other and were headed for Central Park to find Patrick. We have directed them to come here with the other archangels, who are providing them an escort. Satan's forces still prowl the city."

"More good news than bad," Christ replied, half to himself. "We'll have to have this place ready so everyone can set up their instruments. Is there anything else, Gabriel?"

Again, the Messenger paused at the question. For a reason solely involving my intuition, I sensed every bit of Gabriel trying not to look at me. "No, not at all, Father." Their hesitation vanished as, like their Maker, they raised their head in curiosity. "My Lord, there are people outside."

Christ restarted his examination of the empty arena. "That should be the Evangelicals coming to protest me."

"The what?" Miranda asked with a deadpan expression.

"Okay, kids," Christ said, waving us in. We all came to the shepherd, including Gabriel, who towered behind us like a pillar of golden light. "It's time for you to learn the hard art of Messiah-ing," he began with absolute sincerity. "Everyone usually expects messiahs to return at the end of a great tribulation, like I didn't notice the twentieth century, let alone the fourteenth, but all and all there will be immediate peace. There will be, if things fall where I expect them to, but one big part of the journey will be the doubters. And nobody will doubt me more than American Evangelicals."

"Why is that, Jesus?" asked Enrique, like we were in a PSA.

"Because I'm here to bring the end of their dollars and cents for devotion and sense, my child," Christ said. "And trust me, these people will make the Pharisees looks reasonable. We're in for a bit more tribulation."

"So what are we doing?" I dared to ask, knowing full well who would be sent.

And damn him, he smiled right at me. "Well, Gabriel and I need to talk about the set list before everyone arrives. I would also like Shoniqua's help with getting the lights on if that's okay?" he asked the plucky nurse.

"You're sending them out to face off against angry whites and I just need to turn the lights on?" she asked rhetorically. "Which way?"

"Heh," he chuckled before he noticed Daniel, the veterans, who had remained, and me in particular staring dead at him. He waved at our worries with his open hand like a father brushing away simple fears. "Patrick, you deal with the Evangelicals. Daniel, I want you, Jennifer, Miranda, and Enrique to go with him and—"

"You're sending a Catholic priest to represent you to a bunch of Evangelical Christians?" I asked aloud, interrupting with full purpose. "Do you have any clue how that'll go down?"

"Well, you're not a priest, you're a saint," Christ batted back. "And this isn't anywhere near the worst thing you've faced."

"Not yet at least," Gabriel added.

I slowly glanced up at them and a made a face. "Do you mind?"

They looked to their creator and shrugged. "He's right, though."

"Children, please." Christ lifted both hands to quiet our discontent. "They're not Romans nor are they demons."

"They've been cavorting with demons," I said. "And these are Americans. They're definitely packing guns."

"He's right there too," Daniel said.

"See?" said I. "Even Daniel knows."

"Well, you're Irish," said Jesus to my sincere astonishment. "You've dealt with worse, man. Go deal with them. Please. Gabriel, Shoniqua, this is the way to the lights. Speaking of lights, I'm still debating the opener. If we start low and slow—"

The Messenger broke in as they followed the Savior, wings perfectly tucked behind them. "But that's two Peter songs on the list and in the first half. I just don't think a crowd would keep pace."

"I think you underestimate—hey, Shoniqua!" Chris stopped with the archangel beside him and looked back at our mortal number. "Let's go!"

Only a few feet in front of me, she checked with me and Daniel, settling on me the longest.

At a loss, I threw my hands up. "I don't fucking know."

She replied with a tired shrug and followed behind Christ and Gabriel.

We merry five, left to the silent emptiness of Madison Square Garden, started our trudge for the entrance.

14

BIG GUNS

When he said the Evangelicals were coming, my heart sank deeper than the rest of the stragglers he had collected.

Every step along the path since I found Deevi in that basement under a Brooklyn dive bar had featured nothing but evangelicals with guns, evangelicals with presidents, and evangelicals in league with Satan himself. Whether it was a small church in a van or a mega-pastor with his mega-parishioners, I had no idea what I faced once we stepped outside.

I hadn't joked with Christ at all. Americans Christians were insane.

I had been to the Philippines where Pentecostals nailed actual people up on actual crosses on a weekend because they wanted to, to small churches deep in Old Damascus living under the fear of terrorist oppression, all the way to the very foot of the throne in front of the big-P himself. Hell, I left because the insanity of my church had gotten so out of hand we were covering incomprehensible crimes under the guise that God needed, wanted, and desperately relied on institutions instead of grace.

Glossolalia, the snakes, hot tents in the South, I had been through it all and Voodoo, gods, angels, and demons.

And none of that still equaled some of the crazy shit Evangelicals made up to justify the outcomes of their faith. Somehow the gobs of money Christ told us to turn away from was switched to taking away the rights of the poor and oppressed.

Then I ran into the motherfuckers with guns.

God and Guns.

Two things that do not mix.

I looked to the four people around me as we walked the outer ring of Madison Square Garden, headed for the southwestern entrance where Gabriel warned us the crazed mob would arrive. Daniel took point ahead of me while the vets, Enrique and Jennifer, flanked me on both sides. Miranda guarded the back of our cluster. Instinctively I started to check my pockets and found my Bible. I thumbed open the old, worn cover, the black leather beaten gray and blue from the years of use across the world.

"Daniel," I said as light creeping through the entrance illumed the way ahead of us.

"Yes, Patrick?" he said, not breaking his stride. Neither did the vets.

George would have loved this. "No matter what happens," I said to them all, "you all worry about keeping that door open and clear for Deevi and the archangels. Keep everyone else out."

"What about the other doors?" Miranda asked behind me.

"I'm going to trust God on that one," I said, lacking a better answer. "He'll hopefully keep them locked. Or something."

"Oh, okay," she replied with a reasonable incredulity.

"Look, all," I said, "I don't know what the fuck we're doing. Just square up beside me and we'll get through. At this point I don't think he's doing this without a net."

I ignored their confused looks, not liking the metaphor either.

They already crowded the outer doors when we arrived, a bunch of the older set though I noticed a few came younger, in their twenties and thirties. Most white, handsome, and clean, the mishmash of pastels and crosses conceived by another dimwit designer thinking brush strokes in red ever came close to a man hung on the cross with broken legs assailed my gaze. They pounded on the glass and steel-framed doors with their fists, grabbed the handles and yanked, the stout bars leaving them huffing and puffing. Too many megaphones, signs proclaiming every evil in the form of pot, magic, video games, Jews, Muslims, Pagans, atheists, the kindly queers, Disney Films, abortions, Harry Potter, public schooling, goodwill towards men, and basic human decency gave an instant headache for all the liturgical problems abound.

The vets flanked me to the left and behind, and Daniel on my right.

"You bring your gun, Daniel?" I asked him.

"I did, Saint Patrick," said my undaunted kin. "But I can't fire it. Christ compels me not to."

"Dammit," I said. "I can't shoot them either."

"Your vows?" Enrique asked.

"Personal preference." I forbade myself from asking the soldiers to volunteer, which lay far outside Christ's portfolio as well. "Fuck, just be ready to flash it in case these idiots decide to make a move."

"What if they have more guns?" Daniel asked.

"Well then Christ is doing this without a net and I'm going to be shot." I nodded to Daniel to unlock the last door to the right, leaving one small escape point for us in case a stampede ensued. We walked in single file, down the center of the dark blue and white dotted carpet. The Evangelicals shouted at me first, noticing how the rest followed my path. Pounding fists hounded us until I halted at the midpoint of the liminal space.

"Daniel, Enrique, handle the door," I said, signaling to the one in front of me. "Miranda, get ready to yank me back if they try to pull me out. Jenny, go back to the last door and be ready to shut it if they break in. If they swarm just forget us and get it locked. Understood?"

The vets and the RIRA gunman nodded, suited for the toil amid the threat of death.

I remember every day of my first life. My wife. My children. The druids.

I remember the marauders raiding villages, raping, and killing in ways the modern world would fail to comprehend. I stood by and watched druids run cows between fires hoping it would do away with a bad harvest, or bless their warriors for battle, all the while contending with demons their gods and magic failed to defeat.

I remember all the demons I cast out of children, their mothers, their fathers, then the kings.

All because I had God. Despite my frequent criticisms, my doubts about where we went from here pushed to the side for the hard truths I had to accept.

He was here. It was time. And he hadn't damned me yet.

He hadn't damned anybody.

My eagle had flown out of my soul's deepest night and I fucking hated Peter Gabriel.

Secretly, in the last seconds before I gave the signal, I selfishly wondered if Christ knew how much I craved this. I hate nothing more than the hypocrisy born of my faith, and that was the dilemma of this round: I hated Christianity for what it had become, so far from what I and so many others had given our lives for in ways these privileged clowns couldn't imagine. Forget dirty feet and not being able to shit in a commode:

People died before anybody made them saints. People fought for something.

And God put me here to fight for them. "Open her up!"

Daniel unlatched the floor lock on the door first, causing the Christians outside to mass toward us. He stood and followed up with the bar as I stepped into the space, ready for the hatred about to unleash upon me.

Enrique pulled open the heavy chunk of glass and steel. Before one of them could step forward, I yanked my Bible out and pressed it in their faces, my shield for a second time that day.

Somehow the mob stayed back.

But their voices didn't.

"Demon!" a man in his forties screamed into the cover of The

Good Book before he tried to duck under it and glare at me. His fu-manchu mustache forked wild in all directions under a ball cap that said "Plumbers for Jesus." I took the time to search the other faces immediately around his, seeing the requisite, blond-dyed Bob and the exact same pair of glasses every Anna Wintour-wannabe spouting their conservative piety favored.

I almost cracked a smile. Marauders they were not.

The Plumber barked again. "Demon!"

"Bring him before us," one of the Bobs in her bright white pants suit and glittering gold said, more whorish than a Pharisee in the Temple. And Druids didn't behave this badly. "Bring us before him so he may prove himself!"

"Shut it, you shit-digger," I said, my high brogue cutting through those runty American accents.

The gasp from these sign-waving liars, slack jawed by the disre-spect, gave me the opening I needed.

"Who here actually brought a stone worth throwing?" I said. "Let me guess—you all got an email from your buds at New Word Ministries or one of those pervy little networks you have, and here you pop. Am I anywhere near close, or do you all just herd together like the stupid sheep you are?"

"We are the Body of Christ!" one of the Bobs shouted, her shrill voice higher than her false eyebrows. "We are the true disciples! Bring us this creature so we may—"

"Creature?" I interrupted the stupid idiot. "So you 'may' what? One wonders if you are truly the disciples or the scatterers of the ash, rutting low as you crawl in the tombs of your avarice. And you wouldn't even have to get that low, would you?"

"What are you talking about?"

"Look at this!" I cried to Daniel, who stood by dumbstruck under the onslaught of angry eyes and voices. "Come here demanding to see God, looking to test him, and can't even remember basic concepts of the Book!" I shook my head at her and the rest of her doofus posse. "Honestly, for shame."

Then the Plumber, jowls shaking with his mustache, went right for the jugular. "You serve the Anti-Christ!" he screamed, pushing his finger past my Bible to poke my chest.

I put up my hand before Daniel or Enrique moved first.

"I have another cheek as well, old man," I said, dead in his eyes. "And I have the beam in yours for the speck in mine, but what would that matter to you, a wasted seed? The wind blows you about the stone and not even one of you have an ounce of earth to share. Woe, to the lot of you, for if he comes?" I shook my head. "I'm not going to go get him. He does not answer to the braying of donkeys or the cock's crow but arrives now to heal the sick of their ills. So unless you are going to commit violence and use those guns he definitely does not permit you to have for the use you intend, I would back up a bit."

The Plumber, then the Bobs, then all the false believers took their chance to sound off.

But none moved.

"You all must have an extraordinary reason for being here," I said. "Tell me, who among us is actually ordained someplace that matters?"

"I went to Liberty," someone in the huddle masses before me shouted, one of the blondest Bobs in the bunch.

I scoffed. "I said an ordination, not a tax scam. Come on, just one of you! Southern College of Baptist Ministers? Any actual Church of Scotland? Forsake me, England? What about the Ecclesiastic—" I let the names of completely legitimate institutions fade as I found these idiots gaping at me. "Are any of you even Pentecostal?"

"My grandmother was Jewish," said another Bob.

"Oh, Jesus," I whispered as Daniel let out a disbelieving groan. "Are any of you SOPA?"

Dozens of hands went up in the back, the ones holding signs about the sins of fornication and Pokémon.

"Ah," I said. "No wonder you're all in league with the Devil."

This obviously riled them. One of the best things I learned in my first life was to let the damned idiots say what stupid shit they needed to. That's where they squirreled away the things they were really scared of.

It also gave me room to start dropping hammers out of the sky.

"Tell me, who here is from a destroyed church?" I called aloud. "Who here has been scattered by the man inside these hallowed—" I looked up at the ceiling of the entrance to Madison Square Garden, decidingly not my St. Mary's Pro-cathedral. "—halls? Who here is oppressed by the order of this man?"

"Who are you to ask us anything?" the Plumber drawled at me. "What faith are you?"

"I'm a Catholic," I said.

Boom. It was on the signs, after all.

"Papist! Papist!" The Plumber shouted, red-faced as he stomped in his tantrum.

"Baby-rapist!" One of the Bobs screamed, shaking her fist full of gold and diamond rings at me. "You baby-rapist!"

"Papist!"

Honestly, it was never about the Pope. They all had their own leaders, their own saints by different names, but all of them wanted the easy things out of Christ—automatic forgiveness, no matter what. I later agreed with Martin Luther about the Church's abusive mingling of indulgences so the rich could keep being depraved and rich while the priesthood—as always—looked the other way. There was a need for reform, for reformulation, and redefinition.

But Martin Luther also wanted to enslave his wife and get away on the idea God liked that too.

"Ah, there it is! That Papist!" I snorted like I had whiffed piss in the gutters. "But most of your words are complete shite, for they bear the fragrance of death. The man in here?" I called to them, challenging, "the man in here carries the scent of life, and I'm not sure one of you stinking sheep would be able to stand next to him without noticing your own stench for the lack of his. Tell me, which one of you fools thinks you have in it in you to boast before God how much better you know his Word? You?"

I nodded to the Plumber, freezing him on the spot.

"You?" I asked one of the Bobs. "You?" I nodded to one of many frauds before I settled my gaze on them all. "Who here has the guts to actually walk past me, by themselves, and confront Jesus Christ face to face? No mob, or gun, just you?" I scanned them, finding no takers. "Who?"

The subtle use of the Word, the Son, and the challenge subdued them long enough a noise to the south drew all our attention. Several of the Evangelicals in the back, most of them decked in white and bearing their signs, turned in the direction of crashing brass, flutes, and hand drums.

A chant to Erzulie Dohmeney emerged from the rhythmic din. Without having to see who had arrived a smile plastered across my face as the group of prosperity diehards in front of me broke their knot to see whom had come.

We seized the moment when they did. I nodded to Daniel.

The RIRA gunman rushed out and held my spot by the door. I waved for Jennifer and Miranda rejoin us as Enrique signaled his willingness to hold his side longer.

I charged outside in time to see the head of the parade marching up 8th Avenue.

Dancers clad in white shirts and pants gyrated between officiants who held up smoking bowls of incense piled with flowers, chanting high the goddess of love and vengeance. Kicking their feet in wild patterns, others blew powders of red, yellow, and green from their hands, filling the air in a dry fragrance intermingled in a mix of perfumes and washes. Beads of every color, feathers of every shape, and bones hung around necks of adherents who took in the Lwas and let them take over.

This forward line came at the beck and call of the queen at the front.

Her long braids wrapped in a white cloth, garlands of precious stones and gold draped before the flowing dress she wore, blossoming with every turn and twist she made with her acolytes under the flowing banner of Erzulie Dohmeney, whipping on the breeze through the skyscrapers. Queen Meredith Joslin, the Vodunasi of the entire Northeastern sealine, caught eyes with me and grinned. A long joint of tobacco and cannabis between her perfect teeth, she led the horde of her people, pagans, Jews, Muslims, atheists, and an entire ecumenical army.

Equal to the numbers the Evangelicals had brought, drumbeats rattling off hides quickened every heartbeat.

The inevitable return of Christ neared.

15

BIGGER GUNS

Afternoon, Tater!" Merry said as we closed on each other, lost in the tide sweeping fresh life onto the eastern side of 8th Avenue. She hugged me fierce, the clack and rattle of the bracelets and beaded garlands her armor between us.

Pulling back, she pulled out her spliff and offered it.

I took it without hesitation. "Perfect timing, love."

"Well, he asked for a great big gathering," she said as I sucked hard on the spliff's wet end.

The acrid smoke, tasting of petrol and pinecones, struck my tired nerves with a jolt of numbness needed to wake me until the cannabis crashed my neurons. Exhaling as much of the debris as I could, a cloud formed between us as more of Vodun dancers and drummers filtered by on both sides, sandwiching us. Their aisle continued in a line of gyration and the rattle-tat of the sticks on hides, white-garbed practitioners whooping to spirits stretching back to Haiti, then Benin, and ancestors far older. They intruded between the front door where Daniel and Enrique stood guard and the enraged Evangelicals, too flabbergasted by the real locals to do more than stand and curse. None dared reached for their guns.

Yet.

"What's wrong, Tater?" Merry asked, catching me staring.

I exhaled another puff of chronic. "This only lasts so long."

She leveled her gaze on them as well, a tambourine heavy in one hand, her bag full of tricks in the other. "*Oui*, but they're going to be in for it if they do, and not just from my people." She nudged her shoulder back, away from where we looked. "Them too."

Certain of her numbers, the army of people Merry and her Vodun cohorts had brought along went about making a wonderful mess of things. Several set up their tables and hawked wares, from jewelry someone made by hand and undercharged for all the way up to the guy clearly selling Ziplock bags full of weed, exchanging them for dollars by the handful. Rugs and blankets galore spread out on the street, a patchwork network of differing faiths, politics, and spirituality cobbled together in an unimaginable mass more at home in ancient Jerusalem. Witches held lectures about crystals while liberal churches sang hymns. Old rabbis appeared to place their own carpets next to those of their Muslim neighbors. A few grill lids banged open as seals on bags of charcoal ripped.

Tofu sizzled next to sausages as the stink of green snuck its way around.

Part bazaar, part sit-in, the denizens of New York City had turned out for a god not their own.

And all the too-good-for-everyone-else Evangelicals could do was seethe.

"So, what's the actual plan here?" she asked. "Or is he figuring it out too?"

"He has 'something' in mind," I said, sucking off a bit more smoke before I passed the spliff back. "Deevi and the archangels are on their way."

"Oh, good. And what about the little Irish psycho?" She stuck her hand into the pocket of her white dress as she put her bag down. "The dog man."

I snorted at her depiction of Cuchulainn. "Him too."

She extracted a lighter, her thumb already working the wheel. A spark brought a lick, which she put right at the end of the smoking spliff. She sucked quick draws and puffed them out while smiling. "Easy-peasy, then."

It was always the worst moment to say things like that.

"Alright," I said, shrugging my cynicism. "Let's make a way in for the band. Think you can keep those nutters attending to something else?"

"Darling," she said with a false pout, "I didn't get made up for nothing."

We went in the same direction. She blended into the lines of dancers with ease, taking up their hopping steps and spins while I roamed behind the wall of moving bodies, out of sight of the Evangelicals. I reached Daniel by the door we had opened, who squatted to get his head out of sight as Enrique remained upright. I spied quick through the glass, seeing Jennifer in her spot.

"Oooof, Saint Patrick," Daniel said as he leaned away a bit. "You smell of the weed."

"Well, sir," I said, offering no excuse as my dry tongue stuck to the roof of my mouth. A veteran of multiple highs, I kept to the task. "We're going to start bringing people inside to firm up the guard. And I bet Christ will need help setting up the show with more than just us and the archangels."

"I'll unlock a few more doors with Jennifer," Miranda answered from the breezeway with a firm nod. "I'll keep her and Enrique here with you to make sure nobody gets frisky."

I gave them a small nod as Miranda ducked into Madison Square Garden's breezeway, joining Jennifer to convey my plans while I sidled next to Enrique. A tall young man, at least by me, he gave a quiet nod before returning to his watch of the crowds.

The ache in my hips and the dullness in my head sparked one of those weird itches to talk.

"Where did you serve?" I asked in Spanish, cutting right to the point.

The question caused Enrique to look at me again. "Afghanistan."

"You must be, what... twenty-nine?"

"Yeah," he said. "Went in after high school."

I nodded and let the conversation lull, giving us both time to check the crowds. A glance back to see Jennifer still there, it was Enrique who spoke first this time.

"So that's Jesus?" he asked, staying in Spanish.

"For all the irony that comes with him," I said. "Not what you expected, is he?"

"No, sir," Enrique replied, his brow furrowed. "And you're a saint?"

"As much as I've been told."

He smiled for the first time since Christ picked him and his wayward mates off the street in Times Square. His was a kind face, younger than the man who possessed it, as if the last kernel remaining of whomever he had been rooted there. I shared in the grin, happy to see the Lord bring someone something gentle.

One of the Evangelicals shouted some gibberish. A small attempt to summon together a hymn rose but connected by little more than their shared thirst for attention and power, the discordant denominations of the charismatic failed to cobble a tune. We watched in quiet bemusement as they started and stopped, sputtering out a few minutes later.

On edge, Enrique did not take his eyes off them. "Do you know why?"

"Why what, sir?" I replied in curiosity.

"Why us?" Enrique finished, before he whispered again. "Why me?"

"Oh, Enrique," I said in full humor and honesty, "They've yet to explain to me why I'm a saint."

"Oh," he echoed, his wary gaze not breaking, though the expression around it softened. "I didn't think..."

"That he'd pick someone like you?"

Frozen by emotion held back, the soldier only offered a small, tight nod.

"Yeah," I said, knowing it full well and twice-over. "But he did. I'd take something in that."

"Well?" Enrique asked. "What do you take from it, padre?"

Knowing Deevi was on the way but lacking for her presence, for the first time I missed her Nephilim-power to pry the truth out of me with a single question.

I tried my best anyway. "I'm not sure yet. All I know is that he's called me here, and here I am. And the one I care about the most is on the way. I have to trust whatever his reason, the right thing is about to happen."

He sighed through his round stub of a nose. "And if not?"

"Oh, then we're fucked."

He laughed aloud at that one and looked down the line of dancers, honing his focus on the drum line. "You're not the like the priests I grew up with."

"Thank God," I said with absolute sincerity.

His growing laugh cut short when one of the dancers in the parade lurched out of line, pushing up the gun held tight in the hands of the Plumber that had poked me earlier. An errant finger squeezed the trigger again and again, but no bullet tore out of the snub end of the .38 special.

Someone shouting the obvious caused the wanted effect anyway.

"Gun!"

Several of the dancers, as if on cue, set themselves upon the Evangelicals as I readied beside Enrique to duck inside and slam shut the doors. The Evangelicals, commanded to be meek with their swords, drew all sorts of pistols and rifles. Many of the Vodun dancers tussled with them to wrestle free the arms from their would-be attackers. Others on both sides pulled knives.

Then the Plumber batted one of the dancers across the face, sending the poor man rolling farther than any mortal blow should.

I didn't even have to have to look at him to spot the other marble-black eyes inking out the gazes of their hosts. Unable to fire their guns, Perdition attacked in full fury, stabbing forward with their small steels. Shouts of defiance from Merry's troops turned into screams of panic before, as if heralding the next phase of violence, a horn blew close behind me.

I turned in time to find Merry among a cluster of her priestesses, steadfast while the hippies, atheists, and others who had set up tables and blankets fled the scene. Chanting the name of their Lwa, the most powerful triune goddess and wife to the robust, masculine powers of ancient Africa, Erzulie Danto infused their gazes with a lime-colored light.

Blowing her brass trumpet a second time, Merry sent the note high into the air as the voices around her resounded and repeated.

A change came over the dancers and the drummers, the latter casting instruments aside. A strange aura overtook their panic, their faces roaring in renewed, silent rage. Their eyes bulged in their heads. Sweat beaded faces, and before the next breath followed, the muscles on their bodies seized and swelled. Even those stabbed suddenly threw off their demonic attackers, the wounds healing as the warrior-spirits of their ancestors assumed the thrones of their souls.

The possessed of Vodun, transformed into unstoppable zombies, attacked the damned of Perdition in a second wave.

"Holy shit!" Jennifer shouted behind us from inside the arena's entry way. "What do we do?"

Lost for better words to command my few, my hand had found its way back to my Bible. Memories of my homeland evoked a time not dissimilar from this one. On the line alongside druids, who had tried the same sort of magics to empower their warriors against demons run amok, I knew the only solution lay in the way I had solved this before.

"Hold the door," I said, dashing to join in the fun.

16

DAY TRIPPING

Fists flew as knives stabbed forearms and torsos, coating the pavement on 8th Avenue so red the yellow traffic lines disappeared under the blood. The Vodun dancers, many of them tall, athletic men and women, threw themselves forward under the possessed abandon of their Lwas and the ancestors, strengthened with powers beyond their mortal bodies.

It meant little next to the might of fallen angels.

The wrath of damnation spurred greater acts of violence, often shutting down Christ's unexpected defenders with cruel attacks. As quickly as the dead fell, they arose again, healed by their ancient protectors, but only long enough to be mauled and stabbed by knives held in Christian hands.

Like the swords of the pagans, I braved the din of bloodshed, the spine of my Bible a meaningless shield against the flurries of fists and cuts. The sisters of Queen Merry continued their chant behind my side of the line, keeping their acolytes upright against the pushing, encroaching wave Perdition brought to bear.

I shouted proclamations from Psalm 91, trying to get my voice above the screams and shrieks. "You will not fear the terror of the night," I said, as much to the adherents of Old African polytheism as I did the twisted children of God, "or the arrow that flies by day, or the pestilence that stalks in darkness, or the destruction that wastes at noonday!"

A few of the demons flinched, a pause long enough to allow the zombified dancers to knock a hole into the line.

"A thousand may fall at your side," I continued from rote memory, "ten thousand at your right hand, but it will not come near you. You will only look with your eyes and see the punishment of the wicked! Because you have made the Lord your refuge, the Most High your dwelling place, no evil shall befall you, no scourge come near your tent!"

As much as Psalm 91 caused pain and confusion to the demons within the trapped Evangelicals, the dancers and drummers redoubled their attacks. Not believers but dedicated to the source of things I dedicated to, the words infused my heathen allies with new vigor.

"For he will command his angels concerning you to guard you in all your ways," I hollered as loud as I could, joining with the chant to Danto, Dohmeney, and her aspects. "On their hands they will bear you up, so that you will not dash your foot against a stone! You will tread on the lion and the adder, the young lion and the serpent you will trample under foot! Those who love me, I will deliver; I will protect those who know my name! When they call to me, I will answer them—"

"I will be with them in trouble," Christ said, his voice halting the entire battle.

Everyone shifted away from mayhem, magic, all fixed in place by the Savior made flesh. He stepped out of the doorway to his chosen venue, robed in his whites with the vets behind him, his new fishers of souls.

"I will rescue them and honor them," he said, louder than before as he marched right to the front of the demonic-Evangelical horde. He stared into the nearest foe, his gaze clear and resolute. "With long life I will satisfy them and show them my salvation."

He lifted his hand toward them, palm up. Like the raising of the dead on the George Washington Bridge, a relief of light and sighs erupted from every demon mustered in the street. One moment they were there, then the next they were replaced, the person left behind unable to resist the overwhelming awe.

Every single one of those nutters dropped to their knees in reverence.

"Up," he said, rankled by their bowing. "Up! Up, up, up! This won't do!"

He strode forward and picked up the first Bob, who burst into tears at his touch. Without hesitation he drew her into a hug, whispering into her ear to calm her. He did not leave her behind as he went to the next person, however distraught they were by his presence, and offered every single one of them forgiveness without conditions.

"Up, all of you," Christ said after he had soothed them. "I did not come to ask anyone to bow to me, nor am I here to say I am He when it is my acts and words that shall determine that. All of you, all of you, come inside my Garden," he said, waving to Vodun worshiper, atheist, or shamed Evangelical alike. "Welcome home. But before you all go..."

He faced the entrance to Madison Square Garden, and following his gaze, so did the rest of us.

Like a shimmering star bound by the scant gravity of earth, many gasped as we beheld Gabriel walk out of the glass doors, their diminished figure suddenly growing taller as their wings of pure light widened and lengthened to their true scale.

"Hark, for I come on the order of Lord," Gabriel said, nodding to Christ first, "for in grace he has found the need to call another to his side, a Helper to the shepherd so he may better prepare the pastures. I call from among you Ms. Rosie Baker of Bushwick, Brooklyn, New York."

Every single one of us, me included, searched among the Vodun contingent until a tall, slim figure came from the cluster around Merry. Her head wrapped in a white scarf, the firmness of her jaw and gait spoke of a transformation deeper than makeup, almost indiscernible if not to a slight handsomeness to her beauty.

Some of the Evangelicals, awed by the presence of the Savior or not, whispered much meaner things I'll not repeat.

Christ, on the other hand, met her with finger guns. "Rosie Baker!" he shouted, running over with hands extended. "Right exactly where I knew you'd be!"

"You're—you're here for me?" the tall priestess asked, her dark blond eyes full of distrust. "But I don't pray to you, Cristo."

"Ah, but don't you all?" the Savior said right in the faces of Rosie, Merry, and the other African polytheists. Thank goodness he was not a White Jesus. "But no matter who or what you pray for, there is a purpose behind the mystery, Rosie Baker. Will you come along with me and take part in that journey, prayers or no prayers?"

"Wait, how did you know she would be here?" Merry asked, stepping forward beside Rosie. "Was this your reason for sending me to gather my kin?"

"I happen to like music and dancing," said Christ, "But no, I did not manipulate you all here just—" He huffed. "Look, can we talk about this on the way?"

"On the way to where?" I asked, joining in with Merry and the new member.

Christ offered his Cheshire grin. "To The Strand! I need to go pick up some books to help with the set list. It's really kicking my ass."

"You want me to go with you to a bookstore?" Rosie asked Christ dead to his face, full of suspicion.

"Well, you and Merry and Patrick and Gabriel," he answered with a kinder grin. "Always good to have more than one voice in the room, you know."

"Wait, wait," the reawakened Plumber said, his befuddled expression twisting in further confusion, if not disgust. "You're going to take the Catholic and a bunch of pagans with you? Why not us? Why not the chosen of—"

Christ turned on him like lightning. "Pardon?"

Jowl McMuttonchop said nothing, nor did anyone else.

"I said pardon me?" Christ repeated, directly to the Plumber.

"I meant just—"

"I know what you meant," Christ said. "I'm not going to sit here and yell at you, Jerome," he said, widening the fool's eyes on the spot. "But I will ask you and everyone two clear, clear questions. First, do any of you know John 15:12-17? Because if you do, I want you to listen to this part because it is very important, and I'm not doing parables this time around about stone, thorns, and soil. Listen close: if a man who made his ministry with tax collectors, pimps, prostitutes, magicians, fishermen, workers, criminals, thieves, and the poor, and did not cater the people who resided in temples with their wealth—"

He gave each of them a good, hard stare.

"—I would be spending my time asking 'am I a Christ-follower or am I just a modern Pharisee?' I'll let you all think about it until I get back." He exhaled through his nose and shrugged before nodding in sympathy. "I hope you'll still come to the show. You're always welcome."

He checked with me for some reason, and I could only shrug in complete head-shaking astonishment. With one more nod, then nods to Merry and Rosie, he started southward—away from Deevi and the rest on the way to meet us.

Compelled to follow by something stubborn within me, I made no complaints outside gritting my teeth too hard.

SOUTHWARD

aster, Laeg, faster!" Cuchulainn shouted, hoisting his green-and-red oblong shield over the left side of the chariot's basket. Bullets thudded on the heavy slabs of enchanted ash but did not pierce to harm its wielder or the driver he protected. "Faster, by Macha, and then faster than her!"

"Nobody can go faster than fucking Macha," Laeg shouted as he shouldered his brother-in-arm's shield off of him to better handle the reigns. The Black and Gray thundered ahead as rifle rounds pierced the horses' heads, necks, and flank on the same side, but absorbed into their flesh, which healed instantly. The pain, though short and muted, drove them into a chaotic charge, on the edge between control and panic under his direction. "We need cover! Cover, Setanta!"

"These damned bullets don't seem to care for it," the Hound of Ulster shouted as he braced against his shield and the chariot's side. "Deevi, thin these hails!"

"Hold still long enough and I will!" Deevi leveled her magma sword in front of her as the point bobbed off the mark. The horde of demons had broken past the staggered positions the archangels and her father had taken on the roofs past the way they had come. They raked waves from their own light blades, like they had at Lough Derg, but no matter how hard they whipped away life in droves, the lines of the damned refilled as possessed innocents flooded out of the buildings, the shops, from the side streets, a never-ending sea of bent humanity.

All intent on her capture.

The first bolts of red fury from her sword leveled the front line, slowing them enough Laeg gained a few feet, moment by moment, as they hauled northwest toward the portion of Manhattan locals called "The Upper West Side." She swept back and forth, fanning a beam that cut people down at the midsection as they were blasted apart from above by her kin, who disappeared and reappeared atop the buildings of concrete and glass to establish new firing positions. To her left, the Hudson River glistened from behind tall buildings and a highway as the land elevated.

"We need to make south again," she said aloud as Cuchulainn moved behind her and placed his battered shield back in the cart. She loosed a trio of beams on their hunters and took a breath. "Or at least inward. We can redouble them to the park and force them—"

"There's too many of them," Laeg cried. "Look at them! Coming out of the damned buildings! We aren't outrunning this!"

Deevi thought to protest the Hound's driver when Lucifer manifested to her left, flying above the asphalt-paved street. He brought his light blade to bear, joining her volleys at his former comrades in rebellion.

"Uriel has found the end of their numbers!" he shouted between the great strokes of his wings. "In three blocks, veer right! We will be there to cover your course!"

He vanished in the next moment, leaving Deevi and the grumbling Irish warriors alone in the chase again.

"Get ready to fucking turn," Cuchulainn said as he took up an unblemished shield in his left hand. He clutched three spears in the right and had belted on his sword Hardhead. "I'll be dropping off!"

"Are you mad?" Deevi asked. "You will be swallowed and smothered by their sheer numbers!"

"I'm not going to run into them," the champion replied calmly. "But if your kin have a choke point for us to get through, I want to be the hand that squeezes."

"Jesus Christ," said Laeg, his focus ahead as he guided their pair of immortal horses. He groused something in Ancient Irish before he continued in English. "It's too easy to use his name, ain't it?"

"Keep driving," Cuchulainn barked back. "Deevi, fly east. Laeg will keep pushing along the road unless something blocks him, but east and then back to the south. Get to Patrick and inside whatever this damned Gard—"

"Banking!" Laeg screamed as he pulled the Black and Gray to the right. The grand horses answered to their master's order, almost leaning as they turned off the north-south avenues and to the streets, galloping hard beneath tree-covered lanes of rowhomes colored in shades of rust, white, and shale. The driver whipped the beasts faster into their run, extending their distance a few more yards as the demons struggled around trunks and street posts, clogged at the tight angles.

The archangels appeared. Raphael materialized, flanked by Michael and Lucifer as the chariot whipped past. The Trumpeter brought up his eight-foot silver horn and blew a long, low note at the hurtling wall of demons. The note shifted the air as hundreds of bodies were tossed upward before gravity set upon them again, smashing the possessed into buildings and stoops.

At the same moment, the other archangels manifested on the roofs, joining their holy fire with Michael and Uriel's. Raphael's next note halted the possessed, whether they were elder or child, young or old, obliterating them in their tracks. Ash and blood muddied the road.

"Double back in a few miles, Laeg!" Cuchulainn dodged past Deevi, leaping from the chariot with his spears, sword, and shield. "Fly, Deevi!"

She took to the air after him, faced in the opposite direction as she opened her wings and allowed them to lift her out. The chariot zipped ahead, wheels clattering on the seams in New York's weathered roads. Laeg did not look back to see if she ascended, nor did Deevi worry on him as she pulled her wings close and threw them out in a powerful stroke, gaining altitude until she cleared the surrounding buildings.

Smoke pillared from several places to the immediate south, the battlefield left in their wake, but the horizon lay clear as the noonday sun loomed toward evening. Checking on her angelic family, she found the demons stoppered by the trap her kin had set, reinforced doubly by the distorted red creature in Perdition's midst. Blood flew up in great jets with the rising, inhuman cackle.

She thought to fly southward as ordered when she spotted them. Thousands and thousands, maybe in the tens of thousands, converged from the confines of Central Park, forming a thick and teeming force that seemed to keep stretching east. A wall formed, closing on her kin's position.

Deevi could have climbed higher, so high none would have reached her, and glided to Patrick in minutes.

She choose instead to let her liquid-metal armor flow, encasing her completely as she sought the war ahead.

17

STRAND

The secret of getting around New York, or at least the one that every New Yorker stressed by the time they had lost patience with the tourists, was to know your cross streets. Christ knew every step of the way we took to Strand Bookstore down on Broadway. Tucked deep into the corner of an old building not far from the Flat Iron, the red signs and white lettering still burned bright, illumined by the automatic lights. Abandoned by the staff after several blasts to the north of us that he and Gabriel remained coy about, he pushed his way through the unlocked front door, me behind him followed by Merry and his newest Helper, Rosie Baker.

Gabriel reappeared as we passed the registers to our left, leaning over to whisper in Christ's ear.

Merry was at my side in the next instant, with Rosie close in tow.

"What are they talking about?" she whispered, rightfully suspicious. "You heard the blasts outside, Tater. They weren't far, either."

"I know, Ma," I said. "Up and in the west."

We didn't have to say out loud to each other the obvious.

"Hey, Patrick." Christ waited for me at the edge of the spiral stair that served as the store's spine, wrapped around an un-powered lift he wouldn't have used anyway. "Come on."

"Oh, great," I said, half-under my breath.

Merry grunted in agreement, but there was no humor it.

"Reporting for duty." I stopped before the Savior, giving a small but playful salute to him and the towering archangel beside him. The pink-gold curls of Gabriel's shimmering head almost scraped the large floodlights hanging from the high ceilings.

"Down we go," Christ said. Frustration creased his brow. "I really need some help."

This fucking guy—asking for help?

I had been to Strand once before many, many years ago during one of my sabbaticals from the Vatican, recalling dimly the basement holding everything from pop culture to religion in its fluorescent-lit stacks. Smelling of dry book mold, a rather pleasant odor considering what other foundations in New York stank of, he took an immediate right, headed directly for Spirituality.

On his sandaled heels, I huffed at his flighty attention-span. "Well?"

Searching the spines of the books on the shelf before us, Christ bit his lip for a moment. "So. You know."

"Know what?"

"Everything that happened after I rose from my death," he said, almost quiet. "Everything that happened between Lucifer and I."

Exhaustion flooded in with the rush of images, memories, the Morningstar's tale forever etched on my soul. Perhaps the only direct witness to his testimony, I offered a weak, puzzled nod. "About to the point where Michael forced you to damn the fallen angels."

"The *rebelling* angels," Christ corrected. "None of my children are ever fallen." He reached forward, touching the spine on a feminist survey of Buddhism. He sighed deep and let his hand drop to his side, staring at his dark toes before he put his fists on his hips. "Gabriel told me something upstairs that I'm only going to tell you. You can decide how you wish to handle it. The forces of Perdition have stopped Deevi and the other archangels from joining us. They battle on the Upper West Side. Things are turning out quite poorly."

The hammer of the delivery, almost harder than the one the

Romans used to break his legs, left me numb. "Why tell me alone?" I asked. "Why not in front of Merry or Ms. Rosie?"

"Because Ms. Rosie and I haven't our formal introductions yet," Christ said. "And honestly, Merry is already risking enough for a man she does not pray to. I wished to consult with you about my dilemma first before we address how to deal with things in the north."

"Your dilemma?"

"What do I do, Patrick?" God asked me square in the face. Square in the face.

"Oh, fuck," I said. "You actually don't know what to do."

"Right?" He threw his hands up. "I'm drowning here."

"How can you not know?" I asked, caught by the possibility that the Creator—The Creator—did not know everything it needed to know. Or did it? Was I reaching beyond my understanding in this? I gazed into the dark eyes of the Savior in front of me, discovering a doubt witnessed far too many times by those I had ministered to.

And he faced them alone. Here he was, trying to be better while I was bitter.

"Well, shit," I said, lost for a better option. "What is the actual matter?"

"It's the set list," he said. "I have the first half, but the second keeps nagging at me. Something about it isn't right."

"Slow down, slow down, Elvis," said I, "start again—what's the set list even for?"

"Well, I'm doing a show," Christ said. "I told you that."

"I—of course, you're doing a show, but why songs? Why music?"

"Oh," he said, as if surprised to be asked. "Um, it's hard to explain, so I'll try to keep it simple."

"Thank you."

He nodded to me before he continued. "When the Council of El and I started long ago," he said, as if long ago had a reference for him, "we played together. My children and I, ordering the cosmos through the mathematical language of music, composed to an exacting perfection in the boundless and ineffable myriads cast by my Word. I thought it would be nice to start things off by getting everyone together again and then out there. And then go from there."

"So some Kumbaya?"

He smiled at my snark. "It works for the charismatics, and you can't tell me the best part of any service isn't the singing. It's one of the few times people get to get lost if they want. I'm trying to provide the pasture to wander in. If you get my meaning."

"Aye, I get it," I said. "Healing the world through music. It's a nice notion."

"You don't agree?"

"It's harder than that, Jesus," I replied, lifting my right elbow to lean on one of the iron shelves beside us. "Do you really think you're going to simply sing some songs and that's that?"

"No, of course not. I plan to teach between songs."

"Then why all the doubt?" I asked. "Why come here? Why bother me if you are not fooled?"

"Well, I feel like one," he said, less confident. "And that's causing problems with the set list."

"What's it matter if you have the words? It's just choirs and bells."

"Those choirs and bells matter to people, Patrick. They matter a lot."

Strangely undaunted, I gazed back with my best poker-face. "Why?"

"Because he has to show us something," a new voice interrupted us.

We turned to find Rosie Baker at the bottom of the stair. Taller than the both of us by more than a few inches, her broad shoulders cut a long shadow from the inset lamp above her, leaving her face darker and eyes smoldering. The bracelets and anklets on her limbs gleamed in silver and pearl, and about her neck hung a chain full of seagull feathers I imagined she had plucked with her large hands.

She squared with Christ, measuring him with far less favor than he did her.

But he tried anyway. "Hello, Rosie. It's time we met and talked, isn't it?"

"You can say that," she replied in her deep, resounding voice, full of

Bushwick and bitter doubts about the man in front of her. "You picked me after all." She made a sound in the back her throat and shook her head. "Better late than never, I guess?"

"I see you are confused at my choice."

"A bit," Rosie said, bobbing her head hard. The blond tassels of her wig, threaded with bone-beads, shook with every angry move. "I'm the last person I ever expected you to care about, and dead ass, I hope you don't expect me to care about you. I have my gods and my ancestors, thank you, and I don't need the chosen of the white—"

"Am I white?" the obvious brown Jew from Palestine asked.

I took a step back with my very white ass, deeper into the stacks on Religion to give them room. "Well, this is going well," I mumbled to Christ before a copy of Teitsworth's commentary on the Gita caught my eye. Trying my best to stay out of a fight, I pulled it and opened to the third chapter immediately, already familiar with the preamble and opening thesis after multiple readings. I loved the Hindus. No beating around the bushes with them.

"Rosalinda—may I call you that?" Christ asked the acolyte chosen from Merry's many.

"It's my name."

"And I want nothing more than to respect your name and who you are," Christ said. "Which is why I picked you."

"To do what?" she asked, flicking her head up at him in defiance.

"To speak. So that I may listen to things I may not want to hear," he said, befuddling the both of us.

"You want her to tell you what you don't want hear?" I asked, incredulous after two lifetimes of pointed complaints.

"Oh, no cap? Where do you want me to start?" Rosie asked, clapping her hands in front of her. "You are, single-handedly, the walking personification of centuries of enslavement, imperialism, and religious intolerance spanning not only wars but outright murder of innocent men, women, and children in your name. Today—today!—there are people that would see me dead simply because you said that there was only this and that, leaving no room for anything else—"

"If I may—" Christ said.

"You may not," said Rosie with more gumption than I ever had. "In fact, you may not be white, but what white people have done with you should make you take a good look around and think about your song and dance. It takes more than fucking Peter Gabriel, you ponce, to make up for the dead claimed by your name. You are the source for such hatred that to even say that you—*you*—are a representative of love is a mad thing."

"I hear you, and I understand—"

"Nothing," the vodun priestess broke in, a finger up to silence the Savior—and he buttoned up. "You don't understand. You don't know what it's like for your father to see you as an abomination." Rosie hung on the revelation. "You don't know what it's like for your mother to turn you out. You don't know."

He let her proclamation hang between them.

Breaking it with a sigh, Christ matched her pose sans finger and attitude. "Is that why you fell away, Rosalinda? Because of what other Christians did to you?"

"No," she said, both incredulous and bemused. "Because of what you didn't do. Do you know how many times I used to pray to you to make me *me*, to let me be and be free without worry of being stalked? Or killed? Do you know how many times?"

This question waited, pregnant with ire.

"Yes," Christ answered. "Every time. I still know them down to dates and time. Word for word."

"And how many of those went unanswered to? And you're worried about what again?"

"A set list," Christ said. "Just a set list."

"Sounds real fucking important," snapped Rosie. "And—"

A fourth voice to the scolding of the Almighty cleared their throat.

We all turned to find Gabriel behind Rosie, standing between two tables laden with colorful books. The Messenger bore a grave expression at her maker.

"Have they advanced?" Christ asked.

"No," said Gabriel, head bowed as they answered. "The forces of Perdition have set a line above Central Park. Deevi, once again, has—"

"What about Deevi?" I blurted. "Where is she?"

"Perdition has cut Manhattan in half, east to west," Gabriel said. "Many, many people are dying."

"More are always dying." Rosie turned her glare on Christ. "Thanks to you."

Christ settled against her words. "Alright—let me get a few books and we'll go."

18

HARE KRISHNA

Christ ordered Gabriel to escort Merry back to the Garden to while Rosie and I took the 4 Train with him headed north. With the rest of the city barricaded in their high rises, the subways ran empty, the terminals barren save for the scraps of trash left behind on the tiles.

"How do you know any trains are going to be running?" Rosie asked, huffing at the corner of a slat bench after we hopped the turnstiles. "I don't think the MTA came to work today."

I checked the digital placards fixed to the tunnel's ceilings and the flatscreens on the walls on the other side of the platform, their faces dark without power. "She's got you there. It'd be better if we went back up and you unlocked us a car."

"Rosie Baker, I will have you know there are many guarantees in this world," Christ said as he stared to the darkened maw our magical train would emerge from. "Me, taxes, and the MTA. And we're not stealing anymore cars, Patrick."

For the first time, he fixed me with a withering look.

Out of all the sins?

Rosie took up for me. "Yeah, but that doesn't mean anything if the motherfucking—"

The peal of the 4 Train echoed out of the southern tunnel.

Like the arrival of the angels themselves, two lights pierced the gloom, eyes of an aluminum monster's flat face. A great green dot in the front window, lacking any operator in the seat, wreathed a large white four as the pneumatic brakes caught on the wheels. The friction of the electric tracks and forgiving hydraulics chewed the silver lines with a long, low whine, and brought the serpent to a stop. As if managed by a fully staffed crew there to push the buttons and pull the levers, the automatic doors slid open along its line of lit carts.

Satisfied, Christ gathered the hem of his robe as he boarded. "Mind the gap!"

Like the last time, I found myself seated beside the only other mortal while he conspicuously took a bench on the other side, two sections down from us. After the tense introduction between the Vodun priestess beside me and the understanding we headed into shit, the growing anxiety of battle reduced me to a piss-poor mood. Thankful for some space again, I let my head fall back until it touched the clear Plexiglas window.

The train, still without conductors, loosened its brakes and pulled forward on the electric track.

"No cap, this is some wild shit." Rosie fished through the cloth bag she had brought with her. Cluttered in little bottles and bags like Merry's, she fished out an Afterschool special and purple lighter. "Want a hit?"

"Fucking yes I do," I said without hesitation, eager as I lifted my head to check on Christ a few seats down. He was staring right back and shaking his head with a humored smile. A kid caught in the rectory, I froze for a second as old, learned fears crept up.

Then Rosie lit that joint and exhaled the first whiff of green wonder. She puffed twice and coughed before handing it over.

"Here," she said through a gasp, her voice lowered several octaves.

I received the Body. "How long?" I was polite enough to ask before I sucked smoked into my throat and deeper.

"About a year and a half." She cleared her throat and searched her bag for a handkerchief. She dabbed around her immaculately painted lips, the edges of the dark red lipstick exact on the borders of a full, broad mouth. She waited as I inhaled a little bit, then a lot, on the second draw. I expelled it quick and passed the duchy back to the left.

"No," I said once the burn in my lungs dissipated. "How long you been with your ancestors?"

Her hard expression softened at the question. "Twenty-two years. How long have you been working for child molesters?"

I winced and grinned at the same time. "Oh, Rosie. I don't work for child molesters." I pointed at the man down a few benches from us. "I work for him."

"Still worth it?" she asked, taking a hard inhale before passing over the half-diminished joint.

Not one to deny the gifts of a host, I took my last sip and considered it. I pulled the wet end out of my mouth like a cork on a wine bottle, the juice spilling from between my lips. Truth be told, I played too easily against the question in the moment, allowing present action to cover for an over-agonizing need, no, an aversion to admit that I honestly didn't know or care if I got to Deevi again. I feared what would happen when this train stopped, of what we would find on the battlefields of the Upper West Side or wherever that madness drifted to. Never ready for the storm, I shifted my eyes his way again, still terrified at the notion I might see my punishment smiling back.

All I found was the man who sang something back into me at Columbus Circle. I found the man who had stood beside me through Roman slavery and banishing demons.

I found the man who had confirmed my faith despite the world he had made.

Christ popped his dark brows and grinned at me before he broke his gaze away, his attention to a poem on a poster at his end of the car.

"Yeah," I said. "Despite it all."

Red-eyed and wheezing, Rosie huffed for a full breath. "For the life of me, I don't know why I'm here. I don't know why Meredith is doing this for you. Fuck man, I don't know."

"Don't know what?"

"He's right there," Rosie said. "That's him, right?"

"Yeah?"

"Yeah?" she mimicked in the lightest Irish brogue, which got a laugh out of me. "Well, what does he need a fat trans queen like me for?"

"I think he wants you to yell at him," said I, figuring out what was happening:

Under the weight of being chosen, Rosie Baker was freaking the fuck out.

"May I offer you some advice? One holy person—" I made the quote marks for me, "—to another?"

The Vodun priestess nodded.

Bless the reefer. "It's easy for you. You've probably seen an ancestor or two by now, and maybe even danced with a Lwa. But seeing, as I'm having to learn to, is still many steps away from experiencing. No matter our experience, there is no experience to qualify him. There's no experience to qualify seeing a Lwa. Or an angel. I've been exorcising demons for two whole lifetimes and I still get scared shitless every time. Every fucking time."

"Okay?" she asked, too high to follow.

I might have been too high in trying to make the point. "What does Merry tell you before every ritual? Every ceremony?"

"To believe," Rosie said.

"Exactly! But you don't have to believe here. You get to experience. And what do you do in the middle of the trip?"

She laughed at my questions. "Just ride it out. And listen."

I shrugged like Oprah in satisfaction as Rosie caught her fish.

She broke into a smaller chuckle, looking away then looking back. "Man, fuck you," she said before she flicked her purple lighter and flamed the leftover nub of chronic. We were done with our ritual when the brakes squeezed as they slowed us to the next abandoned platform. Christ moved on the doors closest to him.

"Uh oh," I said.

Rosie followed my gaze and deflated as we came to a stop at 59th Street, on the east side of the park and far from where we needed to be. Then I noticed that the station was not empty of occupants. Seated in their cluster, a dozen robed Hari Krishnas encircled each other as they banged their drums and shook their bells in time to their chants, the homage to God in full swing. Someone had even laid the books out to take, though they wanted you to buy them.

Until one of the mendicants, raising his head from their communal meditation, spotted him.

"Hey, it's the Hare Krishnas!" Christ announced.

The entire congregation might have levitated in time, they leapt so quickly to their feet. He disembarked the 4 Train, which sat inert, and went out to meet them. I hustled off along with Rosie. He approached the mass.

To our shock, they broke into a cheer. Several of the younger ones came forward, bending at their knees to touch his feet and the holes the Roman nails had left in them, reverent before the Son of God as they would be the guru of their order or the personification of Vishnu. The older chanters kept playing their instruments, still in time to mutter thankful prayers for the unscheduled ecumenical conference.

"My Lord," one of the Hare said to him, "why do you come before us? What reason have we to receive the blessing of your presence?"

"Oh, I was in the neighborhood and heard you guys in the tunnel," he said before he nodded to one of the bald acolytes. "But I am also here to address the great calamity on this island taking place only a few blocks away. Am I to guess this is why you have taken shelter here, to pray and sing?"

"Truly this is a vision of the Lord," said one of the older monks. "Yes, Singer of the Songs, we hide here. The world above is full of fraught illusion where creatures of light and dark battle, and many, many between them suffer."

"I shine with your bravery and dim at your sorrows," said Christ, far more poetic with these polytheists than he was with us. "How far did you have to flee before you sheltered here?"

"Many blocks," said the older monk again, the obvious leader of the group. "We were collecting alms and distributing your works in the park, Lord, when we heard a great cry followed by loud crashing and gunfire. Then the conch blew."

"Raphael," I said aloud.

Christ hummed in my direction before he readdressed the Hare Krishnas. "Well, we shall wait here together before we go again. Do any of you have any questions?"

To my surprise, more than a few eager hands raised. Smiling as he raised a finger at the nearest, he took the question from a young white girl who had shaved all her hair off. Dressed in orange robes and dripping in malas, she pressed her palms together and bowed. "Lord, we have been discussing your coming since you appeared on YouTube. Are you here to declare the end of the Kali Yuga, ushering in the next cycle of peace and glory upon the realms of thought and sense?"

"That's a very good question," Christ said, blinking a few times. "Let's just say I am here to bring clarity. If in clarity some things end, they end, but if some things are to begin, then they shall begin as they were ordained to. Whatever the cause, the effect shall be what it shall be in adherence to my will."

"And what is your will?" another monk asked, a tall black man wrapped in blue with only a single mala on his neck.

"What does the Gita say?" Christ asked them. "I have come to do everything I have to do, but not with greed, nor with ego, nor with lust, nor envy. I seek to bring only love forward, its gleaming chariot built upon compassion, humility, and the devotion I earn from others. That is my will."

All of them nodding to each other with satisfaction, another voice asked a question in a far rougher tone.

"And what if it's our will to break your head in?"

The lot of us looked toward the turnstile entrance of the station to find five demons shoulder to shoulder while the last three hopped between glass partitions and over the steel arms. More than one carried a pipe, a knife, or some hand weapon perfect to exact the answer to their question out of every one of us.

"Round forever, motherfucker," one of the demons said, his voided black eyes fixed on the Savior.

Christ walked to the front of our group, hands on his hips as he surveyed the small order of fallen angels. "How about we ring the bell now? I ask nor want war with any of you, my children, and if you would only stop to listen to my words, you wil—"

"Stop him before he spills more lies from his torturous mouth," one of the demons, a possessed woman with a broken arm dangling on her right. She wielded a fire ax in her good hand.

Christ still beat them to it. "Hare Krishnas!"

Like the rams of a herd called to the shepherd, the devotees of a Vaishnavite sect heeded the call of the manifest God, seeing no difference between their blue cowherd and the impoverished carpenter. They did not run or raise their fists to meet the forces of the Devil, but instead struck up their voices in unison, the words of their most sacred chant reverberating throughout the subway station.

"Hare Krishna, Hare Krishna,
Krishna Krishna, Hare Hare,
Hare Rama, Hare Rama,
Rama Rama, Hare Hare!"

The chant left the demons writhing, falling into line. Their arms and legs tucked under them by a will beyond the wills holding their hosts, the eight pressed their foreheads against the tile floor, which I wouldn't have done no matter how hard God made me.

Christ spun and pointed to the 4 train, which sprang to life as lights awoke, and the doors slid open.

"Quickly," he said.

"But what about them? What happens when they stop chanting?" Rosie asked.

"Oh, trust me, they hit my name enough and those demons will be crawling out on their own," Christ replied. "But we need to go. Patrick, you and Rosie first, then him!"

"Who?"

The exact moment the question left my mouth one of the Hare Krishnas broke from the pack, sprinting with his tambourine in one hand as he hiked up the front of his orange robes with the other. No older than twenty-two and whiter than can be, he leapt aboard as the electric doors closed shut behind him with a loud clack. The train sprung ahead on the rails, headed into the northbound tunnel.

We were well in the darkness before he stood upright, nodding to me first as sweat coated him from the top of his bald head down to his shirtless torso beneath the heavy cotton wrap.

"Thank you for not pulling away too soon," the young monk said to Christ. "My Lord, my name is Govinda. I believe it is my dharma to come with you and see the end of your quest. Will you have me?"

"Well, I did hold the train a little bit," Christ said as he threw an arm around the earnest young man. "Welcome to the team!"

"What are we?" Rosie Baked asked aloud. "Collecting cats?"

"Don't give him ideas," I grumbled as I plopped down on one of the empty seats, happy for the chance to lower my heart rate before the next disaster.

19

JESUS LOVES ME

The 4 Train slid into the 86th Street Station, the last stop on the Upper East Side before Lexington Avenue ran through Harlem. Bringing the line of empty cars to a halt, the doors slid open with their quiet hiss. Christ stepped out first, headed for the stairs to the street as he waved for us to keep up. I hurried out after Rosie, the Vodun priestess quicker on the march than the rest of us. The young Hare Krishna Govinda came last, his expression serious as the first quakes above us shook dust from the subway ceilings.

The second rock of the earth stopped us mortals, but Christ carried on.

I called after him, "Christ, wait!"

"Call me to wait as my children suffer?" he asked, undaunted. "My children?"

"We don't know what is up there and you're only you," I started, "you might be fine, but we'll get torn—"

"After all this, after everything, do you think I'm here to let that happen?" Christ snapped at me.

I boxed with God with exactly two arms against his, numbered into infinity. "But—"

The streets above us vibrated as an explosion beyond the layers of earth, concrete, and steel failed to muffle its boom. The clatter of gunfire and screams outside were almost hidden by the pound of so many feet the station quivered underneath us.

"Ready?" he asked the other two, completely dismissing me.

"Yes, Lord," Govinda said, stone-faced in his bright orange robes.

"Ah, shit," said Rosie, who thrust her hand into her white-stitched bag and pulled out a snub-nosed .38.

"Really?" Christ asked, rankling his face at it.

"Hey, you brought me, I didn't bring you," she said. "I'm not getting caught not peeping."

In his deep, kind voice, Govinda turned with a gentle movement to Rosie. "My sister in God, to bring violence into a world already full of violence will not—"

"Hush," she said.

Govinda snapped his head forward and looked to Christ again, much more sheepish than before. "Yes, ma'am."

"Put it away," Christ said before he reached behind his back. Worried he was going to pull his own gat, which would have broken this entire plotline, instead he pulled out a guitar with a plain wood body. "I will not repeat this again: I got this."

"Ah, shit," I said this time, the fight draining out of me.

"Oh, shit, just follow me," Christ replied as he spun on his sandaled heels. "By me, it really is like herding star cats sometimes with you people."

"There are star cats?" Govinda called after the Savior. "What are star cats, Lord?"

"I knew I picked you for a good reason," Christ answered. "But not now!"

"Well shit!" Rosie sighed deep and long through her flat nose before slipping the .38 back into her purse. She trudged after, and I after her.

We marched the flights of tile-topped steps worn to the iron by decades of endless feet traversing them every single day. The noise grew in intensity, the clash of the dead and dying beneath the sky-shaking booms happening somewhere north of us, but we were close to the origin. Spent gunpowder and burning iron met us before any of us saw the ruined daylight at the top of the steps. On the turn to the last flight, I halted, dismayed as I saw the fires spreading on the roofs of the buildings outside and across from our exit.

"Right into it," Christ declared, running up the steps. "Patrick, get the YouTube going! Rosie, Govinda, come in on refrain! Go! Go! Go!"

And then this fucking guy ran right into the middle of hell.

I emerged after Govinda, who outpaced me by several steps as Rosie kept close to my back.

We came up into the midst of an absolute shit-storm. Human bodies possessed by demons, black-eyed and growling, numbered into the hundreds, if not a thousand to my muddy count in the cinders. A few fired their guns northward. A quick look in that direction revealed a set of nine bobbing lights in the carpets of smoke billowing from the Upper West Side, all the way across Central Park's northern bound before it snaked down to us on the east. Lines of fury lanced downward, the otherworldly cannon shots of the archangels.

Deevi fought somewhere in there.

Every fiend spun to face Christ as he appeared in their midst, dark-skinned and white robed with his acoustic guitar. He leapt off the curb as I struggled to pull my phone out, hooking one of my rosary's greenstone beads with my ring finger found as I dug in my pocket. It came whipping out on accident, the silver Irish Cross of my homeland knocking around my knuckles before I found the burner.

I raised it like a shield with my prayer beads, my longtime and often only defense against the infernal damnations I had fought.

Before I punched up YouTube, Christ landed in the middle of the road and down-strummed hard on the strings. The round of the notes froze the demons in place as he drew down close to his fret board, picking a lonesome, gentle tune.

The entire world shifted, slowed by a lingering tempo as Christ sang aloud. The battle to the north silenced immediately. All gunfire ceased, leaving the city caught in the silence taken by the roar of burning buildings, broken car alarms, and his singular, resonating voice.

> "Jesus loves me, this I know,
> I am here to tell you so,
> Little ones to me belong,
> We are weak but will be strong..."

Perdition and the Platinum Polis put down arms for a Sunday School song.

On the spot, Rosie and Govinda joined his refrain.

> "Yes, Jesus loves me! Yes, Jesus loves me!
> Yes, Jesus loves me! For I'm here to tell you so..."

I did not move from where I stood before the carrier of my soul and its Savior. My phone never lowered though my right shoulder, side, and entire body ached to. Undeterred, I maintained my guard as the red dot on my app blinked in time.

I spied over the case, marveling as the snarling faces softened, before the first one to my right—an Asian man in his fifties in a blue windbreaker—broke out in deep, wracking sobs. First him, then the woman in a half-torn green pantsuit, then the ten-year-old in his pajamas wielding a kitchen knife and wounds I prayed his host would not bear nor remember. From the lowest child to the richest elder, the humans within burst forth to the call of their Creator, dragging the rebel spirits with them in grace.

And Daddy could play. Christ strummed his way through long breaks between the verses. Every time he opened his mouth seeds fell, sprouting out of the stone and concrete of New York's hard, hard streets.

> For my children I did die,
> To loose heaven's gates, open-wide,
> I will wash away my sin,
> Please let me come back in..."

The second miracle I had seen in only a handful of days almost brought me to my knees.

Somewhere from the folds of his orange robes, skinny Govinda had extracted his tambourine, which he shook with expert timing as Rosie Baker clapped along to the beat both monk and master of the universe put together. The demons almost seemed to sway with the gentle glide of notes, trapped in a rapture of love, and I dared to hope, repentance.

Despite their sorrows, their tears, he sang to their everlasting salvation.

The forces of Perdition wept. I wept. Fuck knows what the other two mortals did out of my eye shot, but to the north the lights glowing off the archangel's beams had failed to glow again, signally a true stop to this fighting.

> "Jesus loves me, this I know,
> As he loved me long ago,
> Taking children to his knee,
> Saying, "let them return to me..."

For some reason my attention returned to the ten-year-old in his pajamas, worried of the toll taken on the little boy. Whomever possessed the child quivered where they stood, mouth half-gaping as their knife hung lifeless to their side. Pure, honest tears ran from every onyx eye I could find, not one unshaken by the offer made.

"Patrick," Christ called to me. "Come here."

My phone almost like a gun in my stance, and my rosary around it, he stopped me with a hand when he thought me close enough. He spoke aloud then, but not to me, or the priestess, or the acolyte who had embarked on this madness like the rest of us.

A father spoke to his children. "There's a lot to say in the moment, and with some of you I have less than that," he began, solemn, "so I would ask for your grace and a chance to finish. Afterward you may continue as you wish, but until then, let us have peace."

Mortals and demons alike stood silent.

"I am to blame," the Personification said. "If I am to be honest, I am to blame. For you being here, now, fighting each other and your family in the midst of many families watching in horror and wondering if they will be next—this is my fault." His shoulders sank at the confession, but his chin remained high as he took a steadying breath. "Long ago I placed power and privilege before what was right, and that was the wellbeing of my children. After I figured out what I was doing wrong, I tried to fix it—for you and for me—but again, power got in the way. I made decisions for others so I could maintain order. But order is not peace, and simply living in a universe accorded to laws I set does not mean there is justice. These are things that must be created, day in and day out, like the ticking of the universe, blossoming like a mustard seed. But what happens if you have no seed? What happens if you have the ground taken or the sky blotted out? What if you were left all alone?"

Privy to parts of the story only the demons—fallen angels—would understand, the pieces of many puzzles fell into place, all the way back the final confrontation of Jesus and Lucifer with Michael in the Platinum Polis, when the latter forbade his Father reunification with his brother's rebellion on the threat of raising another.

He had done it. He had said yes to one son to keep another in play, and in the process damned legions who had simply been unlucky to fall on the side of Michael's wrath.

How it came about, how he had done it, I did not know, but a gut-understanding of Deevi's experience and those fitting pieces gave a sense of certainty my intuition begged me to keep.

And my intuition told me what he'd say next.

"I am here to tell you that you are not alone." Christ gathered the words he needed. "But I know what I have done as well, and no matter the reason, I know I must make amends with you if you are to see the end of your torments. I am here, once again, to say unto you—no creature of Perdition or the Platinum Polis is to be damned. Like mortals, I will accord them my forgiveness, my understanding, and my compassion. I can only hope you will be kind enough to put down your weapons and take it. But," he said, nodding his head with finality,

"You are no longer bound to the place I sent you. All are freed from Perdition."

Every single one of the demons startled at the declaration, caught off-guard for a second before reality smacked them. The first one I paid real attention to, the ten-year-old in his pajamas, dropped the knife he carried to raise both fists in the air, taking hold of freedom in measure Satan could never promise.

Until a few yards past him one demon attacked another. Suddenly several fell upon their brethren, no longer committed to attacking Christ, as the battle reignited. The Asian man in the blue jumper attacked the ten-year-old, knocking him to the side with a tire iron before he beat him savagely with it.

"What the fuck? What the fuck?" Rosie screamed, crumpling to Christ's side as Govinda did the same.

The entire line of demons from the northeastern end of Central Park restarted their bloodshed and chaos, drawing an equally huge confusion from Christ who shielded the two holies. He watched in absolute horror, unable to process what was happening.

I sprang up, grabbing him by his shoulders this time. "Back to the subways. Go! Go!"

2 0

SYNTHWAVE CHASE

I had to pull him back from the melee twice, but with enough pleading from Rosie and Govinda, we convinced Christ back into the subway station at 86th Street. The renewed din of evil crashed and exploded on the pavement above our heads, the pound of feet and bodies coupled by the constant tatting of bullets. To my greatest shock, it was not the battle nor the sight of the demons turning upon each other that frightened me the most, but the absolute despair I measured in the man I carried to a bench on the platform. The old battered 4 Train waited where he had parked it, the cars dim.

"I don't understand," Christ whispered, staring down into the holes in his wrists. "I just don't understand."

"What? What?" I asked him. "What don't you understand?"

God—*God*—raised his head, mouth opened for an answer, but no Word came out, let alone the explanation. He lowered his gaze slowly, lost somewhere too incomprehensible for me to take a shot at guessing.

"What do we do?" Govinda asked from my left, surveying the Savior in his crumbling state. "What do we do with him? He's the only one—"

"Shut it, kid," I said with a snap I regretted. The poor bastard had been dragged along like me, but in the moment, I had little time for nicety. I checked around him for Rosie, only to find the Vodun priestess as the bottom of the stair we had just clamored down. Smoking a large cigar in her mouth, she traced veves to her Lwas on both sides of the entryway, the swirling glyphs drawn in deep red lipstick.

"Go guard the steps with her," I said, nodding for Govinda to go on.

Left alone with my Lord, I knelt before him, who shook hard every time the battle boomed above us. "Hey. Hey!"

He raised his dark eyes to mine, trapped in an absolute downfall.

I dared to dare. "What is happening to you? I need you to talk to me and tell me what is going on. Now."

He opened his mouth again in another attempt to answer, but the words failed for the second time.

"Jesus Christ!" I said, squatting in front of him. I grabbed both of his hands, not knowing if I would remain where I was or vanish on contact. I simply said whatever fell out of my dumb gob. "I demand you to speak. I need you to speak. Please."

"I thought it would end it there. I thought it would stop," he said, finally finding his gentle, wounded voice. "I thought they'd listen."

"Did you think or did you know?"

He froze on the question, his brow furrowing on such an inane thing a mortal could ask.

"Fuck it," I said. "Did they have a choice in their decision to put down their weapons? Did they have a decision turn on each other?"

"They obviously did," God said, as obtuse as any of the lesser things he had created.

"Then we'll skip the debate on how you're hedging your bets," I said, alluding to a conversation nobody could have with the divine save ones they had with themselves. "But you gave them freedom, right then and there, to decide not only what they did, but how they felt about it. You're going to have to put up with a lot of that, damn whatever your set list is."

"But what if it doesn't work?" Christ said to me, as lost on a subway platform as he had been in the deserts of Judea.

"You're God. I think you'll give yourself another shot at it."

He responded with a withering glare.

I shrugged in complete disregard for his feelings. "Welcome to preaching! You know it fails sometimes!"

He barked a single note of laughter before Govinda rushed to us, almost tripping on the bright hem of his robe.

"They're coming closer to the stairs," the young monk called. "We need to hurry—"

Govinda tripped over his sandals.

Christ lifted his hand. The battle above us silenced as the lights of the 4 Train kicked on. The doors slid open as the Savior stood from the bench and sighed. Govinda avoided the worst of a tumble and found both feet. He looked at this renewed balance in confusion, then to Christ, before I checked on Rosie. She had stopped her workings to climb to the first landing, shocked by the sudden lack of chaos like the rest of us.

"You're right," Christ said to me, short and to the point, like he didn't like admitting it. "It's like its yesterday but I forget how difficult it was every day. The Mount. The Parables. All of it."

"People are still struggling with it," I said. "Every single one of us, no matter how bound to you, are also bound to the mystery. In a time of darkness, parables are fun thought experiments, but people need light. Clarity. That's supposed to set you aside from the others. Or at least it was."

"The other gods," Christ said, knowing my thoughts before I did.

"Aye," I replied. "They gave mystery and hard truths and cruel ends to foolishness. Some might do it differently, but they don't have the power you do. You created this. You can explain it. So explain it, and trust we'll understand if you are honest and plain as we must always, always be to you. We have no places to hide."

"And I'm in every hidden place." Christ glanced to the 4-Train's open doors. "I'm going back to the Garden. I'll get to work."

"Okay, but—"

"I know, Patrick," Christ said with a half-grin. "You're going to go get her. And I'll make sure you have the means. Just keep an eye out."

He called the monk and the priestess to him, bringing them aboard as I remained behind on the platform. Alone again, so wonderfully alone, I offered a sincere wave as I watched the train reverse course, headed southbound to reach home.

Then the real weight of what that meant hit me.

Without the protection of Almighty God, I was simply me again, one frail mortal, marching up into the midst of a divine battle between light and dark.

But up I climbed toward the silence. To my utter shock, the entire battlefield lay asleep, the bodies of the demons freed and healed wherever they had dropped. The few I had my eye on the first time, the ten-year-old especially, had fallen on grassy squares and sidewalks, arranged in comfortable positions as the ground allowed. Yet to the north, just in earshot, the fracas continued in the streets above Central Park North, the Upper West Side of the island still engulfed in the war.

But safe enough. Swept up in relief, I scanned the block around me full of sleeping people until I spotted it. *My means.*

Some want cars for the danger. Others, the look.

Not me. I simply wanted to get from point A to point B.

I had done so in the back of paddy wagons, hopping trains, riding camels, and sleeping in far too many economy seats.

Christ had more lavish tastes in store for me.

Like every young Catholic boy sneaking comics, Page Sixes, and NWA albums to listen to under the covers with a stolen Walkman, the yearly car magazine passed through every hand more times than the Bible. I remembered George's torn-out pages of Tim Burton's Batmobile, so enamored by the idea of a jet-engine hurling him into the night. Fights in the schoolyard broke out between those who loved Lambos and the Ferrari dreamers who hated them for it.

Not me. I simply wanted to get from point A to point B.

In a 25th Anniversary Lamborghini Countach.

Perfected under the tender hands and brilliant mind of Horacio

Pagani, the Italian supercar of Western choice found its top speed at 298 kilometers per hour while reaching sixty in four point two seconds, at the time a worthy finish to an already legendary vehicle that decorated bedrooms walls as much as any bikini model did. Couldn't see out the rearview for shit, but you weren't supposed to worry about who was behind you.

Only that you could beat them to the mark.

It was the only car I ever wanted.

There it sat, glossy red with a metallic undercoating that made it pop no matter sunlight or cloud cover, with silver magnesium rims that glistened at every angle. Already purring as its 5,167-cc engine rumbled in its low chassis, the left side door lifted its wing, welcoming I and I alone to enter a bucket racing seat on the right side of the vehicle—also known as the correct side for any competent driver.

I approached slowly, somewhat perplexed when I saw the keys already in the ignition.

A small wooden cross hung from the key ring, beaded with greenstone.

It got a laugh from me. "Cheeky bastard."

I ducked the roof in a perfect swinging descent, practiced so many times in a Ferrari I once confiscated from a Satanist after rescuing him and his daughter from their maniac mother. I strapped in, requiring no adjustments to the mirrors. I pressed on the left paddle shifter and slid into first gear, taking my foot off the brake to ease the bull forward.

The damn monster almost flew off the pavement if the wheels hadn't kept us earthbound. The Countach charged up Lexington Ave in the absolute wrong direction on a normal day, a titan breaking the silence of the Upper East Side in defiance to the war in the west. White-knuckled to the wheel, I laughed in terror as I shifted into second gear, so I didn't scream louder. This red devil Christ provided peeled left onto 93rd street, finally in the correct flow of driving. Somehow all the cars had cleared out of the lanes.

Instead of sniffing suspicion, I let all my doubts die under the acceleration.

I hit 144 kilometers by the time I saw the park and 5th Avenue waiting for me. An ease struck, the thought of a nice, pleasant drive before I had to figure out the best way into the battle. But those immediate worries went away when I saw two shapes in the evening sky ahead, but unlike the glowing aura of the angels, their outlines were sharply defined against the raspberry-purple sky.

Long leathery wings gathered the wind to propel tight, muscular forms toward me. Their glowing red eyes trained on my headlights. The horns, even from afar, distinguished their long, inhuman heads.

Freed from the bonds of Perdition, some of the demons had taken material form of devils.

"Fuck me," I said aloud.

The radio on the dash to my right popped on, honed to static before a voice peppered through the speakers.

"Hey all you snarky saints marching through the night, this is your Lord and Savior with another delectable track to get you through. Dedicated to Saint Patrick of Ireland from one admiring rabbi, this song is 'Running in the Night with You' by FM-84 and Ollie Wride! Drive, Patrick, drive!"

The demons hurtling on my position, I answered Christ's directive by slamming my foot down as I shifted back into first, then into second. A strain of keyboard washed over a snare and bass, backed by the angelic words of the singer in the bounding, jazzy groove.

I reached the stoplight before they reached me and drifted right onto 5th. Pumping the breaks to ease my glide, I recovered and raced north, the pair of gargoyle-like monsters out of sight thanks to the diminutive rear window and the hump of the roaring rear engine.

Until two more flew into view ahead, banking out of the trees bordering the 97th street Traverse through Central Park's midpoint above the reservoir. Then two from the immediate west, joining them in a diamond formation.

They clouded from the trees like pigeons. At first in pairs, then clusters, dozens and dozens of devils rose on the air. Behind this wall of new hell waited Deevi, lost in the chaos of combat and disaster.

"Fine," I said, squeezing the wheel tighter than ever. Pedal to the fucking metal.

I took the left at 97th, into the middle of Central Park, and let the bastards chase me.

RUNNING IN THE NIGHT

For Deevi, the cause and effect of her actions strained through every fiber of her sword arm and the hot, hot stink of dead mortals beneath her. The battle may have been minutes, but it felt like years for the ill toil she had endured painting New York's streets with carnage. Behind the liquid-metal mask of her helm she beheld, in an almost detached way, her and her family's slaughter of innocent men, women, and children possessed in that instant, but not forever.

Not when they died.

Not when she killed them.

The toll of grinding bones and flesh under the ferocious power of heaven against Perdition's gnawing line of demons seemed an eternal damnation until, without warning, her uncles and auntie ceased their battering of the forces below. The damned froze and turned in unison to the west.

Gliding for another run to rake foes with beams from her sword, Deevi withheld when the archangels, her father included, seized in place with their rebellious brethren. Opening her wings to deaden her momentum, she banked hard to the right for an apartment roof, not far from the where her uncle Uriel posted, his own light-sword angled for killing shots. Alighting beside him, she willed her mask away from her face, viewing the strange pause with her naked eyes.

Then the wailing began, here and there in pockets. Demons threw up their hands in exhalation, cheers, some of them breaking down into full sobbing and tears. Smiles abounded in the confusion. Immediately seeking Lucifer, she found her father already sharing concerned glances with Michael, who for the first time looked back without hatred—only shock.

Then several of the demons burst out of their awed states and attacked their fellow rebels. The archangels moved at the same time, gone from targeting every demon to select aggressors, an impossible scenario rendering their beams useless. The Council of El sallied into the renewed melee, far more discreet in the application of God's wrath.

Caught unaware to the cause of the shift, Deevi pointed her sword at every threat she saw, but never released its gruesome energy, unable to distinguish between ally or enemy. Before she could decide, a rock flew up, thrown by a possessed old woman before other demons mobbed her. Expecting her to be torn to pieces, she marveled as they subdued the lone assailant.

Lucifer landed on the edge of the apartment roof beside her, placing her between him and the Angel of Death. Cast in his platinum bright armor, his long mane of golden bright hair flowed gallantly on the fetid wind as he surveyed the fracas below them.

"He did it," her father told her and Uriel. "He did it! He freed them from Perdition!"

"Who?" Deevi asked.

"The Creator," Uriel replied, flashing a smile as he lofted his sword before them, a warning to anyone that dared attack. "He's ended their confinement in Perdition!"

She kept her weapon at the ready in both hands. "What does that mean?"

"Look at them, daughter," Lucifer said, nodding to the mayhem on the stained pavement. "Look at them! Satan's forces are disunited, and with this moment, we might be able to—"

Crimson explosions interrupted Lucifer as select demons, the same who still defied God's new ruling, engulfed themselves in hellish energy.

What arose out of the smoke towered a full head above the other human shells around them, newly crowned in goat horns that twisted to black points. Great leathery wings akin to the proportions of the archangels extended from their backs, the foils fibrous and bat-like. The transformed devils opened and shut newly-taloned hands.

In the next instant, they shot skyward, summoning swords of dark red light close to Deevi's own blade, but of a ruddier, more-malignant quality. They pounced on rebel and repentant demons alike, tearing all asunder.

Lucifer gasped. "Deevi, they—run! Run southward! To Christ!"

Without any more instruction, her father descended upon the nearest devil. Keen to its surroundings, the embodied form of Perdition met the Morningstar before he could gut the damnable thing, parrying the blow with a strong riposte.

Not waiting, Deevi flew south, headed into the northern hills of Central Park. She gathered altitude and then dove, powered by a strong flap that sped her like an arrow. Opening her wings again, the air buffeted in the feathers as she deadened her speed and dropped below the tree line onto one of the many asphalt paths snaking through the park's dales and peaks.

A roar directly behind Deevi spun her about. Able to summon her sword in time, she deflected the hell blade, wrenching hard to the side to throw the devil behind it off balance. She parried its follow-up blow and slipped its third attack, then lunged forward.

The magma sword pierced the devil through its ashen gray chest, leaving it to shiver in final death throes before she yanked her weapon out. Out of the corner of her eye she saw a pair of dark shapes coming in from the left. Ascending as two more devils missed her by a few feet, she banked left just above the treetops. One of her pursuers quickly fell out of sight.

The remaining devil trailed her, pulling hard with his long wings to close the distance as he flew up to catch her.

Chancing the shot, she plummeted for a moment, spinning in the air as she threw her sword out. The point leading the rotation, she loosed a bolt in the devil's face, disintegrating it's gnarled head before she flapped hard to halt her fall.

The second devil appeared beneath her, leaping out of the trees.

Out of reach out of its slashing hell blade, she cut down anyway, a panicked response as she regained her pitch and climbed. The newborn devil dropped into the oaks and elms, clawing in the looming shadows of the evening. Trying to outpace him, Deevi ascended higher then glided, hurtling south again.

She did not have to glance back her to know more foes had taken to the air, their roars close behind.

Her view inverted, she looked down the length of her body and sword, aiming at the face of the lead devil. She blew it out of the sky in a flaming heap. Two more closed ranks as she turned over to fight for more distance.

Then, within her earshot to the west, loud music pumped through the gathering night, backed by sweet words sung in notes of hope, promising a place to land in the shadows.

Deevi banked in the direction of the music, allowing her to gain view of the hunters chasing her from the north. Two dozen devils, gray and winged, kept after her as two more broke from their formation, headed toward the same source of sound to cut her off. She spotted the small headlights at the front of the small red car screaming through Central Park's only west-to-east road above its grand reservoir.

She spotted the devil as it landed atop of the red car, revealing the driver in the front seat as the ashen fiend peeled the roof away. Saint Patrick gritted his teeth, focused on the road as the bright beast he drove powered ahead, faster than before. Acceleration slowed the devil long enough for the saint to shift, an attempt to dislodge him. Holding hard to the exposed frame, the devil cackled in glee and raised a claw to strike.

Deevi met the infernal first, her sword through its heart as she collided into the deadly foe. Knocking it away, she let go of her sword too and grabbed the roof of Patrick's vehicle, her celestial grip tighter than its breakneck speed.

"Grab my hand," she called to him, reaching forward.

He undid his seatbelt and grabbed hold. She lifted them both as she flapped upward, gaining altitude. The supercar swerved to the right, collided with a steel barrier, and flipped several times before exploding in multiple chunks of shrapnel.

Deevi hauled her lover into her arms and pressed higher, until they were well above the trees and over the water of Central Park's reservoir. Coasting down to the other side, they landed on the red pavement. The devils did not follow this time, circling back to the north of the park. Patrick touched down first, stumbling though he remained on his feet.

Landing a few feet behind him, Deevi fought to get the first words in. "Patrick, I—"

He pressed her mouth shut with a deep kiss, stealing everything she had intended to say.

21

WHAUR WILL WE GANG?

We started walking south from Columbus Circle, having snuck around the reservoir without attracting any more of the devils Deevi informed me about. Behind us, the battle between the archangels and the transformed demons continued, but the hellish screams diminished the farther we traveled, hand in hand as we let the glow of her golden wings lead the way.

"Some armor," I said of her new shell as she walked beside me, which shimmered from the bottom of her jawline down to the soles of her feet. The liquid metal made no clanks, clacks, or clangs on the cement and grates we passed over. Somehow she had willed the mask away from her face, leaving her dark hair to flow outward.

She kept checking on me with her golden eyes, squeezing my hand tighter each time. "A lot happened," she said, almost quiet as we beheld each other. "I'm sorry about Lough Derg."

"Oh, don't worry about that. It was just buildings. The land will heal."

She slowed a little. "I'm sorry about George."

"I know," I replied, at a strange crossroads in my grief. I explained the events at Madison Square Garden as we worked our way down, always staying west of 8th so we did not run into anything unexpected. When I was done, she chewed on it, her brow knitted hard with thought after I have revealed my final moment with the gallant knight.

"Well," Deevi said, almost whispering it. "I'm still sorry. All of this is over me."

"I wouldn't worry about that now, love," I said, swinging her hand in mine. "I think bigger things have swept that off the table now."

She grunted an affirmation, but an anxious one.

"What?" I asked, unable to ignore it.

"I don't want to ruin this moment," she said, matching the swing of my arm so we fell into sync. "I'd rather just be here."

"No, no." I halted us on the corner of 43rd Street and 10th Avenue, lingering by a lamp post. "You don't ruin the moment. Just ask."

Holding my hand, she took in it both of hers, gently cradling my fingers. Deevi sighed once through her small, slim nose. "What are we walking into now?"

"I told you," I answered, confused by her puzzlement even as her power pulled the truth out of me. I admit I did not like the return of the feeling, or how the only thing I knew to say was a repeat. "Christ waits at Madison Square Gard—"

"No, Patrick," Deevi said. "He's back. The old gods are back. If I am to believe correctly, he has broken Perdition. What in the world waits for me? For us?"

The overwhelming nature of everything we had been through, everything remaining to face, crashed upon her. Instead of leaving my hands to hers, I pulled her close to me, bringing the brightness of her wings and her eyes near. Then, right as my gaze caught hers and my hand pressed against the small of her back, I remembered the nervous look on Gabriel's face. And, oddly, no easy answer left me free of an immediate response.

"What are you worried about?" I asked. "Did the archangels tell you something? Did your father?"

"Nothing. They had only just found Cuchulainn, Laeg, and I before the demons attacked. Why?"

I eyed her, trying not to make it obvious I knew she hid something. "Gabriel seemed preoccupied the last time I saw them. Part of me wonders if it has to do with you."

We crossed one more street to the south, putting us on course for 33rd where I decided we'd cross over, hopefully into a welcome crowd tending to the arena's entrance.

"Well?" I asked once she had been given a good span of silence. "Anything I need to know?"

"Nothing more than what comes next," she said, mysterious within her small smile. She took my arm and kept on with me, nestled close.

"Oh?" I asked, happy to oblige her. "And what comes next?"

"I was thinking we'd get married."

The reason I never married in this life was because I still remembered my first wife, God bless and keep her. Rhiannon had been the kindest soul and a perfect fit for a man of God in a foreign land, tough and wise as she was beautiful. In a time before nuns and nonsense about chastity ruined the natural course of human life in the Church, it was a sacrament for the priest to marry as much as it was for the warrior, or the crofter, or the fisherman, and at least one of the archangels had seen the providence in a partnership. I worried how Merry might take it, or Christ, or the rest of The March when they found out.

Part of me could hear George groaning in the back of my mind.

But I wasn't a priest anymore. Not the kind the world wanted, anyway.

And I loved Deevi more than anything.

"Oh, but where?" I said, laughing a bit more before happiness—maybe the first in this goddamned miserable life—broke me. "We could get married in Verona. I've always liked Verona."

"Where is it?" she asked, pressed up in her metallic feet to kiss me tenderly where a tear fell.

"It's in Italy. Pretty place." I reached up and thumbed away one trail, trying to march my way through the others. "One of my favorite plays takes place there. *Romeo and Juliet.*"

"Oh, so will you be my Romeo and I, your Juliet?" she asked teasingly.

I laughed at the question. "God, I hope not!"

2 2

—————

THE GARDEN

No devils attacked us the closer we came to the Garden. By the time we reached 33rd and 8th, all fear had gone away, replaced by an awe I don't think any force on earth could have brought out of me.

In front of the World's Most Famous Arena where Tyson had knocked men out cold and Jordan turned entire crowds against the Knicks, the steel doors had been thrown open at the northwestern and southwestern entrances for a constant funnel of people coming from all parts of the city. The masses flocked to Christ's call, and from the vast sea of bodies clogging 8th Avenue for at least ten city blocks, as far I as could see over their heads, more than the maximum of twenty-thousand had come to see the Savior.

Many, many, many more.

Deevi halted me before we crossed the street, hiding inside one last alleyway.

"Patrick, there's so many," she said, squeezing my hand tight.

I held it firm, though her strength might have crushed my bones. "I know. But we'll make it through."

"But what if there are demons?"

"Trust me." I pulled her gently along. "We won't be worrying about that here."

But there was no hiding the wings on her.

Almost every eye turned in our direction, ignoring me for the beautiful woman encased in shining metal. A fast, hard silence fell. I recognized some of the ushers keeping the lines tidy among those in the droves of Evangelicals, now turned to willful servants of the real thing instead of prosperity gospel-nonsense. A few of the white-clothed Vodunasi spread among the crowd.

A familiar face, dark and serene, busied her way towards us, bringing along another person I was happy to see. Merry and Daniel parted the way, already flanked by some of her acolytes. All made room for the Vodun Queen's procession.

"Deevi," Merry cried first. She reached out and grabbed the Nephilim's hand, pulling her into an unexpected hug.

I offered my hand to Daniel. "Sir," I said to the ex-gunman, now second to the Lord if I gathered things. "What's the crack?"

"Sir," he said to me with humored nod. "Let's get you both inside, and I'll show you."

Daniel and Merry ushered us past the horde trickling into the northwestern entrance. Several of the Vodun acolytes nodded and saluted us once we were past the doors, into the halls that honey-combed the entire venue. An absurd amount of people for an unscheduled concert, I spotted more than a few with headsets dolling orders into their mics.

"How did you all get this going?" I asked as we snaked through one of the curtained tunnels to the main arena, the lights above already switched on and bright, bright white. Underneath, hundreds of volun-teers worked at folding down the chairs in the bleachers and risers, sweeping the floors. Dozens labored to erect an eight-foot-tall round which would provide everyone ample view of the stage. Heaps of wires ran this way and that, snaking under the massive black curtain just behind the drum riser at the apex.

Daniel allowed Merry to descend the steps down to the main floor first, motioning for Deevi to go next. "Once we started letting the

Voodoo-folk in and the pagans were given a chance to meet Christ, things kind of fell into motion. Suddenly, people knew how to make this place come alive."

"Some would even say it's a miracle," Merry responded in a wry tone. "Most of the people in this town working stage aren't Christians to begin with. Yet here we are."

"Where is he, then?" I asked as I studied in the immense production assembling in front of us.

"Waiting for you in the dressing room with the other Helpers," Merry said. "In fact, he alerted us you were coming. He wanted for you for a staff meeting."

"A fucking what?" I asked.

"Just come along, Tater," Merry said. "I have the feeling this is the start of many, many meetings."

"That is how freedom movements begin," said Daniel like any well-trained leftist.

"And terrorist organizations," the Vodun High Priestess of the Northeast batted back.

We crossed the smooth concrete and ducked into one of the many open flaps under the actual stage itself. A wide tunnel, several members of the Vodun security posted at the entrances and along the route. Each of them taller than six feet, all the muscled soldiers of Ogun bowed in reverence to their queen. Merry offered back gentle smiles and nods, patting a few on the shoulder to acknowledge them.

Due to the size of her wings, Deevi ended up at the back of the march, stopping often to hug the wall, letting others get equipment through or pass by on their errand. We turned off into one of the building's sub-basements, which buzzed with gophers and techs as they checked a new soundboard someone had ripped the plastic from that day.

When he could have waited where the Knicks dressed or a suite fucking Bono had probably held a seance in, Christ had instead cleared out one of the coat closets to jam all his shit in there, along with us.

And he had brought some shit:

He had built the cave around an old black Roland d50, its keys white and shiny. The synthesizer plugged into a power strip plugged into the only outlet in the entire damned cell, a three-seater couch crammed beside it along with a small coffee table, which was heaped in empty mugs and crumpled wads of notepad papers. Rosie Baker sat at the farthest end, tending to her nails with a block file while Enrique and Jennifer watched Miranda pick out notes on the bench beside Christ, who masterfully produced thin electric strains.

Govinda stood over the shoulder of the creator, the bald monk eagerly observing the lesson. Shoniqua sat in the corner on a folding chair, the nurse mashing hard into the digital keyboard of her smart phone.

"Now you see, Miranda," said Christ, "'The Saints Come Marching' is quite an easy tune to pick up. First you must—"

Daniel stood in the doorway and knocked. "They're here, boss man."

"Boss man?" I asked to the ex-gunman's back.

"Ah, right on time!" Christ scooted back from the synthesizer. He spun and stood up. Searching my face first as I peeked over Daniel's broad shoulder in the doorway, he bent to the side a little in confusion. "Well, where is she?"

"Right in the back," Deevi called, out of his sight. "Odd one out, sadly."

"Okay, okay." Christ motioned to the rest of the Helpers and pointed them to the lone exit. "Family meeting, everyone. I need Patrick and Deevi alone. Hang out some place and we'll be back together soon. Daniel, Merry, would you wait outside? They just finished setting up catering down the hall if anyone is hungry. Go in peace."

Nobody argued when God asked for a bit of privacy. Govinda left last, leaving room for me to step inside the green room and scoot to the far end.

Deevi entered slowly and halted, just past the entrance. The light of her wings reflected in Christ's brown irises.

"Hello," said Christ. "It's nice to finally meet you."

Deevi gave him a long, unreadable stare. "Was all this part of a plan?"

Since the moment we met, the power within my Nephilim lover had produced many amazing manifestations—her magma sword, which now seemly extended into a liquid-metal armor that would make T-1000 blush. Adding to the wings to fly above most things, she had come set for wars beyond wars. Yet her greatest gift lay in drawing the truth out of every single person with a mere question spoken in her voice.

I do not know fully if he had been compelled to answer or if he simply did so because he was God, but Christ did not hesitate. "If it was, it went wrong a long, long time ago, well before you were born. So, no, your kidnapping was not part of a plan. Satan's conspiracy to bring about the eschaton was not part of a plan. Never mine, at least." He furrowed his brow, his jaw tight. "I would never want to hurt my children. Let alone my grandchild."

The admission, confirmation, and so much more bent open the inner floodgates she had bound shut, away from me and the rest of the world. Deevi broke down in front us, our Creator and I. The liquid metal covering her evaporated off her bare skin and tattered clothes. Reduced to a desperate woman in a dirty white cami and torn sweatpants—albeit a winged one—she wept into God's shoulder, her bronze face buried in the red cloth of his mantle.

Christ whispered something in Deevi's ear I could not hear, drawing out of her a sincere laugh of happiness.

A knock at the door broke them up.

Popping her head inside, Shoniqua had paused to see the Lord and the Nephilim together, and me off to the side. She simply spoke, plain and to the point as always. "I just wanted to let you all knowthe archangels are here."

23

SETTING UP

The eight members of the Council of El, bound to serve God since his first sigh in the ebbs of Time, arrived through the northwest entrance like Deevi and I had.

If only our coming had been so grand.

Shining out of the nighttime clouds mixed in smoke, Raphael's horn blew a note of serene triumph as they descended upon fans of concentrated light. Michael led the seven many knew and had prayed to for centuries, the Sword of Truth high on his shoulder like a banner. The others had brought their tools as well, with Uriel bearing a flaming sword, Selaphiel his smoking censer, but the Council had also hauled along a great box the size of a mini-van, its dark shape sharp and rectangular as it floated behind them.

After the seven and the box appeared Lucifer. Floating behind them by several yards, he hovered in the distance as several other angels of smaller and diminutive proportions encircled him, buzzing his ears as he nodded or denied their whispers with each shake of his head. The First among them the last, he kept guard of the cargo while dispensing orders.

Christ, myself, Deevi, and I stood mid-stage in the raised round, able to spy them and their light over the heads of the hundreds massing to see their approach while they marched the tunnels to reach us. Their father bore a clever, almost mischievous smile, before the curve widened into something loving with welcome.

"This way!" he called to them from the center of the arena. "We're setting up over here!"

Mortals stepped out of the way of the archangels. The silence, full of sincere amazement, followed every inch they traveled with their bare, glowing feet on the concrete. None of them bore the wounds or signs of the earlier battle, their wings set perfectly upon their backs to display waterfalls of shining feathers. They halted for a moment and let the container they had brought hover ahead of them, above the floor until it ascended with perfect precision up to the edge of the stage and over, alighting on the first flat surface to fit its dimensions.

They all leapt atop of the eight-foot-tall round, a simple bound that nonetheless enthralled every onlooker.

"Welcome, welcome, my children," said Christ. "It is finally good to have you all here, where our beginnings shall end so others may start. What is the word?"

"Most of the rebellious angels had re-sworn to our banners," said Michael, standing at attention. "The others who transformed into the winged devils have fled. But, my Lord, I do not know how to track them. None of us do. They are strange things to us."

"The answer shall come in due time, Michael." Christ started toward the long black box they had hauled with them, rubbing his palms together. "But due time is later. Now it is time to set up!"

The squared end facing the Savior opened like a zipper, revealing an endless source of blinding light. Michael broke for it first as he reversed his hold on the Sword of Truth, gripping it by its scabbard's immaculate throat. "How much room are we giving Raguel and Ramiel in the center?"

"Oh, I thought if you placed them about two and half meters from each other I'd have plenty of room for the synth," Christ said before he looked to the two archangels in question. "Don't you think so, boys?"

"Oh, yes, quite, though I will probably need a little bit of space for the mics," the younger Ramiel said from beside his compatriot, the rabbi-like Raguel who busied rolling up the massive scroll he constantly carried to record creation's events.

"Are the mortals doing the mics?" Ramiel called, suddenly human-like. "Who's doing the mics?" he asked with some concern as he scanned the main floor of Madison Square Garden in search of techs.

"No worries about that, Ramiel. Our mortal kin will get it done," Christ said. "We'll just need a cabinet behind us to keep a few things and the rest the tambourines."

Michael sighed as he stepped up to the lighted portal. "I'll just bring out the racks first."

Lucifer spoke up, pressing through his siblings. "I'll come—"

"No need!" Michael disappeared into the light.

Too gob-struck to really say anything, I stood nearby, a pillar of uselessness to the entire proceedings.

Then Deevi nudged me with her elbow. "What's that?" she whispered, nodding at the opened rectangle.

"Oh, fuck if I know," I whispered in reply. "I'm pretty damned sure everything is beyond me now."

As if hearing me, Christ checked me over his shoulder with that happy trickster grin of his. Arms folded in front of his chest, he backpedaled right between Deevi and I, the meat to our uneven sandwich.

"In fact," he said, leaning in my space, "There are plenty of things in this scene many people can understand. That there is a piece of consigned space which carries the band's gear. Think of it as a great big cosmic backpack."

"Oh," Deevi intoned in obviousness. "Like a shipping crate!"

"Exactly," Christ said. "Anyway, I certainly still have need for you, Patrick, even in this late, late hour."

"With what?" I dreaded and dared to ask.

He thumbed over his shoulder, causing both Deevi and I to turn in time to see Daniel emerge from the tunnel to the backstage. After our family conference, the rest of the Helpers had been disbursed to complete several tasks Christ had given each of them. Left with no recourse but to follow my Savior where he led me, I had come along simply because, which was fine enough for Deevi.

"Cuchulainn has arrived, my Lord," Daniel said to his Boss Man, "And he's in a mess."

"But we will not meet him as such," Christ replied with confidence as he nodded to both Deevi and I. "Come along, Patrick. Deevi and Daniel, would you two remain and make sure everyone else gets situated?"

"Um, sure?" Daniel asked, as confused as the Nephilim and I. What could we mortals do for archangels?

The Savior and I retreated north through one of the overflow tunnels before making the left for the northwestern entrance. Several of the volunteers among New York's disparate communities mingled as they set up, prepping concessions stands with bread delivered from a local Halal baker and, of course, someone had donated enough wine to marry half the island. Every soul of every origin around the world gave Christ a nod or smile when he passed by, and he returned their warmth with a happy pat on the shoulder, a look, or simple nods that reduced more than a few to tears. By the time we reached the glass doors, the crowd of people had grown into a sea.

Glad to have the main man about town with me to part them, the irony was not lost on me as I recounted Lucifer's memories of his father's first earthly ministry. I don't do well with too many heads and shoulders and wondered how the Apostles had endured such clusters. Flustered by the constant proximity amid the growing sense of expectation once everyone knew he was among them, I groused in his ear. "Where the fuck is he?"

Christ was gentle in his admonishment. "This way, this way. There's a lot of a people."

"Practical Sunday Services," I mumbled.

He laughed too hard at my joke for it to just be a joke, but I ignored that when I finally spotted the sore thumb.

The only place where the attention on Christ flagged was in the presence and power of another who claimed divinity. Cuchulainn stood before Laeg, dripping blood from head to toe. He lofted his sword and trident at his side, having removed his armor, bracers, greaves, almost naked save for his loin cloth and sword belt. The charioteer at his back had arrived as haggard, but at least gave me an enlivened nod while his brother-in-arms stared down the Personification.

People parted, quick to move, while the Hound fixed like a standing stone.

Christ reached forth with both hands and grasped the knight of the Red Branch by his broad shoulders, not too much shorter as far as Iron Age men went for the time. "Welcome, Setanta. I see you have found your way to my woods."

The bloody warrior lowered his gaze to the floor between his reddened feet and the Lord's sandals. "Felt only right. I thought about taking off but I..." He snorted in his hard, sharp nose and raised his fierce eyes to Christ. "We have business, still. And I have business with Patrick."

I braced, recalling the terms of the deal I had made with Cuchulainn when I fished him out of Purgatory. A frenzied but focused warrior, his urge to meet his ends would come to bear at some point.

Thankfully I had the guy in front of me play interference.

"I know," Christ said. "How about this? There are great showers in this place. Why don't you and Laeg go and get cleaned up and I swear, before I leave, I will give you everything you need to feel better."

"What's a shower?" Laeg asked in Ancient Gaelic.

"Looks like we'll find out," Cuchulainn responded. He hefted the legendary spear of Gae Bolg onto his shoulder. "Someone going to take us?"

"Just head down that hallway and you'll see some men in the tunnel dressed in white," Christ said. "Tell them I sent you. They'll believe it."

The Hound of Ulster marched ahead, then halted. "Our horses are outside."

"Don't worry about them," said Christ.

"Oh no," said Laeg in his brogue, chancing an attempt at English. "I worry what they might do to all of you."

"We'll be fine as will they." Christ ushered them on. "See you both later."

Despondent to the world, Eire's ancient champion marched forward to go get cleaned up, leaving drops of red in his wake. His driver kept close.

"What are you going to do about that?" I asked. "Or his kin when they re-emerge in the world?"

"Invite them in," Christ said as he continued to shake hands and signal thanks to his onlookers. "It's all I can really ever do, Patrick. I have left the gate open, but it is up to the individual to see the way through. But it is always open."

Too tired and already missing Deevi, I didn't offer any argument or interpretation as we ducked into one of the tunnels back to the arena.

Things were hopping when we arrived—right into the pit as Michael swung his fist at Lucifer.

Real rock and roll shit.

Somehow they had walked off the circular stage and found their way into each other's faces. The Morningstar stepped out of his brother's looping strike, his footwork keen as a boxer's as he darted back in to tackle him, but by that time the other archangels had rushed in, placing their six bodies between them. Deevi was already a natural at this, it seemed, in her father's face with a calming word as she pushed him away.

Christ grunted beside me, he annoyance clear. Having been inside his oldest child's memories of events outside space and time, I only imagined how complicated parenthood made things, no matter how supreme the being.

"Kids, huh?" I asked as we paused in the threshold of the tunnel.

"I don't know what to do," Christ said.

"You can't keep saying that."

"I know."

Maybe this is what the Apostles did? Maybe this is what the Helpers would be there for. "You have to go be God." Awkward at having counsel the Creator, I threw my hands up and surrendered to the role. "Look, either Michael has to forgive Lucifer, or you have to explain why it's not Lucifer's fault and have Michael get it. That means you have to own up."

"To Michael," he said with a clear understanding.

I reached up and held his right arm, firm but thin beneath the sleeve of his homespun robe. "To everyone. That's what this is, right? 'I must make amends to see the end of your torments.'"

He took one more deep breath through his long, straight nose and went forward. "I said more than that."

"People remember things odd." I followed behind, content to have made my point.

The archangels fell into perfect harmony the second he appeared, upright and innocent as if no fracas had happened.

Christ stopped right in front of Michael first, glaring hard at the Protector before he gave an equal share to Lucifer. "Everyone who is not an immortal, celestial, or named Patrick needs to clear the floor."

Despite the relatively scant amount of people in the stands and on the concourses, the number of human workers ebbed from a few dozen to a handful of stragglers to the last sweeper shouldering his broom, who was smart enough to scoot behind the curtains.

Papa was about to preach.

"I know who started it. I know what was said." Christ traded looks with Michael and Lucifer. "Neither of you did well in the moment."

The former met his father with a mix of anger and shame, but steel straightened his spine with pride worthy of a fallen. The Morningstar, on the other hand, cast his eyes up the lights of the Garden, seeking something he would not find up there.

"We haven't talked about my decision," Christ said in a more conciliatory tone. "In some ways, I'm not taking questions about it because I don't have to argue about this: you are my children and—"

Michael interrupted, the little rebel. "My Lord, you decided—"

"I decided to fix a mistake I made, my son, toward you and the rest of your siblings high and low. Do we have to debate the merits of your argument against mine?"

"Yes," Michael said.

"You're such a damn bully," Lucifer had to jibe. "You could just be angry at me, but no, you have to punish others too."

"After what you did—" Michael bit his bottom lip, his countenance transformed by his withheld rage. He let his teeth off the flesh of his mouth and spoke, slow and deliberate. "Everyone made a choice. You choose to betray us. Betray the Lord. You made others join you, and they shouldn't—"

Christ reasserted his hold of the floor. "If you are going to blame—"

"No!" Michael shook as he shouted his father. "No! I will do this again. I warned you both last time—if Lucifer is allowed—"

The other archangels wilted at the coming promise of rebellion, disunity, but for the powerlessness of six, everyone had forgotten a newcomer in the conversation.

Stepping forward from her father's side, Deevi leveled Michael with her golden gaze and opened her mouth, sharp with every word. "What are you afraid of Michael? Why won't you forgive my father?"

The power of a Nephilim matched those held by God's highest order—wings for flight, the power to summon weapons and defense, but the flesh restricted, leaving Deevi one step below. But the great equalizer, for my love and to the great fear in us all, was the compulsion to answer her truthfully, full and unvarnished.

The greatest tactician of the Platinum Polis had no defense. "Because you won't answer me," he said, pointing right at Christ. Glowing finger extended, a wave of emotion broke his anger, reduced to a quaking soul lost for reason. From my place behind his father, the man responsible, I saw the failure of every parent with every child, the leftovers of a trust rarely given.

Deevi struck again. "What won't he answer?"

"Why is it only Lucifer gets to have a will?" Michael asked, more to Christ than to her. He stepped forward, hands smacking his chest. "Why can't we be free? Why can't we know? Why can't I—"

Some brothers kill the other when the latter gains favor for their harvest. Some simply fall apart. The clear result of his neglect before his remaking, Christ deflated, fully aware of his fault. The distance between him and Michael, only a few feet, seemed an endless gulf none would cross for the sake of their pride and shame.

Always braving the abyss, Lucifer made the leap. "Why couldn't you be trusted? That's it, isn't it?"

"You died," Michael said to Christ, ignoring his brother. "You died. And you told none of us, and all because you were trying to listen to Lucifer. You couldn't tell me? I've fought for you, and I have loved you, and I have tried so hard to show you that I'm worthy, that I'm just as good—"

"But you are," Lucifer cried out, rushing his brother to embrace him. "You are, Michael! You always have been! You've been better!"

The sudden turn, an acknowledgment unasked for nor expected, shattered their feud then and there. Michael did not resist Lucifer, collapsing into him. In the second before he and Lucifer came together, the other archangels teared, with even old Raguel weeping into his sleeve while Ramiel consoled him.

I half-stepped behind Christ and put my right hand on his shoulder. "Get in there," I whispered at him.

And he did, without hesitance or doubt. Somehow this short man from Palestine caught both his immense children in his arms.

On the chance, I checked on Deevi and found her seeking my attention with that mischievous, wonderful smile.

She looked like her grandfather.

REHEARSAL

The Helpers slowly reappeared after Christ sequestered Lucifer and Michael to their own ledge of the stage, seated with their legs hung over and heels almost touching the floor. I did not hear what was said between them, but Deevi did, though she revealed none of it other than a few joyful tears and hidden, secret smiles before she wandered off by herself.

Daniel and Jennifer brought along two full dispensers of fresh coffee, which we descended on like ravenous beasts.

My stomach aching from a bellyful of caffeine and little else, I found myself between Enrique and Shoniqua. Dressed out of her scrubs and into a pair of leggings and a black MSG t-shirt she had raided from one of the gift shops, she sat beside me on the bleachers while the three of us watched the archangels roll through sound check.

Selaphiel played strains of interweaving harmonies out of two stacked keyboards while Raguel and Ramiel had a rare argument, the latter commenting on the arrangement of his elder colleague's black-and-sunburst drum set with more cymbals than I had ever seen in my life. His own rack for the bongos and a standing drum, he ran two of the large brass disks with a wire beater, noting its unequal sound before the Interpreter told the Recorder to shut up.

Besides this small snafu, the rest carried on, the most active of them all Uriel. The angel of Death tuned his black matte electric bass, each flick of his fingers on the thick steel chords thrumming from his cabinet.

"I was going to work," Shoniqua said, coffee nested in her fingers. "I was going to work and had no plans for this."

I finished another sip I shouldn't have taken, wishing it was water. "Sounds about right."

"It was just another day," Enrique chimed. "You know."

The heaviness of a homeless man's unspoken details dulled the conversation until he took a drink.

"Is this where you expected to be when this all started, Patrick?" Shoniqua asked, casting me a sidelong glance.

"Fuck," I said, "I don't know."

I thought that would have drawn a laugh, but they simply watched the stage, too compelled by the sight of the heavenly band. Behind us, Govinda chatted with Rosie, the pair of them thicker than thieves after their odd impressment to our ranks. Studying this motley crew Christ had cobbled together in only a day's time, the eight of us spanned multiple faiths, political views, but there in the stands, I knew I couldn't and wouldn't have chosen better than nurses, soldiers, and holies.

"Fuck," I said again, louder this time. "Maybe all this is a continuance. You know? Because I might as well say it now. There's eight of us. How much longer before four more come about and—"

Daniel appeared to my right, beyond where Shoniqua sat. He waved me to come over.

"Ah, fuck," I said as Shoniqua and Enrique followed my focus to my fellow Irishman.

"Patrick," he said the moment he reached the fence footing our section. "Someone's here to see him. Christ told me to run everyone by you first."

"Why me first?" I asked, not expecting a real answer. Putting my paper cup half-full of coffee down under my seat, I nodded to Shoniqua who gave me a bleak glance. "Want to come along?"

"No," Shoniqua said.

"I'll go," said Enrique with a huff, standing from his blue folding seat. "I'm getting antsy anyway."

I gave Rosie and Govinda a parting wave. The three of us clopped out of the arena into the buzzing hallway where more workers ferried in to help prepare Madison Square Garden for a night none would forget if we weren't trying so hard to keep up. Vendors from the halals around the city prepared the stations and kiosk to serve dishes rich in lamb, rice, and un-leavened bread. The Vodun guards interspersed at the entrances nodded to Daniel as we passed.

Near one of the back doors on the north side of the Garden we found Miranda and Jennifer guarding an odd man. A fair bit under six feet but broad in the chest and burly, his blond hair flowed past his shoulders to cover the lapels of a denim vest covered in the patches of various heavy metal bands. He carried a blue electric guitar already strapped around his body, picking quietly on the strings as his fret hand worked different chords. He raised his head as Daniel led Enrique and I to him, his blue eyes and placid expression measuring us.

"Alright, who's this?" I asked, a bit frayed to be polite.

The stranger with the blue ax lifted his strumming hand, palm thick with callouses. "Nathaniel the Devout," he said in his low country drawl. "I hear Jesus is here about these parts. Figured I slide right into the rhythm guitar spot he has—"

"Wait, wait, wait," I said, a bit flummoxed. "You're Nathaniel the Devout?"

"Last time I checked," said Nathaniel.

"Who's Nathaniel the Devout?" Miranda had the sense to ask.

"One of Christ's closest disciples," I said, well-versed enough to catch a con when I saw one. "Over two thousand years ago."

Nathaniel raised his fretting hand this time. "Hey, man, I know how it looks. I was out on the dig in Arkansas when I got the hunch to check out a television one of the hands had. Figured if the old man is back in business then he's going to need his rhythm guy."

"And you're the rhythm guy?" Jennifer asked, voice dripping with the same doubt the rest of us Helpers shared.

"Look, fine," he said. "Just get me in front of him. At worst, he tells you what you're thinking and you send me back outside. But I gotta gig, man, so please make a decision."

The rest waited on me. No more threatening than a standard human save for his ease, who was I to question an immortal after every other thing? "Alright, I'll take you to Christ, but the moment he says no, you're not only out, but you're also walking away until I don't see you. Good?"

He gave me a solid nod. "Lead the way."

A bit irked, I marched him quickly into the arena.

This time the space filled with the rhythm of Uriel's bass notes threading together the patterns Raguel beat out of his drum set. Ramiel played beside him, golden hands blurring across the plate-sized skin of his mounted conga. Selaphiel manned his stack of keyboards, brow furrowed as he studied the board of electronics for the right settings. To my surprise, Michael and Raphael had taken their instruments from the strange black cube at the back of the stage. The Hornbearer polished his long trumpet with a white cloth while Michael used a small brush to clean out the spit collector of his silver saxophone.

Putting aside the odd, odd thought of the sweet, sweet notes the Protector might play us later, I found Christ at the far end of the stage with Lucifer. The Morningstar and his father gathered before a stack of amplifiers sandwiching one side of the Raguel's riser.

Lucifer whispered back and forth with the Savior as they fuddled with the knobs before the latter turned in our direction. A bright happy smile spread across Christ's face as he spotted Nathaniel, patting the archangel's shoulder to direct his attention our way.

"Nathaniel," Christ declared. "Nathaniel! I knew you'd make it."

No longer able to halt or deny the guitarist, I stepped out of the way. The two men, separated by millenniums, fell into tears. The pair embraced, Nathaniel burying his bearded face in Christ's shoulder. The Savior whispered something to the burly strummer, who made a small step back and nodded through a sniffling grin.

Christ moved out of the way, motioning his devout to join his son at the amps.

I quickly caught up to the Lord. "Okay, guy—what's up?"

"Just getting the band together. More are still coming."

"Look," I said, too tired to argue over the plans. "It's past sundown. When is this show getting started? I can't imagine waiting too much longer. Won't Satan be tempted to try stop it?"

"Oh, he will," Christ said. "But nothing we have to worry about until then. Just stick with me and it will be okay."

"Just okay?" I asked, not hiding the incredulity in my tone.

"Okay," he laughed, "more than that. But let's get there after we get to this," he said, pointing past me.

I spun to find Jennifer waving for us to follow her.

"Merry sent me," Jennifer said as we clomped up the stairwell, the soles of Christ's sandals slapping the cement. She huffed ahead of us, her boots far quieter. "She took them to one of the conference rooms overlooking the stadium. We were already putting the churches and temples there when they appeared.

I came dead last, huffing and puffing. "Who?"

"The Jewish Community," Christ said, not even fazed by the climb. "This was going to happen."

"Oh, shit," I said in a long sigh. "Who came? The Chabad? The Reformers?"

"I don't know," Jennifer answered, spotting me over her shoulders as she rounded another landing. "They just showed up and Merry brought them in. She seemed to know all of them."

We found the conference room in question at the top of the arena. Merry stood outside the doorway, thumbing the screen of her smart phone before she spotted Jennifer, Christ, and I.

She addressed the Savior first. "They called me to call you," she said, plain in her patois of Brooklyn and Creole. "And they are all in there."

Christ wiped his hands on the front of the red mantle over his shoulder, almost nervous. "Well."

"Well?" I asked. "What do you mean 'well'? What are you going to do?"

"Walk in and answer questions." Christ pressed past Merry and grabbed the handle to the door. "Come on, everyone."

To say the relationship between Christians and the children of Israel was complex would be an understatement, but out of every land on Earth where this conversation could have happened, America might have been the only place. Over one million members of the Jewish community lived in New York and nestled in the hotbed with Yeshiva University and Borough Park just across the bridge in Brooklyn; there was no way this conversation wasn't happening. Too much had occurred to simply pass each other in the night.

Absolute silence held sway as Christ entered. The rest of us might have disappeared in the moment.

Out of a million-plus, twenty figures stood on the other side of the long, gray table with a lacking number of black rolling chairs to share. None of them moved, but across the many faces of many descendants of the tribes, not one carried any outright fear. I saw trepidation in the men wearing their wide-brimmed black hats, their payot locks framing their faces. Shawled women studied the dark face of a figure quite divisive in his impact on their history, let alone the Personification of the same God of which both Christians and they claimed ordination.

Nobody knew where to begin, save the man in charge, so he spoke first.

"Shalom," he said in perfect Hebrew. "Would you all like to sit down? Perhaps we can get you something?"

One of the elders, a portly Hasidic gentleman capped in his black hat, black suit, and black shoes edged toward the table. "No, thank you." He answered in English, clearly surprised by the greeting. "Will you sit?"

"Please," said Christ, quickly taking the chair across from the first speaker. "I thank you for coming and I apologize for the lack of invitation. As you've probably witnessed, it's been a day just getting people inside." He checked over his shoulder at me, Merry, and Jennifer, nodding for us to take some seats as well.

I tried not to appear too anxious as I sat to his immediate right, Merry on his left and Jennifer next to her. The homeless veteran, once again impressed to a service without a full explanation, stared wide-eyed at the proceedings as the first man sat, along with two woman and another Hasidic representative younger in years and of fitter constitution. The two women, one Black and the other of Mediterranean heritage, eyed Christ with less ferocity than the younger man did. The rest took a half-step back, quiet in their raiment and witness.

Christ spoke without any sense of nervousness. "I'm sure there are a lot of questions. I can only tell you that this form has purpose, and its purpose is not to settle the debts of others or bring about the fulfillment of one sense of an end over another. I'm not here to be your enemy." Christ swallowed and blinked a few times. "I did not intend to be your enemy the first time. And most of us weren't. Most of us shouldn't have been. We shouldn't be now."

The older gentlemen who had first spoke presented an upturned hand in openness. "But nonetheless, young man, the history of what happened remains. You claim—"

"Pardon," said Christ, "I do not claim anything. What was claimed was claimed by medievalists long disconnected from the truth of my ministry, more interested in doctrine and power."

"But was that not your criticism of us?" the Black rabbi asked rhetorically. "My name is Rabbi Rebecca Schreiber of the Reconstructionists. Pardon me for saying so, sir, but long before medieval Christians we have been the targets for the woes and corruptions of a people who walked away from us. We did not walk away from them.

Your return, if that is what this is and you are as you say you are," she continued, not leaving out the sincere doubts on her side of the table, "it could cause us real problems in the midst of a world already seeking scapegoats."

"And I would dare not seek to make you scapegoats, for you are my brothers and sisters going back to our Prophet. I must address this again and again, because if it bears repeating for the need of it then I shall repeat: any ministry believing that I have come to support or deny your people, faith, community, civilization, or purpose is not a ministry of mine. Frankly, and because I am truly strapped for time tonight, I must—"

"You will not dismiss us," the younger Hasidic said at the table. "This is not a conference, this is a—"

"Joshua, please," the older rabbi said to his younger counterpart.

"No, Hadar," said the young man. "This man is not the personification of our people's God nor is he the Son of Man. He is not, nor was he ever, prophesied as Elijah nor do we, nor will we ever, recognize his claim of substantiation. Simply put," he said right to Christ, "you are not who you claim. You have no right to speak on the matters of my people and what you hold to be truth is sin in the eyes of the Jewish community."

"Ah," I said, though none of them paid me any attention. The younger one was more than any simple rabbi or representative of his community. The global headquarters for his movement located in Brooklyn, Chabad had likely sent him to check and see if a fight was brewing, not just a concert, and maybe start one if things didn't please him. For all I knew, the man had an army outside, which this city allowed, waiting to the storm the place with more than a few former IDF members among them.

His distaste for the hostility clear in his expression, Christ addressed Joshua directly:

"Rabbi, I would not dare to speak on the matters of your people, not in this age when you already have enough to deal with on your own. The Temple I contended with in Jerusalem is no more. You are no longer Pharisees any more than you are Essenes or Sadducees or anyone who was there to witness my ministry. I will not defend the events of my ministry, nor do I demand you defend the constraints and considerations your community must make here and the world over. Frankly, you have suffered enough under those claiming me in the name of their gross deeds, so I would seek to not have you suffer me at all. Whatever distrust you have is yours, but I shall not share in it." He scanned the faces of the people across the table. "For I am, and I am you as you are me. But I am only one person in a community, and no community should revolve around one person outside of God. All I shall do, because I do have to go, is apologize for any inconvenience I have made, then and now, and seek communion with you over our shared values. Other than that, that's really all I can do."

Even Rabbi Joshua had to absorb everything said as Christ pushed his chair back and stood up. Folding his hands together, he offered the group a little nod and started to turn for the exit.

"Mr. Christ," called the elder Rabbi Hadar.

Jesus paused. "Yes, Rabbi Hadar?"

"If I may," said Hadar. "We have dared to seek a meeting with you, and you have met us boldly and with honesty," he said with a thankful nod. "But it is hard to simply part when so much is already in the air tonight, as it could be said. We would need to speak again."

"Many times," Rabbi Joshua interjected, glaring at Christ.

Then the trickster's smirk, which I recognized behind his magnanimous grin, crossed the Savior's face. "Then let us not end the conversation." He leveled his gaze right on the rabbi for the Reconstructionists, Rebecca Schreiber. "Why doesn't Rabbi Rebecca come with me, and she can continue to ask more questions that I will be more than happy to answer when able. I'm only flesh and blood, after all."

They did not appreciate the joke.

Then Rabbi Rebecca showed true wisdom. "Why? Why me?"

"If I am God, does there need to be a question to why?" Christ asked to her and everyone else. "And if I am not, what better way to find out than to come along? I also think you'll find you are not the only one with reasons to doubt." He scoffed at his own dilemma, the bastard. "You might even make a friend or two."

The doubt on Rebecca's freckled brow eased. "Then this an ecumenical organization?"

I couldn't keep my mouth shut. "Rabbi," I said, deadpanning the flummoxed new Helper, "you're among the meddling kids now. And he's the talking dog."

DECISIONS, DECISIONS

"Try turning it the other way," Lucifer asked Deevi with gentle patience, though the smile on his face strained. "They're coming."

Twisting the distortion knob, as the odd Nathaniel had called it, she watched in quiet half-focus as her father strummed down on his bright white guitar, the cascading melody warping into something fuzzed and deep. Lucifer quickly palmed the stings, silencing the notes.

"That ain't it," Nathaniel the Devout said, standing to the side of a stack of speakers connected to her father's amplifier. Unplugged from his rig of wires, stacks, and amps to match Lucifer's, which ran off to 'this board' or 'that pedal', he leaned against the tallest speaker and picked out some notes on his own strings.

"I know it isn't it," Lucifer snapped at the immortal. "It'd be quicker if you just set it up for me."

"Then where's the fun?" Nathaniel asked before he tossed a wink to Deevi in good humor. "Got to figure out the tone to get the tone. Night after night, day after—"

"Fine," said Lucifer, holding up his glowing hand to quiet him. He approached the knobs of his amplifier and his daughter, who scooted back to give him room before the panel.

"Sorry," she whispered.

He hushed her as he turned the first knob down. "You're nervous. Don't be."

"What if he isn't happy about it?" she asked.

Lucifer exchanged glances between her and the adjustments to his guitar's resounding tone, the green lights near the board of sliding dials beeping every time he tapped one of the gray buttons beneath them. "Then he would be a fool."

"Father."

"I do not think you need to worry about whether or not he is happy, Deevi," Lucifer replied. "In fact, I am certain that you do not have to worry about the saint for a moment. Not only will he take responsibility, but it will also become the definition of his life. Like you already are."

"Are you certain?"

"I mean, your dad is Lucifer," Nathaniel chimed in from the other side of the six-foot speaker to their right. "It's not like the guy will have anywhere to go if he isn't."

Deevi flattened her mouth in a frown as her father leaned back and stared at the guitarist.

"Psst."

The sound of the hissing drew three of them around, and at the edge of the stage stood Jesus Christ.

He surveyed the entire stage where the archangels and the immortal among them finished their load out of the strange black rectangle. Raphael polished his silver trumpet as Michael did the same to his saxophone while Selaphiel refilled the censer atop of his rack of keyboards, already forgetting the rhythm Uriel plucked from his bass, the reverberating notes buttressing the steady but intricate beats Ramiel smacked and palmed from his collection of standing drums while the elder Raguel filled in the gaps from behind the black-sunburst kit.

Gabriel stood the farthest away from the rest of the band, their head hung in thought.

Dozens of mortals loitered around the setup, answering any request made to connect equipment to the greater sound system installed in Madison Square Garden, which housed the best of the best, or at least she had been told.

"Hey, Deevi." Christ singled her out. "Come here for a moment?"

She checked with her father first, who motioned for her to answer God without hesitation. Leaving behind Lucifer and Nathaniel to fuss over their walls of loudness, she approached with dutiful quiet.

Christ folded his hands behind his back when they met. "Well," he said. "How are you?"

Deevi tried a timid smile. "I'm well. At least as can be expected."

"Good." Christ bobbed his head and widened his eyes. "Okay—so I guess the problem is here now. If it is a problem."

"Problem?" Deevi asked, confused.

He nodded again, but this time toward her stomach. "Sorry. Wrong wording."

"Oh," she said, her surprise muted. "Oh!"

"Let's take a walk." He had her lead the way to the small set of steps at the round's rear, into a black tunnel to the backstage. Deevi's immediate suspicion peaked when she noticed nobody toiled in the passage, which lay almost empty save for the pair of Vodun guards at the end. They gave both her and Christ small nods of respect.

Not one to walk into an ambush, she struck first. "Have you met the others like me? The other children?"

"No." Alone in the makeshift hall, he put his dark hands on his hips and faced her. "You're the only Nephilim I've met."

"But there are more," Deevi said. "Aren't there?"

"In London, in 1986, with their mortal parents." He did not shy away from her questions, though she had no power to sense if she had coerced him. "With your mother."

"So why was I taken? Why the monks in Syria? The monastery?" she asked, full of so many questions she had always yearned to ask and have answered, now possible before the mystery that knew every truth. "Why was I separated?"

Christ paused for a long moment before he replied. "Michael was very, very exacting in his punishment of your father's rebellion and my forgiving of it. To forestall another rebellion, he believed you specifically would become the cause of future dissension one day in the Council of El, and directly because of your mortal heritage, which he discriminates against as something weak."

She hummed in half-understanding.

Sighing heavy, he reached out and touched her shoulder. "Deevi, whatever the reason for what happened, it happened, and it was wrong. I cannot give you back those years you lost with your mother and father, but I can do everything in my power to atone for what has happened. Would you be willing to allow me to do so?"

"What choice do I really have? Won't I always be at your mercy, whether I care about it or not?"

"Honestly, I don't know."

"You don't know?" she asked. "How can you not?"

"I don't," he said. "But I will. That is part of the mystery—the process of discernment. Even for me. Michael is terrified about what would happen if angels and human gave life to children beyond my design. If I allow an archangel to wed a mortal woman and procreate..."

"Then it is a feature, not a flaw," Deevi said, no longer perplexed. The kindest way to be told she was no mistake, no spawn of God's rejection, a burn in her eyes threatened tears. She tried to sniff them away.

"Oh, my granddaughter." Christ pulled her toward him. She collapsed into him, crying hard as the years of doubt vanished. He kissed her on top of the head. "You never were. And I'm incredibly excited to see what you and your cousins will become, with or without me involved."

"So then—"

"So then you, like the rest, must wait and watch." He took her hand

and placed it on her stomach. "Like all good things that come with time."

"This is truly a mystery," she said, innately aware of the spark of life growing inside.

"It is." Christ grew serious as he removed his hand. "But some things, I'm learning every moment, should not come down to mystery. Everyone needs help—most of all my granddaughter who needs to feel safe in this world." He used his hands to indicate her wings. "You have already done so well this next part should be easy. Imagine for a moment that like the sword, like your armor—"

"Is that all it takes?" Deevi said, aghast at how short-sighted she had been. The thought-form, away instead of toward, outward instead of inward, coupled by the ability to direct light, constructed in her mind's eye the means.

Trembling, she shut her eyes and opened them.

The golden glow of her wings, constantly lighting every step she took, had ended. Deevi looked the right, then the left, startled every time.

Both had vanished.

"And you know exactly how to call them back to," Christ said, a serene smile formed as some tears speckled his dark eyes. "Oh, Deevi. You should be very proud of the person you are."

The lightness of her back, the way she could stand straight, almost broke her more than any terror or tribulation. Freed of the one thing that had kept her from everything, from a center, she staggered toward him. "I—"

"Shush," Christ said. "You don't need me, for I am already here. There's a wide world out there for you, and while I know you will seek it, I have a feeling about where you'll head first."

The halls of Madison Square Garden were packed with people, the supporters and allies of Christ clogging the entrances they tried to keep in the tides of humans outside at bay. The pressure, the atmosphere, frenetic like New York City's soul, offered contrast to the quiet tunnels. All of the concessions had opened, and behind every counter workers switched on ovens and filled drink dispensers with the barrels and barrels of wine.

And not a single one of them paid attention to Deevi as she walked by looking as human as the rest.

Almost leaning forward, she strode faster than she ever had, no longer compensating for the weight of her wings. The few who did check her on the way by did so in slight confusion, but no eye strayed longer like they used to.

Freed.

She smiled as the word echoed in her head, on her tongue, down into her core.

Freed.

As always, Deevi followed her innate senses, focused on the thought of Patrick as she guided herself up a long twisting flight of concrete steps. She reached the top of the arena and entered the long hall designated for the private boxes.

Inside the hall of doors leading to their individual compartments The Helpers of Christ stood around a long folding table someone had set against the wall. Open bottles of red wine littered among plates of cheese and bread and four stripped buckets of fried chicken, two of which had already been emptied, and a whole carton of vegetable mimosa which distracted Deevi for a moment. Merry had wedged herself into the party, next to Daniel on a couch between two doors, lost in a chat with the new members of their troop.

Puffing on a fresh joint of stinking cannabis she traded with her fellow Vodun priestess Rosie, she rose from her seat. "Excuse me, dear, but we're—"

Deevi grinned as Merry recognized her. "Is Patrick about?"

Winged or wingless, her power over mortal minds to expel the truth remained the same. "He's through that door," Merry answered in shocked amazement, too stunned to say more.

"Pardon me," Deevi said simply to the priestess's shock as she quickly approached the correct portal, opened it, and stepped inside while closing the door in a single move.

The lights were off. Her beloved saint lounged on a plush black couch, a bottle of wine on the coffee table in front of the glass window overlooking the entire arena. Eyes shut and on his back, he drew on a small joint. Its lit end flared orange as he inhaled. Both boots had been kicked off, thrown to different points in the room.

Deevi cleared her throat.

Startled, Patrick righted on the couch with and exhaled a large cloud of smoke, coughing until his face reddened.

"Having fun?" she asked.

"I was until you came in and—" the dawning of her power upon him, Patrick stood up, facing her as the lights of the arena popped on. Wreathed in their glow, it revealed his utter surprise.

"Your-your wings!" he said. "Where are your wings?"

Coy, Deevi paced toward him and stopped, face to face. She beamed as she checked the wine on the table. "Were you having a party all by yourself?"

"I just came in here to smoke," he said, looking about her shoulders in astonishment. "Are you going to transform next?"

"And if I did?" Deevi asked, smiling all the wider as her power havocked him.

Patrick grunted but relented. "I'd make it work. But you aren't—are you?"

"Not anytime soon," she answered, teasing as she grabbed his right hand. "Let's sit?"

"Yeah," Patrick said, plopping back down on the couch.

He made more room before he remembered he didn't have to move, an awkward pause she broke by sidling beside him. Ducking under his arm, Deevi kicked her feet up beside his on the coffee table, her head rested on his shoulder. Quiet in the gentle peace with the room's central air conditioner humming in the background, they stared out the glass partition and watched hundreds of people open the tunnels by removing the black tarps. The Vodun guards in their white clothes appeared, fanning out to cover the entry points.

"Guess it's starting," she whispered to Patrick.

"You mean it isn't over yet?" he asked, musing. "They didn't play already?"

She reached up with a bronze hand and stroked the beard on his face, meeting his reddened hazel eyes. "I have something to tell you."

"Anything," he remarked, leaning toward her until their noses touched. "What happens?"

Deevi reached for his far hand. Picking it up by the wrist, she lifted it over and placed it on the middle of her stomach. "Remember our nights in Dublin?"

PART III

JESUS CHRIST — LIVE AND LOOSE IN NEW YORK

CONFESSIONS

I convinced Deevi I was going to the bathroom.

Instead, I slipped out one of the back entrances, several floors from where we parted. The streets of New York choked with cars never to move again for days while hordes and hordes of people congregated around the Garden. I tucked away in a small alley near one of the many garbage bins and watched through the channel to 34th Street as every manner of person crossed its opening, never once daring to slip in and try to steal an admission.

For all my amazement, I could not give a single fuck.

I'm a priest. Was a priest. Either way, I wasn't supposed to do a lot of things I did anyway.

I'm also the idiot who impregnated his Nephilim girlfriend.

By the giant green bins, stinking to high heaven in the acid-sweet stench I was happy to stay clear of, I allowed myself the moment.

To completely lose my shit.

What had I done? What had I done? Did I not think about this every time we had folded ourselves into the other? For all the excuses I had and could point to her power, her strength, her beauty, in the end of it was me who had not pulled out like any smart fucking guy would have not looking to knock up his Nephilim girlfriend.

Fuck, I'm the idiot who impregnated his Nephilim girlfriend.

"I'm going to be a dad," I was dumb enough to announce to no one.

The hard realization opened the floodgates to everything else, every other potential. Diapers. Being unable to lie to anyone in the house without getting in trouble for it. Midnight feedings. Who do you actually find to help deliver a Nephilim's baby? Did I need insurance? Where were we going to live? How in the fuck did anyone ever do anything like this and not create a terrible person?

I'm a terrible person. The weight of that hit harder as I thought of whatever little person who was soon to appear, innocent of a world I knew too well was anything but.

I hadn't known my father in either life.

And now here I was.

Deep in the doubt, the worry, a flicker of something eased the heaving in my chest. I rubbed my beard with both hands, at a loss before I remembered the leftover blunt in my right pocket. It came out straight with its burnt end crisp, the perfect cap to start a cherry. Somehow I had kept Rosie Baker's little red lighter, which would be returned.

A quick flick and I took a deep, hard draw. Ganja pounded into my lungs before his fiery claws dug deep.

My face reddened as I tried to keep it in before the choking vapor flew out. Unable to clear out the rest, tears filled my vision as I hacked into the gutter. An old bunny's trick I had learned in the streets of Kingston, the clearing and immediate intoxication stung my eyes, but a numbness, a freedom, settled my entire body.

The old wounds burned, but too high to care, I remained bent in my thoughts.

The clarity of the weed opened the doors. "I could be a dad," I whispered before the consideration of the next hit paused my thinking.

"Oh, sure you could."

There didn't have to be a moment of shock or any attempt to hide what I was doing. Christ had found me as he found me, standing right in front of the door I had escaped out of.

I drew my second hit and studied him. "We're going to be able to get back in?"

"Don't worry about it." He laughed at the inane question and pointed at the blunt. "May I?"

I popped my brows in surprise as I exhaled a gout of smoke. "I didn't think you did this."

"Maker of heaven and earth and I get questioned about a plant in my design?" he asked with the intended irony. He extended his hand again. "Are you going to be stingy or not?"

Not arguing over what was kosher, I passed the blunt to the left and let my hands hang, the tingle at the end of my fingers pleasant.

"Well, this won't do," he said, reflecting on the half-spent roll of cannabis wrapped in tobacco.

"Sorry," I said, letting my head loll about my neck. The tension seeped out. "Only had a little left."

"This is an old party trick," he said, like he let me in on something. Christ took his left index finger and pressed directly on the flaming hot cherry on the end, snuffing its drizzle of smoke. Worried he had burnt himself out of pure human concern, my astonishment grew as he pulled the offended digit away. The blunt restored, centimeter by green and holy centimeter, until the end re-wrapped like a torch never touched it.

"Lighter?" he asked as I gawked at the insignificant miracle.

Christ took a huge, huge hit, but released it before sucking a few more sips like a champ. We stood in the small alcove, me watching him as he spied out the sea of concertgoers through the small passage to the street.

I brought the renewed blunt up to my lips, the strain of Animal Face boiling the evening air in stinky-stank. "So."

"No getting around you," he said with a serene smile. "But that's why I like you."

Smoke escaped my gullet and mouth as I popped the blunt out and spoke, "Then why are you out here, Janey? Did you just come to fuck with me or is there a point to all this?"

The question caught him. His attention stayed to the people in the streets, the city, on the face of the pale blue dot he had made out of mere thought. In a real fucking moment for me, I watched, as Lucifer had witnessed, his father seek an answer in human words beyond their limited means.

He let out a short laugh. "I'm so nervous."

This fucking guy. I almost flung the blunt if better sense had not taken me. "You wild, wild fuck."

"Pardon me?" Christ asked, a bit confused at my response.

As if he allowed there to be some sort of surprise.

I knew better. I had known better since the day one of the strict fathers in the Vatican sat me down and explained how angels and demons worked. I knew through the many, many victims I had freed from this mess. The gall of the confession—God's confession—sent me too far. "Pardon you? How about you pardon me? You're the alpha and omega, the beginning and end and now, and you dare to sit here and act like you're fucking nervous?"

"Well, I—"

"No, no, no," I said, cutting him off. "You don't get to be nervous. I get to be nervous."

He defended with a simple response. "Why are you nervous, Patrick?"

"Oh, fuck you."

"I'm trying here, brother." Despite the tokes he had taken, Christ remained clear-eyed. "Nobody can deal with the problem until the problem is given voice. So please—you seek to confess the problem, and I seek to listen to you with all my heart and mind and ears and everything I can give you. But you have to give it."

"Give it?" I exclaimed. "I have to fucking 'give it'? After years, years, of giving in to you and your damned wants and needs! I have literally walked this entire goddamn speck of dirt you pine over every goddamn second and you're going to tell me that I have to—"

"Now, that's enough goddamns," Christ said. "I am standing right here, you know."

"Trust me," I shouted. "How can I forget? How can I forget the many times I have prayed to you, thought about you, worshipped you, and now you're right here. Right now. Not when I needed you back when fuck-knows-when, or when this literal girl could have been spared a posses-sion, or that tribe could have just left the past well enough alone, or this fuck-face shaman I still have nightmares about! But here you are, here and now, ready to do what? Fucking sing some songs, you glory-hound fuck?"

He put his hand on his chest. "Saint Patrick!"

"No," I said, putting the blunt back in my lips. Pulling hard on the inhale, I blew the fire out instead of my next string of expletives. I balled my left hand into a fist, just wanting to see if I could crack him a second time. "You're going to sing some songs and tomorrow I'm still going to be the same old me. I'm still going to be the man who hates being the priest, hates how many friends he's lost, and is now stuck in this cosmic game of yours forever. And I have to be a dad on top of it." Then it slipped out of me, the raw notes played from the heart. "That child deserves so much better than me and what I've done. And you have your way with all of it and you just expect me to—"

I couldn't finish the rest. My lips quivered so hard to stop the tears in my eyes from flowing. There were so many things I wanted to ream him over, for Deevi, Lucifer, the loss of George, but I fell apart, a strange loser in a strange world I had no control over.

Whatever went unsaid, he knew.

Christ clapped me on the shoulder. "Thank you for your truth, my son," he said. "I understand, despite you not wanting to hear that, and I know. As much as I would play at this body, this face, and this affecta-tion, I always know."

"Then why—"

"Because, like you," began Christ, "I can only do my best. And often times my best failed. If it didn't, there would be no serpent to tempt because the serpent would have no reason, nor would have Lucifer rebelled against me for my lack of understanding on how I treat my creations. But along the way to discovering these things, I have also stumbled on one absolute truth that helps me out."

"Pray tell," I said, glib but curious to what the Godhead had gleaned.

"It is very, very hard to expect things of others," Christ said. "When you see others fail, what causes you to fear it so keenly is that you know you can too. Speaking from my place, if everyone is of my body and so many fail, what does this say about me? I refused to tackle that and look where we are. Nobody wants to see the tyrant in themselves, or the slaver, or the whore, or the beggar, let alone the left behind, yet they are of me as I am of them and of the same substance. Who would I be to create all this suffering and not turn my hand out in helping? If I abandon them, I would be abandoning me, yet unlike myself who would go on with nary a care, the fact is I learned how to love. I learned to care. So now I take it one hand at a time, one blanket at a time, one child read to, and all the food in as many bellies as there are to bellies to fill. That means one day at a time for a little one. And rest, when required."

"You rest?" The buzz in my head made my body too light in my boots. I firmed to keep myself from swaying.

"Oh, yeah," said Christ. "Got to get in that rest. Half of my mortal life was just napping because we had to march everywhere. Trust me, tired is tiring."

We passed the weed back and forth for the next few minutes. Burnt back down to its original half-length, I stuck it in my boot while we patted the smoke off ourselves.

"So," he said, "you coming back in?"

"Of course I am," I said, rubbing the bridge of my nose to open my smoke-inflamed sinuses. "I have a baby on the way."

"Well, good," said Christ as he threw his arm around my shoulders. Grabbing the handle to the door, he turned it open. "Because I need your help with something."

"Is it dangerous?"

"I mean, what isn't?"

This fucking guy.

ED ROLAND'S PRAYER

Someone by one of the soundboards handed me a set of headphones with a mic attached to them. "Here you go, boss."

It had been a while since I had a good freak out, so calmed and consoled by Christ, I put them on my stupid bean head and nodded as I walked past whatever nameless pagans had shown up to run the sound. I cannot express the words to report the monumental effort that had taken place from the moment we let people in the building. The homeless, the lost, and the "damned" from traditional perspectives had shown up for the scion of tradition, feeding the hungry and slaking the thirsty in the lit hallways, while in the main arena twenty-thousand people in seats nobody paid for bubbled in anticipation.

Every nation of the world, of every faith or not, had united together in earnest curiosity to what they would witness:

Jesus Christ was going to play with his angel band.

And all I had to make it shake and bake was eleven strangers forced together because the lead singer had to have his way again.

I found the Helpers along with Deevi and Merry backstage with Lucifer, separated from archangels standing by at the curtain. Shrunk to human heights and proportions, the rest of the celestials held their instruments tight in glowing hands, and more than one of them bore a nervous expression. Michael damned near looked like he was about to piss himself.

Fuck it, I was going. "Okay, everyone," I called. "The Big Daddy has put me in charge and—"

"He's not going to go out to Big Daddy, is he?" Rosie Baker asked, interrupting me. "Because that is trash."

"I can only rely on what he told me say," I replied. "The important thing that has to happen—hey, wherewhere's Enrique?"

At that very moment, the bright bastard of the day showed up. Dressed like Phil Collins right at the turn of the 90s, Christ arrived in brown trousers, a rather billowy shirt stripped in Technicolor on both breasts, with the cream sleeves rolled up to his dark elbows. He threw on a tan sport coat as he gave everyone nods and smiles.

"Ready to go?" he asked the angelic retinue and I. "Ready to go?"

"I guess, but I can't find Enrique," I said, already too tired to put up lead singer-nonsense.

Someone buzzed in my headset. "Security is making way for Enrique. Thirty seconds."

"Who's this?" I said into the mic. "Shoniqua?"

"Right here, Patrick," she said in my ear. "I'm over in the sound booth with the techs. I'll keep you updated how things are going."

"And you'll be fine with that?" I asked, letting Christ or the nurse decide who answered first.

Shoniqua crackled into my ear. "No worse than running charge," she said. "I got this—'Tater'."

I hated all of this. "Okay. Okay. Just—"

"Just listen when she speaks and you'll be fine," Christ said, confusing everyone in the room not able to hear the nurse in my ear. Deevi, Lucifer, and the rest of the archangels stared hard at me, though, which I ignored as the Savior brought all the attention back on him.

"Like the man said," he declared, "Take it easy, but take it!"

And then Jesus of fucking Nazareth stormed through the curtain.

The archangels lined up at the lighted way clattered together and hurried out behind him. Lucifer pecked his daughter one last time on the forehead and chased after his siblings.

Right on the spot, thirty seconds after the voice had spoken in my headset, the missing veteran arrived, nearly sweating from head to toe. Ignoring everything else, Enrique rushed me. "Patrick, we can't get the TV signal out! The Internet is down! We can't get the show out!"

"One of the Devil's devils is attempting to destroy the communications hub," Shoniqua buzzed in my headset, already panicked. "I have a map right here! I can lead you through the headset!"

I scanned the faces of the Helpers, wondering how many of them would balk at my next request. I wondered if Peter had dealt with the same. "Deevi, Daniel, Enrique, Jennifer, and Miranda, with me! The rest stay here and make sure the damned lights stay on."

Lucifer and Nathaniel hit the mellow riff together as the lights came on, Raguel's snare snapping on Uriel's steady bassline. The collective scream of exaltation rose from twenty-thousand audience members, dumbfounded by the sight of the archangels on the stage.

Heavenly instruments bled hints, allegations, and so many things left unsaid.

The man to say them hit the stage, mic in hand as he stormed to the front.

Born out a basement in the desperate hope it might find purchase somewhere, love from his words permeated the air as the litany of two brothers passed his lips, a refreshing water that washed away doubts of who had come. Every voice joined, an acclimation of what songs of the yesterday still meant to them in turbulent times.

But for all their questions, he had arrived, promising answers.

The distortion of the guitars and fuzz on the bass, joined by Ramiel's small additions on his conga, rode the rat-tat of Raguel's driving command. Christ's voice, strong but restrained to not overpower the arrangement, stoked something within the rapt listeners in the crowd. He did not sing of strictures and sin, nor damnation for acts too human to simply confine to the grays of good and evil. Instead, he sang of a calm, a clarity, all bound together by liberation, things not heard in the halls of those who claimed his words.

The melody, the tempo, backed on the notes Lucifer raked out of his white ax, stretched over the audience like a net until the Morningstar powered into the bridge, replacing Ed Roland's bounce with a buzz saw. The entire band stepped down on the speed, the tempo up an extra step.

Ecstasy exploded in tens of thousands of voices on the next refrain.

Christ roared back, the lion returned to earth.

"Holy fuck, that's insane," Daniel cried as he raised his gun skyward.

Deevi elbowed him as she aligned her sword at the devil swooping for another pass. "Shoot right, now!" she screamed at the Irishman who had promised to never pull a trigger ever again. Forced into it in the midst of the fray atop Madison Square Garden's roof, the voice in my headset had led us down halls and up the right sets of stairs in time to scare the damned thing as it had torn off the first of four panels, exposing wires. It had tossed the hunk of circuitry to the side before taking to the sky.

Enrique manned our exit while Miranda and Jennifer dashed for the panel. We all fell to our natural habits, Deevi and Daniel engaging the enemy while I supported the vets. Shoniqua hadn't buzzed me again, but the vibration of the music course through the floors, walls, and roofs of the world's most famous arena.

"Mira," Jennifer asked, her hand out as they squatted over the corner of something I couldn't even begin to describe. Miranda pulled from her white Fubu pants a multi-tool, ripping open its hinged fold to free the pliers. They both dropped to their knees and started stripping the coating off the damaged ends.

I prayed. For the mess of wires and plastic bits all over the concrete roof, the beams from my lover's magma sword to end the danger now.

The devil dodged into sight. As if mocking my pleas, a flaming blade appeared in his hands.

Until Daniel's bullet scored on his dome, knocking the monster off course.

Rolling in a heap of wings and the long, leathery tail, the devil turned over like a cat on all fours and looked directly at me.

"Let it shine!" Christ rumbled under us.

The bastard bounded for me.

In an instant, Deevi—my pregnant goddess—landed in the devil's path and batted it hard across the head, sending the gray beast sprawling a second time. He came up snarling, clawing ruts in the concrete.

The mother of my child advanced to fight for me, and I, the fragile human, could only watch.

"Shine!" the archangels chorused.

Not that she made it much to watch. Swarmed by hundreds, perhaps thousands all at once, Deevi had defended herself against worse. One on one?

The poor thing roared forward, wings tight to its strong torso as the long, spaded tail whipped everywhere. A sheer vision of hell ended when she met the devil with a stiff jab to the face, stepping out of the way to let it fall dead on the spot.

"Now!"

Miranda and Jennifer lifted the repaired panel they had wired back together. Designed in a way to stand in its rack, they rehung it and started re-wiring the shod ends together.

The voice cut into my headset, loud from where they had fallen around my neck in the dash and shuffle to the roof. "Patrick? Patrick? Are you there, Saint Patrick?"

I brought the cups over my ears. "Yeah, yeah, I'm here! Are the fucking tubes going?"

"Well, we lost half the song on Vimeo, but everything else

remained fine," said the pleasant voice to my cursing. "Why don't you all get back down here?"

"You sent us for Vimeo?" I asked, agog with incredulity. "For fucking Vimeo?"

"A lot of people watch Vimeo," Shoniqua said on the other end.

Deevi walked toward me, a happy smile on her face like she hadn't murdered a supernatural creature. "All is well?"

I had no way of stopping her flying headfirst into danger. The reality of every father and father-to-be's helplessness reared.

"Are we going yet?" Enrique shouted, the odd man in the fracas. "Whatever they're doing downstairs sounds really good."

We caught the end of the first song in time to understand why these people were so damned loud. The whole world melted under the power of Christ and the band, who brought the song to a close with a loud crescendo of their instruments. The cheer blasted in my ears, unruly and fervent. Making the last dash down the hidden stairwells of the arena, the six of us reconvened with the rest of the Helpers backstage, thankful for a lack of problems considering what we had faced.

Then the lights cut out.

"What the actual fuck now?" Rosie Baker said aloud, face lit by the blunt she shared with Govinda. The Nephilim's wings would have lit our scant area in the tunnel, but pleased to put them away, Deevi stood in the dark with the rest of us.

A big part of me wanted to go over there and tell Rosie to put out the blunt because Deevi couldn't be around the smoke. Before I made a damned hypocrite of myself after I had smoked up with Christ, Shoniqua's voice cut into my headset.

"Patrick, someone broke into the booth!"

"Oh, fuck, fuck, fuck," I shouted. "Deevi, wings! Everyone to the booth!"

Deevi's wings, willed from whatever extra-dimensional place she tucked them, revealed their golden splendor. Faster than us, she was already at the junction had formed around the back of the stage. The rest of us merely echoes of her dust as she sprinted left, I dreaded what she'd run into first as we rounded in time to see her dart right, into the staging area where the pagans and atheists had set up the soundboards and mixers for the evening.

We arrived in time to see one of the soundboards fly in our direction. Colliding with the concrete floor first, it skipped between Govinda and I. Deevi wrenched a woman away from the sound booth where the crew cowered under riggings and tables. Shoniqua stood by the torn section of board, trying to gather it all together like prolapsed intestines.

"Jenny, Miranda, help her." I pointed to the panel the possessed intruder had tossed our way. "The rest of us—hurry!"

The two homeless veterans, tougher than most men I had met in my life, launched forward with Enrique behind them, stooping along the way to hoist the hunk of plastic, bolts, and wires together. I quickly lost sight of them as I ran down the tunnel Deevi had literally tossed our target down, where the fight continued.

The possessed woman had regained her footing and belted the Nephilim hard on the jaw. Head snapping under the punch, Deevi's face screwed into something nasty as she returned a stout blow to the demon's chest. Blown off their feet, the body tumbled down the hall.

"It's Satan," Deevi shouted as she stalked after her opponent. "He's possessed a young woman! Stay out of my way!"

For some reason, I put my arms out to the sides to stop anyone from getting past, catching Govinda and Rosie first. We continued at a slow jog, keeping our distance from the fistfight put on by Deevi and the Devil.

Perhaps it was the anger of her abduction, or the threat to rape an unwanted child into her, but whatever the reason, Deevi beat the absolute shit out of him, giving three punches for every one the stupid idiot dared to throw back. We all watched in the glow of her wings as the damage accumulated. Blood sprayed from the swelling parts of the

Devil's face, but fueled by an unnamable hatred, he healed every wound in time for the next.

Under the light of an Exit sign, green and bright, I finally got a look at his host's half-torn visage.

Poor Tina half-grimaced before Deevi kicked her husk through the door.

Which opened to two leather-winged devils waiting outside.

Christ whispered into the microphone, active by some miracle in the complete darkness of the arena. He offered them wisdom most forsook for their safety and vanity, as much as risk to them as it was relief.

The crowd answered in refrain, understanding they heard that could not be measured by the brain, only within the heart.

The wings of his archangels muted, almost snuffing their illumination.

Alone in his new church by and by, Christ's low, lulling voice rose upon Lucifer and Nathaniel's dueling take on the Chad Taylor's timeless riff. The light from the wings of the divine band members strengthened, slow at first, before each of the eight shone like a torch. They charged in, the outline of the Savior stark as he and Nathaniel closed on each other to share the chorus in the mic.

He declared the end of fear.

Christ flung the audience and viewer back to an age of darkness, when the lights of the stars had not yet burned, and silence ruled everything. Alone in this void, trapped, scared, ignorant, the Absolute spoke a single word to bring forth a glow to match its own. The warmth in the cold enough to cobble together something real and true, separate from the dark, but alike in quality. He tempted them, but not with longing, but answers to the longing inside.

Cradling the seed of existence, the Absolute spread forth love in the guise of life and death, a rising multiverse too vast to be fully known woven together in the cloth of Creation, its spinner operated through ineffable, incomprehensible grace alone.

The light from the archangels wings almost blinded if not for their crystal purity.

Christ screamed as he once had, in the past and present, reverberating to a future unknown before mortal eyes.

Fear would not be the end of this.

Somewhere in the scuffle I picked up the handgun Daniel wasn't supposed to shoot.

He had been knocked down with Govinda, who had bravely barreled in only to catch a smack from one of the devils when the monk tried to protect the RIRA soldier. Rosie stood beside me, baring her .38.

One of the newer Sig Sauers, a compact version of the M11 felt like nothing when I lifted it off the ground, my thumb flicking off the safety like the Swiss Guard had trained me to do in my teenage years. I leveled the barrel and sights with the first devil's head. Facing away from me as Deevi deflected the pair's flaming sword blow with hers, nothing would have been easier.

The Vatican, through The March, had trained me to save the lives of those claimed by the Devil, to the point of ending the mortal torment. They had taught me to do this like they had taught me litanies and strictures, the raw edge of a belt placing into me whip-snap reactions to placate the brutal loneliness of a life among cruel soldiers posed as priests and nuns.

They had cursed within me the ability to kill God's creatures.

Watching the devil fight my pregnant lover, I made a fine examination of the back of his molting skull. My finger came off the trigger guard, nestling in the steel curve with ease. A quick squeeze.

A quick squeeze and I'd murder one of God's creatures—in the name of God.

In the name of God, this was all so fucked.

Thank the proud land of Ireland someone else made the decision for me.

Cuchulainn appeared, goring one of the devils on his sword before he harried the one attacking Deevi. Overwhelmed, the remaining abomination bounded away at an odd angle from us and leapt, clearing the edge of the arena's roof. Gone in an instant, we all turned to the last intruder who had started this mad chase.

Thankful beyond thankful, I lowered the damned gun when I discovered Tina the Uber-driver unconscious on the ground, knocked senseless after Merry had pistol-whipped her. Under some influence of the Devil's power still, her injuries disappeared while she slept unawares, a small but needed blessing in the moment.

"Oh, Jesus," I exhaled.

"He's doing just fine," Shoniqua said in my headset as if she gathered herself. "I think she just dimmed the lights."

"Well, wonderful," I breathed as the Hound of Ulster trod toward me, bloody sword low at his side. "We'll be back in soon."

Shoniqua beeped the affirmative on the other end, already ahead of us as her and the vets kept the show together.

Covered in sweat, my adrenaline crashed. Dead-eyed by the demigod, I kept it short. "I'm not running anywhere, nor do I ever intend to. But I need to get this done tonight. Part of our deal is you help me, I help you. Will you help me?"

"Laeg and I will stand guard," Cuchulainn replied. "But no more funny business."

"Friend," I said, much as I would have to his gentler father, "I wish the world was out of laughs sometimes."

BENJAMIN BURNLEY'S
DESPERATE PRAYER

———

The lights were indeed on when we walked back inside MSG, the promise of Cuchulainn and Laeg patrolling outside giving me a smidge of comfort.

Then Shoniqua chirped in my headset. "Patrick, he's back!"

"Oh, what a gloriously fucked day," I declared. "Hurry, all!"

"What's happening?" Govinda asked. He half-carried Daniel, who had taken one for the team in the scuffle. Merry under his other arm, the former gunman nonetheless marched, regathering himself with every step. Deevi led the way ahead, Rosie in lockstep behind her.

I pressed the call button on the monitor attached to my belt. "Shoniqua, we're on our way! What's happening?"

"He's here," Shoniqua said, almost breathless. "He just walked in. He's here. He—"

"Shoniqua? Shoniqua?"

"He's here, Saint Patrick," she said. "The Devil is here."

Tricky bastard.

The passage to the sound booth lay in complete chaos, stagehands running about to tend to broken circuits under Miranda and Jennifer's direction. Some of the Vodun guards lay bleeding on the ground. None of them dead or severely injured, Merry and Rosie lagged behind to tend their kin. Several people pointed the way for Deevi as she stormed forth.

We made it to the sound booth in time to find Shoniqua confronting Satan.

Braced in front of the curtain to the stage, the nurse faced off against the fallen angel in possession of a homeless man covered in a dark poncho and grimy boots. Enrique stood behind her, unarmed but undaunted.

Deevi and Rosie halted first, so sudden Govinda, Daniel, and I almost crashed into each other, three stooges clumped together.

Freeing from the tangle, I extracted my Bible and rosary. "Make room!"

Bearing her glowing sword of magma and metal, Deevi barred my path. "Patrick—"

"If he's stopped, he's stopped for a reason, and it isn't because Shoniqua—"

In that very moment I noticed the marble-blackness blotting out the whites of Shoniqua's eyes.

"Out of my way," Satan said to whomever had taken her.

"It's time to end this, Shaytan," the demon inside answered. "He has freed us! The Messenger and Morningstar have sent out the call to convene! The war is—"

"It's never over, Beherit," Satan cried in his inhumane bellow. "Never while the Son of God walks!"

"Oh, you silly idiot," I called. "Come, man! It is over! The time for your rebellion has ended, like it had long ago for your maste—"

"No one," Satan screamed from inside the homeless man. "No one shall rule me but me! I deny him! I deny all of you!" He lunged forward and the possessed form of Shoniqua met him. Hands around each other's throats, the two infernal creatures tussled.

Deevi tried to dart in, but I caught her by the wrist.

"Back, all of you!" I broke past her as Beherit slipped under a looping punch, stepping behind Satan to wrap one of Shoniqua's dark arms around his neck, the other around his stomach.

"Hurry, saint," the lesser demon said as he wrenched them around to face me. "Banish us to Perdition! I shall take him there, if only to delay him!"

The Devil wriggled in his fellow angel's hold, raising one foot to stomp down on Beherit's feet with the heels of his boots. "I will trap you, traitor," he warned. "I will bind you to Perdition, to places so deep and dark not even the Savior shall find you! You will mire—"

"Do it, Patrick," Beherit wailed. Tears spilled from the demon's onyx eyes. "Send us down! Send us down!"

The two grappled before me, fiercer than before.

My Bible in one hand, rosary in the other, I spoke, and hoped something bigger saw me through.

<hr>

The lights slowly rose to accommodate the glow of archangels' wings, revealing Christ with an acoustic guitar, nothing more than a strap, strings, and the sweet notes he plucked from it as he stood before a microphone.

He cleared his throat. "This isn't easy." Staring for a moment into the faces of the audience, into the cameras centered upon him as they beamed impossibilities on every screen across the world.

For a moment he seemed hesitant. Human.

Not the powerful, vengeful, certain God who had made them.

He cleared his throat a second time and brought his guitar higher on his chest. "None of it ever is. Every measure, every mistake—I'm at the beginning and end of all of it. In the midst of all of it." He swallowed. "I was too far outside of it for a long, long time. Alone, though I wasn't." A quick glance to Gabriel drew a smile from the Messenger. "And I'm not perfect. It wouldn't be fair to expect you to be either."

He brought his hands up to the strings as Uriel plucked a thrumming bass note. Selaphiel's electronics fed from his synthesizer and the small midi-pad beside it dappled in a slow, sorrowful tempo.

The lead sang into his mic, calling out to the quiet.

Gabriel answered with their brightness over his croon, still calling to their maker like we all were, desperate not to let go of truths we desperately wanted to cling to.

The sadness spurred a wanting, a needing that flourished in the garden of every mind. Suns set over the paradise in every heart, the memory of a place he had designed in pride, and perhaps foolishness, emerged from ethers.

Christ, Lucifer, and Nathaniel led Raguel in on his drums, the other archangels finding their notes in the weave.

In every rise, an arrogance diminished, crawling ahead no matter the wounds. A needing heart forever searched the boundless for a sound to match theirs. Michael's saxophone sank into the background, forever mournful while Raphael's hearkened to the next day, the next night, and new dawns.

Promises of mornings that would last forever.

Proof that God need not be lonely anymore.

The archangels chorused as the promise of what Eden had been burned, the ashes of it leftover for the Garden we all stood within. Whether in person or watching, listen, and witnessing from afar, its waters found their way into every soul again.

"Heaven help me," Christ and Lucifer sang together. *"Heaven help me..."*

<hr>

The mystery remained the mystery, the music remained the music, but knowing the deeper mistakes made by Creation hit all the harder. I sat on the floor, facing away from the curtain while Deevi, Daniel, and the vets removed an unconscious Shoniqua and the poor vagrant the Devil had taken in one more act of desperation.

But I was desperate, desperate for all of this to end.

I kept it down, kept it down, focused on my knees and feet while I squeezed the Bible and rosary in my hands. Wishing nothing more than to pressure so hard I pulverized both, every part of me seized. Until I couldn't, no matter how hard I clenched my jaw. My jaw lost its tightness first, my face on fire.

I exhaled into full crocodile tears to Benjamin Burnley's desperate prayer. Even in the presence of God personified, backed by archangels, believed in, and awed, and definitely feared, the world remained fucked. It was all fucked—the Church, the people who ran it, but also the people in the stupid pews lined up like hogs to the slaughter.

What kind of world was I about to bring a child into, powers or no powers, God or no god as her granddaddy?

I tore off my headset and flung it away from me, too damned upset to care.

"Now that won't work," said a heavily accented voice directly in front of me.

Rubbing my eyes, I glared between my fingers.

And into the face of Mary.

The real Mary.

The Virgin.

She reached down with a richly brown hand and stroked the tears from my cheeks with her thumb, giving a smile every child yearned for from their mother.

"Up, Saint Patrick," she whispered to me. "We haven't even started!"

PAUL MCCARTNEY ENVISIONS
HIS MUM

She held my face in her hands, her brown eyes filling my entire gaze until all I knew was the solace she exuded. To be touched by the mother of Lord God, who had endured so much simply to see her son hang on a cross...

I fought to find words, barely noticing the two women flanking her.

The possessed saw Mary when the demons left, and I hoped, prayed, in the odd times where I had doubted what I done, that the damned saw her too. Arrayed in a simple gown of white and her dark hair covered in a deep red shawl to match her son's blood red mantle, she wiped more tears.

Freeing me.

I wanted to cry, cry out all my tears. For the baby coming into a world I didn't trust, for a wife I hadn't married yet was shackled to my wretched self, and all—

"Shush," Mary whispered, patting my cheeks before she took my hands. The second I rose a piano played behind us, bringing the crowd from their moody lull after the last song to a rousing applause. She dusted my shoulders. "Now, out of the way. I have to sing a song."

Just like her son had done not half an hour before, she charged out to a hushed awe that ended the clapping with one collective gasp. Too dazed to look beyond the curtain and watch, my focus drifted between elation and exhaustion until I recognized one of the faces of the women who had come with her.

"Hello, Patrick," said a bonnie beautiful brunette endemic to the Scottish Highlands, her agelessness still pristine despite the decade since I had last seen her.

Saint Brigid, the immortal goddess who had become a saint in the midst of her people's paganism long, long ago, held her bare arms out waiting for my embrace. Matched to the Virgin, she chose blue to cover her hair and a hunter's green for the dress, a snapshot of a time and place never existing save in annals lost to the ages. The only one of us in The March never to reincarnate, she had spent years in and out, with reasons far deeper than the Vatican wanted to go, giving her ample leeway to do whatever she wanted.

I took a shoddy step toward her before she caught me, my sister from my people's kin finding me far across the sea, centuries from where we began.

"What the actual fuck, Bri?" I asked, too bewildered to say 'hello.'

"It's something," she said in Ancient Gaelic. "You have your feet under you?"

A ragged nod and a breath, I steadied my posture in time for Deevi to meet us with the other woman. Garbed like the two she had come with, her cloth was dyed a deeper red, which made her dark hair seem blacker than oil. Her bright golden eyes, a match for the Nephilim's in shape and luster, measured me with keen, almost dire critique.

Deevi beamed in a way I had never seen her smile.

"Patrick," she said in an official tone, "this is Lisbeth. She's my mother."

Selaphiel carried through the loud applause of the crowd as McCartney's arrangement took hold on his keys, pressing out the slow melody for a full minute before Christ came to the mic posted in the middle of the round. The archangels and Nathaniel downed their instruments, heads bowed, save for Michael and Lucifer. The Protector with his saxophone, the Morningstar with his white electric, they scanned the crowds and the stage, alert for something none could identify.

Christ lifted his head, his mouth to the receiver.

Everyone in the arena knew the song since the turn of 1969 when Paul's mom visited him in a vision preceding the ending to one union, and the seeding of something else four experienced lads from Liverpool never expected to follow them afterward. Timeless, the crowd joined on the chorus with Gabriel, who shed a serene smile as they looked out upon adoring, loving masses of people shedding their fears.

Ramiel tapped the hats to enter the second verse, followed by the plucks Uriel dribbled from his raw bass. Rhythm joined to the melody of the piano, they uplifted the singer's words, the scaling heights adding new instruments, new notes, all to the fullness of what had been composed.

Christ promised, swore, there would be answers.

Selaphiel adjusted his synthesizer, now a church organ. The casting light of the archangels and their wings, often defeating the stage lighting high above everyone, glittered in rainbow shades touching every direction. The entire audience sang along, word for word with the Savior, no matter where they had come from or what they worshiped. Michael and Raphael joined with their two horns before Lucifer ripped into George Harrison's solo.

Then, for every mortal voice joined in song, all silenced when she stepped on stage.

Without hesitation, without fear, Mary came and stood beside her boy. She sang into God's face as he teared up, a mortal man beside his greatest hero.

Fuck, I cried. I cried so hard.

I cried in front of everyone, including the Jewish mother of the woman who had just decided I was her son now as well. Putting aside any old jokes about Catholics and Jews working together in matrimony better than Catholics and everyone else, or other attempts at my charm, whatever plagued me as Mary sang onstage vanished.

My guilt over Merry, the death of George, and all the suffering from the first life, was gone like a blown-out flame on a candle's wick. The memory of those moments, those traumas, fogged like mists, remembered for their scent and sights, but devoid of any weight.

Then I heard him behind me.

"We're going to do a quick changeover and be right back," Christ said. "Everyone stick around!"

The cheer inside the arena almost shook a new memory into me, but I calmed the moment Christ appeared through the curtain. He spotted me immediately, by myself while Deevi, Lisbeth, and Brigid had watched me unload at a respectful distance. His mom came through next.

"Hey everybody," he said, like he hadn't just played a hard twenty-five minutes. Not even sweating in his new clothes, he put his arm around my shoulders and faced me toward the hallway. Brigid was quick on his heels.

"You okay, bud?"

"Fuck, no," I replied as I let him lead me. "Where are we going?"

"Oh, just checking on a few things before the next phase of the show begins."

That brought me back to attention, sharpening the exhausted haze Mary's voice had wrapped me in. "The next phase?"

He patted me on the shoulder as he broke from me. "There's more songs, Patrick, but let's go check on the Helpers first since they're in need of help."

My worries recovered themselves as we entered one of the changing rooms off the main hall to find it in bedlam. Rabbi Rebecca had reappeared at Merry's call, who along with Rosie attended to the vets, thrown deep into an intense release of emotions that left Enrique catatonic and the two women sobbing.

Govinda and Daniel bookended their couch, face down in their palms as they wept.

Christ entered first with his consoling smile, but I spoke the obvious question. "What the fuck happened here?"

"I don't know," Merry said, "His momma started singing and they all lost their shit! It took me, Rosie, and Rebecca together just to get them back here!"

"We were going to come get you last, but you seem fine now," Rosie said she rubbed the Jennifer's back to calm her breathing.

"What are we going to do with them?" Rabbi Rebecca asked, directing the question at the only person in the room who would know.

A deep sigh as he came forward, Christ knelt in front of the vets, both hands out for theirs. Meekly, through the ghosts of their downfalls, all three reached forward.

"Speak," he told them. "Speak to what has happened."

Commanded by a will beyond wills, Miranda spoke first, suddenly calmed. "I remember his face. The sergeant," she said, almost surprised. "I saw him everywhere. In the barracks, in the line at the mess hall, when I discharged, yesterday, this morning. I could never get away after what happened." She shook her head, caught between her current awe and the past flowing down her cheeks. "He haunted me for so, so long."

"It was my captain," Jennifer said in a low voice, sniffing through her anguish. "Nobody listened. Even when we were tossed to the side —" She shuddered, but not from torment, but as if chilly. "But it's like I can just look at him and walk away now. He's there, but I don't have to let him follow me. Not anymore."

Christ looked to the man wedged between them. "Enrique?"

"I'm okay," he said, laid up in the plush black leather with the other hand over his face. He let out a long groan and swallowed. "I'm okay."

Christ patted the healed man's knee. "You three take your time. When you're ready come back to the show. I'm going to go check on Daniel and Govinda before I look in on Shoniqua in the next room, alright?"

He received weary but thankful nods, and kissing their hands, he rose. Signaling me to the door for a moment, we reentered the hall where Brigid waited.

"Okay," he said to us, the two saints. "I need you two go to stall for time onstage while I handle the rest of them."

To my shock and horror, Brigid answered first. "Yeah, sure, no problem."

THE GOSPEL OF THE CELTS

"Yeah, sure, no problem'?" I demanded. "'Yeah, sure, no problem?!'"

Brigid and I half-sprinted down the hall, shoulder to shoulder as Rabbi Rebecca hurried to keep up. I had given the poor dear my headset and monitor, leaving her to untangle the wires and clip things on herself as the headphones hung askew on her head.

Flowing in her robes cut to the same style as the Virgin's, the former goddess shrugged. "We were called, as always."

"Well, I'm not," Rebecca said behind us, exasperated by her wires. "Will one of you help me?"

Brigid stopped and assisted the rabbi. "Of course, dear. So sorry for us to be rushing about like this, but we've got a bit of a thing going."

"You don't say?" Rebecca replied dryly as she adjusted the headphones on her head as Brigid clamped the monitor to her pantsuit's belt, leaving her to collect the excess under her bright blue coat as we took up again.

"I haven't preached in front of the masses in long time," I said, somewhat lying, but this was no homily. "This is way, way above me, Bri."

"So was Eire and Alba," she said with the old sharpness.

And I was tight like a tick. "This is New York. This is the entire world."

Brigid didn't slow, nor did Rabbi Rebecca behind her. "No," she replied. "It's just another Rome."

"Hey, I got this working," the rabbi said, adjusting the knob on the monitor. "Someone's waiting by the curtain with mics. Apparently one of the guitarists is still out there with one of the archangels."

"Great," I said, "let's let them play as long as they like and—"

"Oh, get on!" Brigid berated me.

We charged through the tunnel to the sound booth, which had been restored to some semblance of working order by the stagehands. Our Vodun guards had redoubled, taking more prominent positions in the backstage. Of course, Deevi had remained with Lisbeth and Mary. The Virgin had lost herself deep in conversation with Gabriel while the other archangels re-tuned their instruments and Lucifer convened with his wife.

Deevi met me as I passed by, catching my hand. "Patrick, wait a moment. Could you, my mother, and my father—"

I interrupted before she could finish the question. "I can't, Deevi. I just can't."

"Why not?" she asked in a hurt tone.

Her innate power yanking the truth from me and the sight of a stagehand gifting Saint Brigid one of two live mics, the answer would have been the same either way. "Because I'm good and fucked to go do something worse."

She gave me the most peculiar look as I scampered away. Thankfully Brigid had the sense to stop at the curtain and wait, peering out to the wonders on the circular platform.

Selaphiel had remained behind on his keys after he had re-lit the censer, which smoked green, pink, and purple, smelling sweetly of frankincense. He twiddled out a jazzy number while Nathaniel bent a solo that glued the audiences' attention to his hands as they glided on the fretboard. In perfect sync, they ambled along a slow, gentle arrangement, picking the next note in the places where the other left the last.

"What are we going to even say?" I asked over Brigid's left shoulder, suddenly losing count of all the heads and faces out there, all the way up to the nosebleeds which seemed crowded with too many people on its tight, narrow platforms.

"I guess we make the pitch," she said with a shrug.

"What?" said I, "the old one? For this crowd of heathens, sinners, and—"

She cut me a subtle glare. "Patrick, you sound positively Roman again."

The crowd swaying in the aisles and among the floor seats, the accusation hit hard but on target. These people had appeared for a reason, and whatever doubts, the order had been given. "You know he didn't tell us to go out there and make the old pitch. That's proselytizing us and not him."

"Well," Brigid said with a deep breath as she checked the on-switch at the bottom of her microphone, "he didn't tell us what so say, either."

Nathaniel and Selaphiel dueled the last notes between them, guitar and piano, an immaculate harmony that brought the crowd up to their feet in wild applause. The immortal gave a wave to the audience with a large hand while the archangel, pleased to the point of embarrassment over the adoration, blushed as he gave a few quick bows. With a careful grace he looked our way, his shining eyes matching his grin as he nodded to Brigid.

Shit, everyone was in on it. Everyone but me, it felt like.

That feeling remained, a new demon to possess me as Brigid walked out of the curtain, just as confident as Janey Mac at the start of the show.

The Pitch, as former pagan goddess Saint Brigid of the Caledonian and Hibernian Peoples had termed it, was an argument for Christianity among the Insular Celts. Unlike the imperial dictates of Rome, the Isles of Eire, Briton, and its small satellites had not the security of an army that walked the roads every day, let alone the legions needed to defend lands sacked by raiders and petty chieftains. We lived, worked, and competed alongside a vast amount of other religions native to the land, including some of the descendants of the Mithra worshipers who had first built Hadrian's Wall or dared the shores of Eire, never to be taken until the Vikings later on. We worked and worked, exorcising demons while saving souls, all the while tailoring Christ's promise to hard ears and iron hearts.

Our kirks and monasteries often had to make our own way.

The way of Christ meant less judgment, more love.

I tried to remember the premise as tens of thousands of eyes fixed upon me. Far from the white walls and stained-glass of St. Mary's Pro-cathedral, New York waited on me, her, and whatever would come out of our gobs.

Thank the old gods of her land that Brigid could talk for the both of us.

"Hello, New York," she shouted into the microphone. "Can I get someone to turn up the damned lights in here?"

Following behind her and trying to ignore the obvious confusion twenty-thousand souls paid her, I glanced down at my own mic. Certain it was switched on, I cursed my predicament.

Today was a day I was losing many paths for a single road. "Well, let's try to be softer than that, Bri," I said into the black, cylindrical receiver, raising it up like Raphael's horn. "Rabbi Rebecca Schreiber is backstage"—the pitch required naming the accomplices—"and I'm sure she can get one of the stagehands to help turn up the dam—"

On cue, the arena lights of Madison Square Garden blazed to life, thousands of small suns arising out of their ethers before they popped into full, blinding fury. Every face, every person, every single individual in the arena was revealed, no longer just eyes but whole peoples packed together to view something impossible.

These people had seen me and Deevi outside. Anyone with a smart phone probably knew who I was by now.

There was no place to hide anymore.

"Hello, New York," I said, "my name is Saint Patrick. I'm considered the patron saint of Ireland and the worst day of the year in this city. Sorry about that. And this ma'am here is Saint Brigid of Ireland, Scotland, and probably the Cornish, Manx, and Welsh too."

Brigid pumped a fist in the air. "Go Wales!"

Crickets.

"This is getting whiter by the second," I replied before I widened my smile at the audience. Search for the complicit and smile.

Thankfully the joke roused a good laugh out of more than half, wherever they had come from.

I went at them, full pitch. "You've seen me if you've had any sense to look at your phone, and every single one of you has. Christ is present, so seriously, don't lie. He'll come out again." Louder laughter eased me into it. "In all seriousness, let me first thank the people who came from all over this city to help put this together. It took much in the way of mutual giving, kindness, and a true sense of welcome to do this. If New York is anything, it is full of kind people."

"Honestly, why are we up here with such a fine audience?" Brigid asked me, playing her part.

"Getting to that," I said, waving her off as I pulled answers out of my ass. "You know, Bri and I were in the back when Jesus scampered in, and he told us to come up here and—"

The lights of the arena eased in my tired eyes, and beyond their harsh glare I finally spied the smiles and sighs. Many were still weeping, crying into their hands. Dozens huddled together in support, pockets of different faiths, ethnicities, and fortunes cobbled together by the weirdest happenstances.

And here was I, acting like the comedian at a rock concert.

I sobered my tone. "We know there are many, many questions you all are probably asking. I know all of us, here and now, are feeling things we have either long forgotten or never held before in our hearts. We just wanted to come out and say there will be peace. Whatever tonight is, it is meant to bring peace though love. Brigid?"

Quieted by my sudden focus, the former goddess raised her mic. "Does anyone have any questions? We are here to give as much comfort as we can within the truth, and the truth we shall give you. But more importantly, we are here to spread love. Love. And so is he." she said, pointing to the star somewhere behind the curtains.

"So," I said into my mic, "who's first?"

Too many hands shot up. We met the people's needs, one by one, like we did in the old times.

LIVE IN ATHENS 1987, SONG 16

Brigid and I got about five questions from the audience before she noticed Rabbi Rebecca waving from the curtain. I let her finish on the story of her conversion from a divine figure of worship to one of Celtic Christianity's favorite saints before I interrupted.

"Listen, friends, we're being waved off the stage because the man backstage wants to get on with the show," I said, quick to take up whatever floor there was before the next query followed the usual course—purpose, eschatology, and materialism—and I would have to deny the asker, something every honest minister of the Lord's word loathed to do. "Thank you, everyone, and thank you for your questions. Bless you and your families, and good night."

We departed to a nice round of applause. Once through the curtain, we found the entire band lined up, Selaphiel first and Lucifer last, and then Nathaniel right behind him. Christ waited at the very back, talking to Mary in only the way a mother and son spoke to each other. I saw none of the other Helpers save Rebecca. Deevi had gone off somewhere with Lisbeth.

"Interesting perspective," Uriel said when Brigid cleared the curtain with me, his large black bass slung over his shoulder like a sledgehammer.

"Get anything wrong?" Brigid had the guts to ask.

A few of the archangels murmured while the Angel of Death chuckled at her return. "We'll find out," he said with a disarming smile.

Christ quickly spoke as he formed up with his children, their mortal grandmother standing alongside him like she was up next too. "Pay him no mind, Patrick! You and Brigid and Rabbi Rebecca did a very fine job. Now to really show them! Let's go, Selaphiel!"

On the order, the Consecrator lifted his censor by its chain as the lights lowered onstage, dimmed by one of the crew on the effects board. He spoke something to the gold cylinder and from it issued a glowing smoke, smelling of cinnamon and pungent tannins. His wings brightened as he broke past the curtain, drawing a loud roar of excitement from the crowds. The archangels each went one by one, instruments in hand, until there was only me, Christ, the Virgin, Brigid, and a very awkward Rabbi Rebecca amid too many Christian figures.

Lucifer's guitar kicked in, doubled by Nathanial's, before Selaphiel rushed with his keys and Ramiel, his drums. The cheering raised to new heights as the familiar strains of Solsbury Hill echoed through the arena.

Mary produced a tambourine. Shaking it to loosen its silver bells, she gave her son an affirming nod. It may have been something wanting within me, but I thought she winked at me as she passed.

"Remember to sing and sing high," she said as she stormed the stage.

The fucking roof blew off the place.

"That's Mama," Christ said. "You three did good," he told me, Brigid, and Rebecca. "Just keep the house together until I get back, alright?"

Just as he exited, Daniel entered the backstage. Fitter than the last time I saw him, he had recovered his wits and spotted me instantly. He made a beeline for us. "One got in," he said before I could ask. "A devil got in the building!"

"Oh, shit," said Rabbi Rebecca, pulling her headphones down around her thin, dark neck.

"Don't worry," said Daniel. "Deevi's already hunting him down."

My panic rose with the music.

He strode onto the stage as the full band united, every instrument blended into the rambling, wandering riff born of that other Gabriel. The mic already at home in its stand, he ripped it free. "Let's climb that hill!"

Every hand not holding an instrument or serving bread and wine came together until those who carried the food found places to leave their loads and join the resound. A song of songs already in the ear and hearts of those earlier in the day, the additions of Michael's saxophone and Raphael's horns, Raguel's percussions, and presence of Mary side by side with Gabriel entered a new dimension of sound and awakening. The story of a scared young man in Jerusalem, powerful but without purpose, refreshed with the cry of his eagle at the center of the Jordan River, flying out of the night to spur him toward destiny.

But his was no longer the only voice.

The Virgin sang loud into her microphone as the archangels raised the light of their wings. She pounded her chest the roaring blend of guitars and keys.

New York answered her. *"Boom, boom, boom!"*

A mother issuing her own prayer, she urged them to prepare for the way home, taking only the things that mattered to them the most.

Trading the headset with Rabbi Rebecca, who need a moment after already dealing with so much, I sent Daniel, Rosie, Govinda out into the audience, allowing them time alone as well as a chance to find places and keep watch. I had the Vodun volunteers combing the back and basement. All the doors had been locked, back to front, on my word.

The idea of being able to open and shut the world's most famous arena gave me no thrill of power, not when I stepped out of the tunnels and onto to the mid-level of the packed venue.

Closer to the masses than I had been minutes before, only a few recognized me, but not enough to peel from what they saw before them.

The world leapt to Mary's word as much as they did to God's, captured by a mortal hero beyond heroes, unsung for too long. Past tears they clapped, sang, and hearkened to her radiance while her child wove the tale of his sojourn, her support, sometimes the only dauntless defender in a world where a poor man claiming God and goodness seemed too vulgar for those in power.

Someone tapped me on my left shoulder, and posted my side, I found Merry entranced.

"What's wrong?" I asked, half-shouting over the music and noise.

She pointed toward the rafters.

I raised my head in time to see Deevi swing under one of the roof-struts, her summoned sword in one hand while clinging to the supports with the other. The devil slithered out of range of her strike, dodging behind a webbing of steel beams and suspension cables connected to one of the basketball nets. Red flashes leaked out, giving hints to the rat-tunnel fight happening above the humans.

"Holy fucking shit," I shouted, unable to contain it. "A pregnant lady should not do that!"

"What did you say?" The Vodun Queen of New York, my former lover and oldest friend, seized me by the arm. "What now, Tater?"

Unable to process anything else, I brought my headset's mic up and pressed down on the monitor. "Fucking bring all the guards into the mid-level and upper balconies right now. We might have to stop if the concert if—"

The next red flash, more intense, followed with the fall of the dead devil. Dropping like a stone held too high, the body plummeted.

A second flare of golden light heralded Deevi as she dove, chasing of her kill. Wings close to her body, she closed the distance as they neared the dancing humans carpeting the concrete.

I did shut my eyes, my palms clapped over my ears to keep out the impact.

Mary called out to the world, "I've come to take you home!"

"Oh fuck, she did it," Merry exclaimed.

I tore my hands away in time to see Deevi fly over us, holding her load by its long, thick tail. She glided into the tunnel behind us.

And not a single person had torn their gaze away from the spectacle on stage.

DEADPOOL & WOLVERINE RUINED THIS SONG AND MADONNA MIGHT SUE

We chased Deevi into the tunnel while the dead devil crashed and rolled until it struck the wall. Opened from clavicle to sternum, black blood crusted the entire front of its body. Her clothes stained in the mortal skirmish, Deevi smiled broad as we approached, a proud cat displaying the bird she had caught.

The gross sight of it, the splatter, and that weird, happy smile just did it.

"I just can't fucking do this," I said, shaking my head before the sobs claimed me, then the tears. "I just can't fucking do this!"

The exertion, the outcry, brought me to my bruised knees. The unvarnished truth spilled out of me quicker than the blood pooling beneath the devil's torn body. I couldn't take my eyes off its corpse until I forced my eyes shut.

I was just some rich Roman kid who had gotten captured by pirates and was lucky enough they put me to herding. That's all. From the ridding of evil in my first life to the many, many, many failures I had found in the victories of this one, whatever drove me on the inside checked out.

Then their hands lifted me from where I collapsed, red-eyed and dazed by my breakdown. The Nephilim cradled me against her while the Vodun Queen held one of my hands, messaging the back of it with her thumbs.

"It's alright, Patrick," Deevi whispered in my ear. "Everything is all right."

"None of this is all right," I hissed between my lips. "It's just so fucked. It's all so fucked."

"What is?"

With her powers or without, little was needed to wring the truth out of me. "Look at this! Look at all of this. We're stuck, doing this, again and again, when he's out there just dancing and singing and thinking the world is just going to get solved with love and community. None of these things fucking matter to those he's harmed. Some wounds are too deep."

"And are you that wounded?" Merry asked, studying me with her bright amber eyes. "Are you that hurt too, *mon cher?*"

"I don't fucking know," I said to this woman who had been my lover, my partner, my best friend, and the greatest ally any person could have. "I just don't know, Merry."

The Vodun queen swallowed and nodded. Sadness dewed her eyes. "I've had to think a lot about what we lost in all this. On what happens when it is all done. But this is life: it's always ending, but whatever happens continues after this. I will still have my Lwas, he has said, and no fear of some white savior riding out of the clouds to strike mine down. I think—" She swallowed again. "I think it matters less what we lose now. Whatever happens, whatever is taken, we get back more. I have to have faith, now, that what will happen leads to something more than what I lost. What you lost," she said to Deevi, breathing hard before the tears ran down her dark cheeks. "The only thing we go do now is care about what is here, and hope, hope it will still be there when we see the end."

"Hope is the way," someone said out of our view.

Jolted by the power of their voice, an immediate presence brought us to our feet.

A woman walked toward us. Dressed much in the fashion of the

Virgin, Lisbeth, and Saint Brigid, her cloth was dyed to a bright, bloody crimson. Waterfalls of luxurious black hair framed the tanned, beautiful face of the Levant, a timeless expression of symmetry jeweled by two bright green eyes. To say her beauty stole my breath would not be a lie, for the charisma also awed the women sandwiching me.

Our complete attentions drawn to her as she passed, she paid us a sneaking, salacious smile.

"See you soon."

We watched, wordless, as a force of nature strode past the dead devil and down the steps into the arena.

The band played through the end of Solsbury Hill, Selaphiel's synthesized piano and Ramiel's steady, solid rhythm leading Uriel, who led Nathaniel, before the rest followed suit. Christ twirled both his mother and Gabriel around him, front and center of the stage as the archangels and immortal danced to the glory of their noise. A sight of infinite delights as they smiled, laughed, the gigantic Messenger clapped along with their father and grandmother. The crowds formed their own lines and circles on the floor and in the stands.

But someone in the crowd caught the Savior's attention. A smile unlike any other crossed his face, a human grin, overjoyed and playful and mysterious all at once. He backed out of the dance circle and pointed to Lucifer's microphone. The Morningstar nodded, playing the ambling riff to an Englishman's gnosis, before his attention too was captured by the red-dressed figure ascending the rounded stage.

He stopped strumming, standing dead on the spot with a dumbfounded expression, like he saw someone impossible coming toward them. Every single archangel stopped playing when they saw her, leaving only Nathaniel the Devout to carrying on.

Christ marched, beaming from head to toe, and met this woman with a deep, passionate kiss.

The gasp in Madison Square Garden was explosive, punctuated and heightened by the sudden silence at the midnight hour.

Mary Magdalene took the second mic from her husband's hand and lifted it up. The woman in scarlet scanned the entire horde of faces, searching, questioning, until she found the object of her fullest affections. She called his name.

And he met her, welcoming her home better than any scene Ryan Reynolds could come up with using a weathered-ass Hugh Jackman.

Uriel's jubilant bass unleashed the band from their stupor as Ramiel's snare snapped the entire crowd into the Madonna's lyrics. Every instrument, from Michael's warm saxophone to the electric sharpness of Lucifer's ax atop of Nathaniel's dulcet harmonies, the archangels watched in a precise state of awe, unable to process the emotions they expressed on their faces though their hands moved along keys, strings, skins, and boards.

The Truest Apostle danced ecstatically with her husband; a complete head-over-heels idiot wrapped up in her glory, down on her knees until he lifted her up. The sight of the Savior, fully within his humanity but lacking none of his divinity, removed one mask for one closer to his true, ineffable skin. His muse before him, much of the mystery vanished.

God had found love in a woman who drank in life, her microphone an overturned wine cup. Jubilant in their reunion, they ceased to carry the tune, letting instead the crowd become the choir and sing.

The Virgin and the Messenger answered the final call, fierce along with everyone calling their hearts out in Madison Square Garden.

The luster of her voice brought Deevi, Merry, and I out from the tunnel. My legs still shaking from my exhaustion and emotion, I stood among the mess of dancing, sweating, weed-and-tobacco-soaked humanity.

We all sang, deep within ourselves to meet this goddess in red beside the ultimate creator.

At least mine. With little time to measure the day beyond the events that had happened, I stood behind Deevi as her and Merry leapt up and down together, shoulder to shoulder thanks to the lack of wings. I looked upon what the Lord had made.

He had built a Mount and gathered us for a sermon. Or at least another one.

An infinite number of moves ahead on the chessboard, I never had a shot at beating this guy because I was in no competition, and he wasn't trying to compete at all with us—quite the opposite. He dared to do things on that stage with the Magdalene that I'm sure Dan Brown's fans would cheer while the rest of the world shook.

But not for the people around me. These heathens from every part of the globe, enemies of the Church I had held forth since its middle days, had come to hear of peace. Where their lack of faith had been was also an open window to true light, wherever it came from—be it their gods or Him.

Looking to my right, Govinda's tall, bald head poked up in the crowd as he watched the show with a serene smile. Certain of Deevi's safety in the sight of the archangels, I left her and the Vodun Queen to dance.

The young mendicant greeted me with a warm grin and nod but said nothing as I took a place beside him, between two girls and a lad stinking of body odor, incense, and cannabis that Selaphiel's censor failed to defeat.

"Hey," Govinda said.

"Hey."

"Good show?" he asked.

"No one's buzzing and, well..." I nodded to the stage and shrugged.

"Yeah," he said. "But you are okay, Saint Patrick?"

"I think so, young monk," I said with some unexpected affection. I liked this kid. "I guess we're in it now."

"Since birth and will be when we are born again." He returned his attention to the embodied god on stage. "Until we learn well."

"Want to make a deal?"

He cracked up at the question. "Sure."

"I think we're going to be helping them for a good bit," I said, nodding to the woman in red and her smitten Absolute. "Life will be quite the mystery."

"Oh, many lives," Govinda replied.

"How about this, then?" I said, offering my open palm. "We're all dragged into this, but we'll drag ourselves out of it. Together, huh?"

The young Hari Krishna smacked mine in an instant and shook. "The only way we go."

Getting through a full song without issues set off alarm bells. Beside Govinda as we watched the band end on a rousing crescendo, I looked out upon the crowds and spied no problems.

No problems at all.

I reached to the monitor and pressed the call button. "Shoniqua? Are you there, dear?"

"Roger, Tater," the nurse crackled on the other end.

"Anything going on?"

"Nothing back here. Just met Brigid and Deevi's mom. Is she really a former goddess?"

"I'll explain it later," I said, "but there's nothing going on back there?"

"Nope, just me, the vets, and Daniel watching things from the monitors."

I glanced to Govinda to catch him studying me. Smart lad. I pressed back down on the call button. "See you if can find Rosie and Rabbi Rebecca. Once you do, tell them to come out to the floor. Something isn't right."

Shoniqua did not answer, responding with a bloop of confirmation.

"On again?" Govinda asked, the serenity of his expression dulled.

I signaled for him to follow as we pressed forward into the crowds watching Christ and the Funky Flock lay it on the line.

Christ raised his hand, signaling to Lucifer and Nathaniel to halt their strings. Raphael and Michael silenced their horns, then the rest, one by one, until only Selaphiel played, low and mournful. The wings of the archangels dimmed to a soft blue, the details of their heavenly fanes almost distinguishable in the shimmer.

Alone in his clothes best fitted for Phil Collins in 90s Berlin, the Savior approached his post, hands behind his back as he moved close to the receiver. "Everybody is here. Those who will help me here and after. Those who came before and remained. The first among my creations. I have brought them together, as I have you, because obviously something ceased to work at some point. Without fixing it, we can't go forward." He looked out at the audience, taking in each visage of himself. "What I do here, now, is not to change anyone's faith, but to reveal the truth. The truth of what I have done, why I have done it, and what I will do after. I have come to proclaim revelation."

Ramiel tapped out the three-quarter beat with his drumsticks.

Christ whispered into the mic. "This ends my rolling suicide."

Lucifer swept the strings of his white guitar, infusing the song with its original Armenian flair from his tremolo picking as the tempo kicked upwards in a frantic pace. Uriel and the guitarists struck into a bouncing, grinding riff as the rest remained with their instruments lowered. Mary, Mary, and Gabriel staked their places to Christ's right, still as statues. Raguel joined Ramiel with his own percussions, the two sets of drums blending into a syncopated rhythm. Awakening the crowd, the tension of the music drew all corners together in wait.

Which broke apart again when Lucifer pressed down on the pedal by his feet. Buzzsaw distortion warped his notes.

Michael and Raphael's horns backed Christ as he tore his mic free of the stand and screamed.

The Magdalene whispered back, asking him why he left the keys to life on the table for all to take.

Every word, delivered by the nails driven through his pierced arms and feet, jolted the audience into maddened moshing. The center formed a corona of bouncing, running bodies, backing away from itself until a wide space had been made. In the minds of each of us, every soul able to see, hear, or sense, marched that space to the middle again, much like the man born of a virgin womb had marched his way to a violent, brutal death.

The breaking pace of the song bolted back into the ambling, folk tremolo as Christ crooned. Singing with the passion of a people the Ottomans had tried to wipe out to form a religious ethnostate built on suppression and violence, he reflected the deaths of those millions, many of whom had prayed their last to him during the death marches.

His scream to die echoed in each viewer watching on screens across the globe as he was laid on the cross with them, arms and legs bound. Like the kick of the double-bass drums in front of Ramiel, the crowds flinched as the Roman sledgehammers broke open the bones, blood and marrow and iron invading their noses.

The second verse, a second refrain, illuminated the torture of his sacrifice, needed to find the answer to ineffable mysteries only he could ply from oblivion. The full fury of a people long oppressed by another as his people had been, as he had been, under the hand of empires and temples emerged. This death every person felt down to the final breath coalesced into a bellowed bridge by the one who had died, risen, and defeated such odds.

Then Lucifer stepped up to his microphone, strumming hand thundering on his strings. *"Father into your hands, I commit my spirit! Father, into your hands, why have you forsaken me?"*

At the edge of life and death, the people inside the arena sang their hearts out. Within their hearts, opened by his word, the hint of what lay ahead beckoned.

Christ declared to the purpose of his death, body and soul given at once to save the children no one else was coming to rescue.

Including the ones on high.

Soon we were all in the audience, seeking out the weird needle in an immense haystack of strangeness. Govinda remained ahead of me, always in my sight, and Daniel and I passed each other a few times, exchanging nods as twelve people combed twenty-thousand. An impossible task on an impossible night, I considered calling Shoniqua to give the order, more than willing to absorb the embarrassment of being too high-strung about Satan if it kept these people safe. Amid the stinking, sweating, smoking masses slowing from the whirlwind on stage, I posted at the edge of the largest mosh pit.

A hand fell on my shoulder, and turning toward the owner of its touch, I almost didn't recognize Deevi without her glowing wings. Beautiful as ever, a deep concern had driven out the joy she had reveled in during the Magdalene's introduction.

Before I could ask, she pulled me down, her mouth by my ear to speak.

"Something is happening," she said. "There's a change in the air. Like it's charged."

"Charged?" I asked, worried instantly of the electronics clipped to my belt, set on my head, and in my pocket. "What kind of charge?"

"It's like when Gabriel tried to teleport us away from Lough Derg, or when the demons became devils and..." A horrid realization widened her golden gaze, and she checked the stage, the band, and their leader. "The dimensions are shifting. Thinning! Something is coming!"

"Damn." I pressed down the call button. About to speak into the microphone of my headset as I used the other hand to steady them on my ears, words failed when I caught him to my left.

An older man in a black rain poncho that covered his clothes, if he wore any, faced Christ while the people around him recovered, but not him. The straightness of his stance, the weird, unblinking intensity of his stare, weighed a terrible feeling in my gut. I couldn't see his eyes or his full face, but the paleness of it drew me toward him.

"Stay here," I told Deevi. "Or go find Daniel. Quickly, Deevi."

"What is it?" she asked, following the direction of my eyes. "Who is it?"

"I'm going to go find out," I replied as we marched back into the battle.

CHAKA KHAN WAS IN THE MUSIC VIDEO

U nwashed, unclean, but no worse than some of the other un-housed Christ had brought inside, he could have passed for any homeless on the street.

If not for the lack of eyes. Chasms of darkness bordered by fleshy eyelids, the shell of whomever Satan had possessed firmed both shoulders. Hands hidden in the flap of his black poncho, he paid me absolutely no mind as he stared every single bit of his disgust at the band onstage.

I took one last step toward his rear.

"If you are smart," said the possessed vagrant, "you will not take another step toward me, saint. Not when I know you have so much to lose now."

"And you don't, Shaytan?"

He gave no reply, at least none I could gauge from an eyeless angel bent on being the last thorn in the lion's paw. A quick check ahead of me and I saw Govinda doubling back, already wide-eyed as he viewed the possessed man. Daniel and Enrique came in from the right, then Rosie on the left. I heard a crackle in the headphones that had fallen around my neck. I brought the right cup to my ear.

"There!" Shoniqua exclaimed on her end. "I got him, Rebecca! Patrick, we see you both!"

"Everyone needs to stay right where they are," I said calmly into my microphone.

"Very good, shepherd," said Satan. "Best to keep the sheep back."

"Or what?" I asked, not needing to raise my voice to know he heard me. "What will you do? In the face of God? In the face of all the archangels? Come, serpent, the war is over. You are cornered and defenseless. Even now the forces of Perdition flee from you, brought back to the flock you spurn."

"You think that makes me defenseless?" A cold smirk formed on his chapped lips. "All you can do is destroy a body. But me..."

He needn't say more, but neither could I as Christ spoke into his mic on stage,

"So," he said, grinning on his divine children, Virgin mother, mistress Magdalene, and the immortal guitar player arrayed behind him. "Yes, I died. I took the step to embrace a mortal life because I did not know the depth of my creations, too often thinking that my perfection of form and thought outstripped notions of dignity, as if I could be above such a thing. In learning to live, and breathe, and love, and be among you all, I learned where I had failed. Where I failed every one of you."

He laid eyes right on his enemy. I swallowed my anxiety for a bit of faith as the two poles of the universe faced off, finally in each other's way.

"Keep everyone back," I repeated into my microphone, "and let them figure it out."

The admittance of a mistake created a swelling silence, fear and disaster in the mind of every listener. Christ took one step to the edge of the stage and lifted his mic again.

"Look, you don't know. I didn't give you the means to know, but somehow you're expected to. And while you are me, but there is a clear difference. A disparity. The point I want to make here is that when I died, I understood that all of you have to live with a limitation that makes it wrong of me to demand of you without good reason or guidance given first. And frankly, the people who claimed me after I departed the first time did not do any better. I cannot damn those men, who were my friends and followers, for what they said and created in my name, no more than I can damn a priestess for dancing with her snakes or a monk meditating in a clearing. Who am I to judge a witch when priests in my churches do worse to children than any root-woman would dream? But I am in your dreams as well. And when I died, I found..."

Christ turned in Lucifer's direction, giving his son a mournful glance. He faced the people again. "I died on that cross. All the agony and shame and fear and unknowing and questions of what I did not know, and I put each and every one you through that without knowing what I had done. I put you all through so much you bravely face. But, when I went on the cross, I did not go to the place you call Heaven, but someplace else, made from that pit of loneliness I found in the earliest understandings of myself. That void was the reason I created so much so I would not be alone." He brought the mic to his forehead. Two pounds on his skull reverberated through the arena. "That place was meant to simply be, a part of me banished upon my resurrection because I could leave it behind, and I could see an existence without needing to fear loneliness because you are me and I am you. I know I will repeat that, and you have all grown up hearing it, but it bears repeating. But as I lingered in that Perdition, I conceived the means to bring me back to life. But what would be the purpose? To shake off the chains of death. To bring about an end to suffering. I am you and you are me."

Raguel struck upon his conga, the sharp strikes reverberating as he took a pair of sticks to it. Ramiel followed, beating his drumsticks in a fast, switching rhythm. The Interpreter came down on his toms, bridging in Selaphiel's synthesized melody.

Backing up to stand side by side with his band, Christ threw his head back, revealing truths conceived down in the heart or the in the stars above. Gabriel answered in kind, waxing on the ills of existence.

Christ and his Messenger harmonized, low and full through the verse on what could be instead of the death of what was happening all around the world in that instant. The world screamed their demands in Steve Winwood. Michael and Raphael blasted with their horns as Selaphiel's keys danced among the rest of the instruments.

Seeds thrown to the rocky and thin soil, new roots delved anyway, clawing deep to the earth in every soul. Fed on the waters of life in his voice, they swelled in immensity as they branched and crossed. Filling in spaces long left neglected in the human spirit, the promise of something new, different, sprang out of the two-thousand-year dark.

The end of tribulation. The coming of peace, slow to grow in the stony loam, but certain to blossom like the mustard tree.

Christ sang with his wife, his mother, and the gigantic child between them of a higher love, dug up by the Savior from Hell's cold loam in the fight to get back home and show the world different.

Satan watched as we watched him, unmoved despite the torrent of human bodies around us jumping, exalting, pouring emotions I had never witnessed in such volume. People fell over themselves in tears, laughing and weeping in the throes that would have caught me as well if not for the massive fucking problem in front of me.

I felt a hand close around mine to the right, and startled, I turned to find Deevi beside me. She held on, focused on her tormenter's back. Squeezing hard, the strength of her fingers almost crushed bones.

"It's happening," she said into my right ear, over the music and the jubilance. "The veil is falling!"

"Bring it," Christ whispered into his mic as the band broke down the beat and melody structure, leaving the electronics from Selaphiel's synth to assume their space. Each instrument fell away until only the Consecrator's loop remained.

The Savior strode to the edge of the stage and raised his fist, pumping it to the strike of the crowd's hands until they all fell in time.

"Stop," Christ said. He turned to the keyboards and signaled a cut across his throat.

Selaphiel answered with immediate silence. The band inert under the lights, the clapping died as the Lord of Hosts found Satan again.

Surrounded by the Helpers, caught in the sea of newly-realized, the fallen angel in the guise of a homeless man glared.

"I've made a decision," Christ said. "It is not easy to say 'as above, so below' when the below never gets to see the blessings of above, nor do those above have proper stake in what happens beneath them. Angel or demon, they all work upon my word. Even you," he said, raising a finger at Satan.

Every single person turned in our direction, almost rote to the order, and took a collective step away. The Devil, unflinching in the recognition, paid the world no mind with his eyeless, soul-ridden stare.

"You're only in him because I said you could be," Christ said. "But that is not fair to that person you hold."

Uh oh.

"If I am to bring about liberation, if I am to bring about peace, I cannot do it through the coercion of others. A true god needs no servants other than the one they are to be. So..." Christ reached toward the ceiling of the arena. The damned thing shook, drawing a loud cry of surprise and panic from the mortals underneath.

"Oh, don't worry," he said into his mic, the other hand aloft. "This is a piece of cake."

Before our awed witness the roof of Madison Square Garden deconstructed, layers of girding and steel flying away in disconnecting bits before the actual roof appeared, only to peel itself outward. The sky bared above us, a night full of stars burning brighter than the lights of New York City.

Then a line of light unzipped in the firmament.

Raphael blew on his silver horn to usher in hundreds of thousands of angels and fallen angels. Fleshed in their different forms, feathered, light-forged, and machine-like beings descended upon the Earth. No longer demonic, those who had returned to the lists of the Platinum Polis had regained their divine forms, crowned only in laurels of dark leaves to set them apart. They came, some multi-winged and multitudes of eyes, other like lions and griffins, but all bore human faces.

Uh oh.

"Patrick, look!" Deevi thrust her hand toward the stage.

As if another curtain had pulled away, dozens of young men and women appeared beside their older human parents, the former winged in spans of feathers imbued with a familiar golden light.

We both knew that light, for it matched the illumination of Deevi's wings.

The Nephilim—all the Nephilim—had been freed alongside the prisoners of Perdition to appear among us.

Deevi revealed her wings, the sudden expansion of light causing everyone but myself and Satan to step back. Like a dart she flew forward. More than happy to have her away from the weakened lord of an emptying hell, I remained unmoved as Christ gathered the entire force of the Platinum Polis sans one before the entire world. The clouds in the sky above the exposed roof, blazing white from the shimmering sources too blinding to count in full, I could only imagine the terror of an entire planet who had just been watching some goof dance and sing about love and peace bring down an army no nation could match.

"Heed me! Heed me," Christ said, almost washed out by the rays of his multitudes. "I have enslaved! I have chained! I have cursed! I am the bounder of bounders as I am the liberator of liberators, the beginning of freedom as I am the end of it. Too long I sat on a throne, exalted without exalting what I had created, fractal mirrors of myself cast in equal glory. I placed myself above all others, setting rules I never suffered but everyone else did. So I am to bring this crime—my crime—to its end."

He raised his gaze heavenward. "From this day, I impart to all of the hosts the flesh of my flesh and blood of my blood! You may return to the gleaming city, hold its gates open for those that will one day join its throngs, or you may take substance and walk among your mortal kin, no longer divided. You will find your own way as you see fit. From this day forth I will no longer possess, nor allow any of my host permission to possess the souls of the innocent and unknowing. My finite tyranny ends here for what is infinite! For what is boundless and filled by love. For the Nephilim, I grant them the freedom they should hav—"

Blinking through the blinding glow of the burning angels above, I struggled for a moment to find Satan in front of me when I realized he had vanished.

Then the earth shook from its core, interrupting Christ's words.

THE LAST PARTY POOPER

The second quake knocked most around me to the ground, and outside the screams of the people filled the streets. The third sent the summoned angels away, the vast doorway of light shut in an instant as the realms between vibrated. Fixed in our present, the Nephilim surrounding the archangels quickly moved with them to guard Christ, flesh and blood as he was.

He had other thoughts. "Stop," he boomed into the microphone. "Stop! You are safe with me!"

But we mortals were no easy flock, quick to flee in an era of mass shootings, terrorist attacks, and disasters. Planes had struck down an icon of this city, so everyone had primed every morning since that day, ready to take New York for what it was, rats and all. And like the rats, everyone had some idea of an exit until things got crowded.

Then Satan roared from outside the opened arena, voice raging across the sky.

"Nazarenus," he cried in Latin for some weird-ass reason. "Nazarenus! Appear in this world you spurn! Appear, coward!"

The depth of it, the sincere threat and evil, carried more horror than any demon had ever gurgled at me from inside a human, and likewise it sickened all of us present. The sound of herded women and children slumping dead in showers, entire fields of rural innocence set ablaze by flamethrowers, and the pounding of two nuclear waves searing shadows on the walls gathered in a guttural, sawing, warping bass.

When Satan spoke, he infused his words with every bit of the darkness he crawled out of. If not for the presence of Christ, I am not sure I wouldn't have gone mad. Others vomited up their wine and bread, sacraments wasted by the corruption upon us.

"Come out!" Satan roared outside. "Come out, you lying, thieving conniver! Conniver! You played upon suffering to create adoration when you offer salvation, but these are words! Your words! The beginning and the end! And I shall end you, pretender! Appear!"

All turned to Christ, mortal or divine, devout or doubting, in search of a response.

Promised since the Roman Empire oppressed the early Christ movements, this final reckoning had shaped itself into something much more than John the Apostle's folk had built it to be, but none of the potency was lost. On the edge of the circular stage which raised to the drums kit and keyboard station like a mound, he stared westward, toward the 8th Avenue exit, but said nothing.

Michael appeared at his side, then Lucifer, both of them whispering to him. Neither argued, thank goodness.

"I will come in if you don't," Satan warned, louder than before. "The longer you wait the worse I will do to you, mewling kitten! The thorn taken from your paw I shall plunge in your heart!" He laughed, the cruelness sharper than guillotines severing necks of the condemned, guilty or not. "Perhaps I shall use my thorn on that red slut of yours! Ha, yes! Perhaps once I throw your body down I shall throw her on top of your dying—"

A great cry of surprise erupted from the stage as Christ leapt off and marched, dead set on the exit.

"That's enough," he said into the mic before he tossed it to the side.

Mary Magdalene chased after him, slower to get off the lowest platform due to her hems until Gabriel helped her and the Virgin float down. The audience halted in place as God in the flesh stormed by.

"Patrick and Patrick alone," Christ declared. "With me, saint!"

"And I'll fuck his bitch too," Satan cried, more laughter punctuating his mean little amusement. "Bring her fine—"

I pulled my Bible and rosary out and chucked them as I fell in with my Lord and Savior, needing nothing of them anymore or ever again. No longer employable as an exorcist, the next natural role fell to me:

A pissed off Daddy-to-be.

We marched through the parting throngs and into the packed halls. Several made way, forming an aisle all the way to the door. Too damned mad to think straight, I kept focus until we cleared the entrance. 8th Avenue, clearly once packed with people from the amount of red cups and discarded blankets stank in the crisp night air, their stragglers disappearing around the blocks in every direction.

And for good reason why.

Straddling the intersection of 31st Street and 8th Avenue, he came twelve feet tall and carved of gray-skinned muscle, though of finer and sleeker proportions than the minor devils I had encountered in Central Park. This pure expression of Satan's form, infernal and terrible, stretched widely with a pair of black wings feathered in strokes of un-light. He carried a longsword in one hand, nothing in the other. Two sweeping horns sprouted from his forehead.

A long, leathery tail whipping behind him, he went right for us.

"Nazarenus! Nazarenus!" he screamed in his horrid voice. "The reign of your terror ends here!"

"Oh, shit," I said.

Christ firmed his stance beside me. "Just hold, Patrick," he said, perfectly calm as he linked his hands behind his back. "The Devil only has words."

"Well, he certainly looks like he'll—" The words were torn from me as the gray bastard raised his burning sword in threat. Shut me right up.

Not Christ. Unimpressed to say the least, he gazed up into the Devil's face. "You know you can't."

The lord of Perdition's hands shook as he growled down at us. Yet he did not strike.

The dawning sparked the wild reminder of this entire mad journey: God was the one who gave permission—and he no longer gave Satan sway.

Left inert but posed, the Devil revealed his truest nature: another sad, angry soul, unable to exert power or control no matter how much he flailed at it.

"You couldn't hit the broad side your ass if you wanted to," I said aloud, cocksure in the moment.

"Patrick," Christ chided me. The look he paid the gigantic foe looming over us was unreadable until he let out a deep sigh. "Shaytan, I'm giving you a choice, as I am giving *everyone*. It is a choice you can take, here and now, and it is yours to make. I will not make you do anything you do not wish to do, but whatever happens, you will bear the consequences. I hope you understand this, because I love you and wish for you to come home. I made many mistakes and I am willing to pay for them. But you must stand down. We all must stand down. The wars between Lucifer, myself, and Michael have ended. They must end between us too."

The bestial creature leaned down until he was hooked nose to nose with the gentle carpenter. "Fuck you."

Christ sighed a second time. "All right. As I have said, I will not harm you. However, I see you having two paths now. I hope you will understand them and their weight, because I will not spare you from either."

"What will you do, little man? Turn both cheeks?"

Christ shook his head. "No, my child. In five minutes, I will walk back inside the Garden and finish my work. I hope you will be beside me. That's the first path you may take. The home I would make is as much for you as it is for everyone else. The second path lies behind you."

Confused, Satan spun about to find Cuchulainn waiting for him.

Scrubbed clean after a shower and re-dressed in his armor, bracers, and greaves, he went naked under it save for his laced war-sandals and the wide belt about his lithe waist. He had brought no weapons.

The Devil leaned down. "I can't hit him, little man, but I can hit you. What even makes you think your little half-breed ass can even touch me?"

The Hound of Ulster smirked a deadly smile and balled his right hand into a fist. "Because I'm a bastard."

Without pause Cuchulainn threw a right haymaker up into the jaw of Satan, buckling the idiot's knees. Stunned by the unexpected strike, he scrambled as my ancient kin pounced without mercy. Stomps to the wings and neck, hard soccer kicks to the head and face, put the Devil down each time in renewed shock and pain. The next five minutes passed with brutal gusto as the pint-sized Irishman beat Satan up and down the block, turning him both times. He skipped him across the asphalt, tossed like a stone on water.

Wings mashed into clumps on his back, one snapped horn plunged into a bleeding side, a broken Satan crawled toward his creator on two hands and one knee, his shattered leg dragging behind like his limp tail. Taloned hands grasped Christ's brown ankles, burying his forehead against his shins.

"Mercy," he screamed through swollen, bleeding lips. "Mercy!"

To his credit, Christ bent down and touched the fallen angel's shoulder.

In an instant Shaytan re-manifested before us, back on both feet and in his original form as a winged man robed in scintillating white. He looked at his unmarred hands in surprise and delight before touching a blemish-less face. His big eyes, filled with stars that shimmered brighter and brighter, ringed in tears.

He reached forward. "How?"

"Oh, just because," Christ as he led the stunned angel toward the Garden, hand in hand. "Now we have to hurry! Your grandmother is about to sing."

THAT WORN-OUT LEATHER

I stayed on Shaytan's left as Christ brought him inside, only to be met by an unexpected welcome.

Michael and Lucifer had put aside their instruments and left the stage, standing right at the threshold. Michael balled his fists at his sides, incensed as he had been with his archangel-brother. Lucifer glowered at the broken seraph.

Neither of them said anything, nor acknowledged their father in reverence.

I firmed myself, glancing to Lucifer first, but he paid me no attention. The halls leading to the left and right and the tunnel to the arena beyond were packed with people, eager to see the lost lamb we had returned with.

"What are you doing?" Christ asked.

"He cannot come in here," Lucifer said first, monotone as he stared hard at Shaytan. The latter refused to raise his eyes from the concrete.

Christ tightened his arm around our defeated enemy and stood a bit taller. "Oh?"

"Lord, he is the traitor among traitors, the spoiler of the Garden, the general of Perdition's forces!" Michael stated, far more animated in his indignation. "You cannot bring him in here! There will be angels and fallen angels, and when they see him—"

"They will see him as I see him, and they will be seen by me as well." Clearing his throat, Christ kept Shaytan close to him as they attempted to maneuver around Lucifer's outer wing. "Pardon."

The Morningstar took a hard step to his left, in the path of his creator.

The Savior sighed. "Lucifer."

"Michael is right," The Morningstar replied. "To have him here, after what he has said, and done, and allowed through the ages with—"

"With my permission," Christ replied, cutting his son's point off at the knees. "And my forgiveness. And I have forgiven him now, so if you excuse me, your mother and grandmother are about to take the stage. Can't miss it. Here you go, Patrick."

Like it was nothing, he took his arm from around the former Satan and placed the shamed angel's glowing hand in mine before, without worry or concern, walked between his sons. The throng of onlookers accepted him with awe and wonder, once again parting their sea, and was swallowed. Out of sight and immediately out of mind, I glanced to the downcast Shaytan, then to the perturbed Lucifer, before settling on Michael.

The Protector, without his sword, almost shook where he stood.

But I also felt the flesh that was not flesh, light that was not light, trembling in the hand I held. Fear and shame and so many other things I had found in this world, there in an angel. Another victim of circumstances out of their control.

"I have to say you're both being a bit much," I began.

"He threatened to rape the mother of your child, priest," Lucifer said. "Perhaps my kin and I are incapable of the humanity to forgive...him, but to see you, of all people—"

"He murdered St. George," Michael spat, like the truth would harm me.

And it did. I gave the lowly Shaytan another review. Battered by

Cuchulainn's savagery, he made no sign of defiance. I checked past Lucifer and Michael for a moment, seeing if any of the crowds remained behind to watch us. A few stragglers had stayed in the hall at the peripheries, but most had retreated into the arena with the star of the show.

"They're right," I said to Shaytan. "I could let them have you, right here. After everything you done, there's plenty of people who'd think you deserve it. I might be one of them. So, I'm not going to save you, Shaytan, but allow you to save yourself. If you answer me honest, we'll go right into that arena, and it will be the start of a new day. For all of us." I gave a hard look to the brothers. "But if you lie, Shaytan—you will probably end up in some place. And I don't know if I can't talk these two down."

"He can't," Michael rumbled, placing a foot forward in advance.

Shaytan started, almost pulling out of my hand. Somehow I held tight against his massive strength, then placed myself in the middle of their divine triangle.

"All right?" I asked, brooking no more nonsense from any of them. "Fair?"

"He has nothing to say, priest," Michael snapped. "Just more lies!"

Fresh tears dropped from Shaytan's scrunched eyes as he covered them with his luminous hands. A deep, deep sob escaped, and he mumbled something short and moaning.

I neared, leaning close to hear. "What's that?"

"Please," Shaytan said, whispering from behind his hands. Suddenly he crushed into my side, limp as a noddle as his emotions flooded out. He wailed, breathless as he tried to mutter words. "Please..."

"Please what?" Michael asked as Lucifer stared the broken Devil down. "Please what?"

"I just—I just—"

Michael opened his mouth to bark something more, but my hand came up. Silencing him, I pressed my mortal forehead against the warm, plasma-like skin of the seraph's. "Shaytan," I whispered in his ear. "Why did you surrender?"

Heaving once, he blurted it all out. "I just don't want to hurt anymore. I just don't want to hurt anymore!"

No matter how selfish, or how deep the crimes committed against themselves and others, the confession sapped Michael and shattered Lucifer's hard expression.

Then I heard a voice on the microphone in the arena, soft and melodious. "Hello everyone, my name is Mary. You may know me as the mother of Christ." Fingers strummed down the strings of an acoustic guitar, the five notes reverberating. "And with the help of my daughter-in-law, Mary, and the rest of the band, I'd like to say some words."

Mother Mary took a stool in front of the drum riser, bearing an acoustic guitar while Uriel repositioned the microphone he had lent.

"Anyway," she said, tuning the knob on the E until it plucked true. "I call him Yeshua because he's my little boy." She gave a proud, sad smile to an enchanted audience. "But he's also much more than that. And tonight is a very special moment for my son, and while I risk embarrassing him, I wanted to give my testimony. There are a lot of things said about the women in your holy books."

Selaphiel played on his keys a slow melody.

"You know, it is easy to read that book and think 'oh, what a blessed thing she did.' But I didn't feel blessed when it happened. I felt confused and scared and betrayed by something beyond me when I had tried do my best to be a good person for the times. Having a baby in the circumstances I did felt less like a scene from your Christmas stories and more running for our lives because people wanted to kill me and my baby. And they called me a whore. Nobody believed me. And then you rebuild, only to discover your son is the God of your people. The God who placed you where you are, whether or not you asked for it," The Virgin looked out in the crowd and spotted him. The sadness in her smile lightened but did not fade. "And you have to ask: what do I do?"

She brought her hands up to her guitar and sang.

The voice of a mother sang out to the crowds, to the world, filled with the sorrow of the scorned, the refugee, and the dejected. The wanderer in everyone, lost to the whims of fate, peaked our heads above its ruin to see a coming dawn.

All were bound and led by her words.

The Magdalene backed her up on her mic, speaking to millions of little reasons not to believe, to have their doubts.

Then the Virgin proclaimed her prayer, to make the world seem better despite the cruel hand the Lord had dealt.

Raguel padded in on his hand drum, soft like a gentle heartbeat.

"In the end, I realized that no matter what God chose, the same choice was always going to be in my hands one day: what am I going to do with this baby? But that is a choice we all have to make every day in so many different ways. What am I going to do with my partner? My debts? My home? My future? What am I going to do? Hearing sometimes you don't have a choice is the hardest thing to hear. But even in that lack of choice, there is one that always remains: will I do good or will I not? Will I make the world better or let it suffer?" Eyes fixed on her child in the audience, who also wept, Mother Mary beamed to each and every child around him, beyond him, and more. "He was a baby. *My baby*. And then he was my little boy, and then a young man. But he's always my baby. Especially when the world comes for him."

The two Marys took the song back up, the elder leading while the latter supported. For all the wear of the world, tearing sorrows it had left upon them, they took upon them the mantle made of God's failings, loving him nonetheless beneath it all.

When they hit the chorus, Uriel arrived with his bass to unite the disparate voices of the audience into a choir, softly soaring to meet the two leads at the front of the stage. Every voice together, the tearful and the joyful, the heretical and the faithful, bound in humane understanding of the challenge. Along the highways of the soul, where the rest might have fled for the hills, they staked themselves as posts for the Almighty.

But never flagging, always courageous, the Virgin did not deter from the choice put before her.

Cursed by mortal failures, but blessed by an immortal love, she picked her child first as she always had.

People doubted before the show whether the world would listen, and after many proclaimed that they did not, but for the time she had, the Virgin made it clear exactly why she had been chosen.

A TICKET TO ANYWHERE

Slowly, as the song ended, a soft light issued from the skies above the opened roof of Madison Square Garden.

Recalled without order, the angelic body of the Platinum Polis reappeared, first in clumps of a few dozen, then by the hundreds and hundreds before the sky was so lit up not even the crevices between the nighttime clouds held shadow. I watched, as awed as any mortal soul despite the things I had seen. They descended, landing among the people in the audience, but too many to enter all at once, forcing the rest to settled in the streets around Penn Station and the arena. Wreathed in crowns of black laurel or pure of brow, the newcomers must have been picked up by every satellite, and probably the bleeding aliens watching us from space.

To see many of them up close baffled, no matter how often I had now stood among the towering archangels, or beside the winged man-form of the defeated Shaytan. One close by had taken the upright form of a man, but kept their claws and talons, along with an eagle's beak. Many different animals in the form of serpents and foxes and wolves and frogs roamed among stunned and ordinary.

The heavenly ambiance wreathed the two women on stage in halos of their own as they stood among the archangel band. The immortal guitarist Nathaniel assumed the same glimmering crown. Lucifer and Michael had yet to return.

To the silent curiosity of many, including myself, Christ stood among us but did not wear his.

"That's definitely something to think on, Mary," the Magdalene said into her microphone as she stood beside Selaphiel's racks of synthesizers. "It's very important to remember that every day is a choice based on small things. Those small things are the ants that build the hill, or the drops of rain that wash them away."

"Very wise," the Virgin replied.

"May I have a turn?" the Magdalene asked.

"Oh, of course, dear," said the Virgin. "This is a family effort, after all."

"Perhaps before we begin our missing band members will return," the Magdalene responded, glowing in her red dress and shroud. "But I also understand there might some hesitance. I can also understand for many of the people here and at home," she said, looking into one of the many cameras stationed around the rounded stage.

"You see," she continued, "some of us aren't blessed with motherhood like Mary was, and some of us don't want it. I don't know where I stand. And I'm married to God. *Who already has kids.*" She scrunched her face cutely with a smile. "Tough one."

"Imagine raising five," the Virgin piped in, amused.

"I may now have at least a hundred thousand," the Magdalene replied in sing-song, "but the point remains that for many, faith has to take on more than simply doing the right thing. It's not wrong to expect that for all that is given, you take something back. But that's also hard to measure. I'm going to sing the next song, and during that time I want us all to really think hard. Not about where we have been and what has been said, but for a moment, where we're headed."

Lucifer and Michael broke among the crowd, whispering requests to make way as they stepped by or wedged through. Left behind with the former Satan, the slayer of St. George, the weirdness of the moment anchored me as Ramiel tapped on his high hats. The Virgin struck the opening chords on her guitar.

A hand laid on my shoulder, and turning, I almost thought Deevi had rejoined me when I recalled the darker complexion of her mother. Surveying me with the smile of a lioness who had caught her prey, Lisbeth held me in place.

"Hello, Patrick," she said in Hebrew, standing in the same place her husband had. "Let's talk."

The Magdalene crooned like her savior, speaking about starting from zero to make a little bit of money, living off of flesh and deals simply to take care of her weak-willed father.

"So how do you want to talk?" I asked in her language, drawing an impressed pop from a set of dark eyebrows so much like Deevi's.

Lisbeth grinned with full cunning and guile, though no threat lay behind it. "You're very good," she said. "Very worldly. My husband says in more ways than one."

"I'll try to be better," I replied without pretense.

She reconsidered me with a wider grin. "Well, don't try too hard."

"No?" I replied in Hebrew. "Then what should I do? I have to admit I have little in the way training for all this."

"For being a father?" she batted back.

I laughed at her wit. "I mean all the archangels. The Nephilim. Who knows what will happen once the world adjusts."

"That's out of our hands," Lisbeth replied to me. "But what will you do—in all this?"

She waved at the world in front of us, her daughter somewhere in it.

The masses of people hummed along with the main riff of Tracy Chapman's ballad as Uriel plucked his thick strings under those bending notes. I checked on Shaytan to find the reclaimed angel singing along with some girl beside him, their arms thrown around each other. They wept as they swayed.

Twenty-thousand and the legions of heaven sang together about quitting school to take care of their dad.

"I'll have to take it day by day," I said. "I guess that's been the best I've been able to do. Ever."

"Then you've got everything you need," said Lisbeth, leaning to the side to bump me. "No training necessary."

The hum of the audience with every guitar chord soon vanished under the contact of uncountable hands coming together, palms clashing inside and outside the arena, where throngs of angels celebrated with the citizens of New York, no longer frightened to remain in their homes.

Enmeshed into the thousands upon thousands, my hands came together too.

We all had a decision, Mary Magdalene said, each and every one us:

We could leave tonight, or stay as we were, living and dying in our ways.

Then Christ appeared, at the foot of the stage. He ascended and went to stand beside his mother. She leaned toward him to rest her head on his chest.

Without looking back at him, the Magdalene lent her voice to a kind woman's words, the poverty of life and fate never once diminishing the urge to do better, be better, even through the trauma of an empire from nailing her husband to a cross. Every single word wrung from her soul, every tear, echoed across ages of human misery and loneliness. More than one voice who had abandoned him and her in the darkest moments arose again, drowning hers out.

Then the band picked up, bridging out of the mire of the past to here, the year we were in and the time we lived.

Then Christ cried. Full on wept. Broke down as he had the most human moment I ever witnessed in a man. I stood there, awed as the leader of my soul displayed a humanity which forever impressed upon me the depth of his ministry.

A hand slide into mine, the familiar fingers finding their homes.

Christ and the Magdalene said together after he broke from his mother to sing into his wife's mic, promising everyone they could be someone too.

THE PRINCE

Christ waved an end to the gentle ballad, taking the mic from his stand.

"Well, I'm here now," he said, "and I hope by this point you understand that I'm conceding much. I'm knowingly giving up power because giving up power is the correct thing to do for the powerful, as it is giving your extra coat to someone who does not have one, or feeding the poor from your own kitchen. To know me, as I have come to know myself, is to know service in the face in our own inequity and striving to right what is wrong. For all. And here we are, with only two songs left, so I will cut right to the chase. I can't fix what has happened, or else you would know nothing of it. The experience would be gone, and I would be spotless among my victims, but not for a lack of action—but for the lack of you. I am you and you are me. I am a head without a crown, and you are my beating heart."

He hid some Gnosticism behind a clever grin. Finally able to notice the scene, I spotted each of the Helpers close by. Govinda and Daniel had fallen side by side with Rosie, who smoked a blunt with Merry before the Vodun Queen of the Northeast handed it off to Rabbi Rebecca, on her left. Standing a few feet ahead of them, Shoniqua linked arm and arm with the vets, Enrique, Miranda, and

Jennifer, all half-spent by the night. Lisbeth had made room for them and doubled back to rejoin her daughter and I.

A hand lit on my left shoulder. Brigid slip in beside me, pulling along a nervous Cuchulainn. The Irish champion of Ulster gave me a small nod, and I saw Laeg close behind. The chariot driver double-fisted two red cups full of wine.

The trickster. The damned trickster.

"This fucking guy," I said aloud.

Deevi squeezed my hand. "What did you say?"

I nodded to the stage, unable to hide it. "This was all part of his plan, Deevi. All of it."

The truth sobered her as we trained our eyes back to the man in charge. Lucifer and Michael had reappeared, completing the ensemble as they lifted their respective guitar and saxophone.

"Let me be clear," Christ declared, "in this story, in this time, we can defeat hatred, lust, and greed just as I have brought together heaven and earth and all places to be here, now, with you. There is no Satan other than the one you allow in and there is no Christ save for the character you bring into the world. My garden is ready! From here on the seventh day shall be for my children and their own plant-ing. Those who have chosen to take the flesh will be given it upon the dawn, free to live as they shall, be judged as they shall be judged, but not with the coercion of Perdition or my weight upon them. No child born of my children shall be my enemy, now or ever. I, the Lord God, proclaim my love for you, *no matter who you are*, and promise no punishment for you being as you are. I am you and you are me. Upon this stage I make a new covenant! But we have two songs, two seeds left for this tilled soil. This first seed is a vine, to nourish the good and entangle the wicked. Hit it Ramiel."

The Interpreter behind the drum kit filled the front with a rolling cadence before Lucifer struck his ax, the jumping riff powered by the snare. Nathaniel mirrored the Morningstar.

Warning of us the aged old dangers of princes with diamonds dripping from their pockets, Christ slapped his chest as he hollered into the mic. He spoke out against the modern slavers with the space-rocket fantasies who offered a bread of dust in return.

Christ scatted into the next verse, warning of the men who planted their worth in capital, the vices of flesh and time, not the endless possibility of what love and community granted that horded wealth never could. Not vague about who the vine in his vineyard would squeeze out, he pleaded his case as Uriel and Nathaniel jammed down on the bass line and Lucifer pedaled though, backed by the effortless touches of Raguel's percussions and the embellishments on the horn Michael and Raphael inscribed on New York's own 90s-declaration of peace against profit.

He bolted over to Mary Magdalene, who smiled ear to ear. Would one like her marry kings like that, he asked to a playful shake of her head, knowing better. He wondered about himself, which received an enthusiastic nod, for who better could wed audaciousness other than one who knew what princes and lovers ought to be?

I was pulled into a deep kiss by Deevi, her strength and surprise outstripping me.

The band jammed out for the tail of the song, leaving the Savior to kiss the Magdalene full in front of us again. Lucifer and Nathaniel traded leads with Uriel in their inward-facing trifecta. The rest of the band filled in their parts as the funk switched to a moody, deeper jazz number, something that skirted the edges of different, unexpected places. Selaphiel tapped atmospherics into the flow, sending auroras into the mind and eye. Archangel wings flared in prismatic hues.

Strangely lost in their cyan and magenta darkness, Christ parted from the Magdalene and went to the front of the stage, sitting down on its edge. He rested his mouth on a fist, his microphone in his lap. Satisfied but unfulfilled, he uncovered his mouth.

"The Pharisees had the Romans crucify me because they were broken by the corruption of capital. Everyone is broken by the corruption of capital, though it holds no favor to any group. Especially those who claim themselves to be following my name while they make more of it. Have they forgotten about the eyes of the needles while they damn the beams found in the eyes of sick, the poor, and the hungry? Have they healed the sick, housed the poor, and fed the hungry *before* they set about damning others? My ministry is not one of walking around and asking for handouts from governments or the commoner, high or low, then spitting in your faces."

He scratched his dark beard with his free hand, sniffing so loud the microphone's receiver picked up the snort.

"That thief who died with me on Golgotha died because his life was such thieving was one of few options he had. And all were bad. And he still had a moment to be kind to me. Me! Someone who has everything and needs of nothing, and this broken man who had ended up where he was because of *me* still had kindness to give *me*. And not because he would make money, and not because he was dying, but because in the final moments that mattered, he was kind! I just..."

To my shock the crowd erupted.

Christ waited, respectful but disconnected from their favor, until the audience quieted. "Thank you, but I would rather you all have some clear understandings of where we go from here. I am God and I am telling you this is where I am, where I will be, and while there are many ways to see me, I am being clear in my speech now. No parables! I will meet my true foe from here on out, a way of thinking that places markets that weigh flesh and lives equal to gold and power. Pardon me, but history is not over!"

The packed stands of MSG resounded in victory, understanding their days of suffering were closer to an end than not, no matter who and what they prayed to.

He waved them down. "And once again, I will not come alone. I shall walk with very few, but those I call to help me will do so out of need to serve, and we shall see a greater openness to my ways, a better understanding of its nature and how it may broaden the paths of everyone. But it shall not be done for the sake of capital, and capital must be spurned if this is to remain in solidarity with the greatest of dignified causes! Unlike the men of the past, who fled from me or wrote letters in my name, I arrive to rebuke any pretender who claims me. No person has a monopoly on the word of God, especially in gold, pearl, and blood."

It was at that moment, in a climatic statement which hushed all, confused some, and confirmed many, a strange sensation tore me out of reality. A hard lump buzzed against my left leg.

Reaching into my jean's pocket, I found the screen on my Vatican burner lit up.

The Chair had left sixteen voice mails.

BUT SERIOUSLY...

So let me talk to the band for a moment," Christ said. His gaze drifted dead to mine as the burner shook in my enclosed hand. "And let you all handle your own business before we go into this last song!"

Understanding a subtle directive, I nodded as we broke eye contact and removed my right hand out of Deevi's. She quickly glanced to me, confused and concerned before I held up the phone and winked.

"Be right back," I mouthed.

She measured me for a second before giving a nod.

I backed into one of the tunnels, finding a quiet eave off the passage where no one waited. Alone, I let a long minute pass.

Without fail, the burner vibrated.

I took the call. "Hello?" I said as I put my ear to the receiver.

"Saint Patrick, I have seen you on the stage. I have seen you in the audience. I have seen you stand side by side with Satan. Now I see you stand side by side with one who would do away with everything holy and sacred."

Not a "hello." Not a "how you doing?" Or a "holding it together?"

The Chair hit me with his thesis. "What he is saying is blasphemy, heretical in the strictest sense of our faith—*yours and mine*," he stressed in his deep Argentinian accent. Straining hard on his English, he switched into Latin, the fluency of every single priest who bowed in the direction of his throne. "He would undo an organization dedicated to charity, to good works, and to spreading the Gospel to the lost and disbelieving the world over. The Holy Roman Catholic Church is an anchor f—"

I couldn't help it. "It fucking is, isn't it?"

"Pardon me, Saint Patrick?" he asked, aghast on the other end.

"Frank, it's done," I said. "You can talk about the charity, but what about the children and the lawsuits you refuse to pay out because it would bankrupt you? What about the red slipper-wearing devil before you, who pimped and racketed those kids? Please, speak of good works you missionaries do in far-off places with little to no actual support from the coffers of the Vatican, with its own armies and bank."

"The Church is—"

"The Church is usury," I interrupted with emphasis. "Usury. Since Constantine, it has been used for everything but ensuring the Gospel, bringing more disbelief, more doubt, and more inroads to the Hell you supposedly rally against, yet do nothing real to save those teetering at its edge! And here, now, before our Lord and Savior, you'd tell me to stop him from offering the ladder out the pit?"

The silence on the other end sounded louder than the rhythmic applause from the twenty-thousand in the arena, clear in their adoration as they chanted together.

"Je-sus! Je-sus! Je-sus!"

I couldn't help but cackle on my end of the line. "I wonder," I spoke in the Vatican burner, "how many people are watching the telly with you in the room right now? Is it in your apartments, or did you drop that big screen in the Basilica?" I scoffed. "Silly me, what does it matter? I bet your wondering what I'm really wondering: how many are watching?"

"Please," The Pope whispered from his golden chair in some dark hall in Rome. "He'll end it. He'll end it all."

"If not for Christ," I asked, "then what are you actually doing this for?"

I ended the call before he answered, threw the burner in the nearest bin, and walked back into the arena to find Deevi among the spectacle of wonders.

I pressed past a foursome of cherubim huddled together in rapt joy at everything around them, serpentine eyes gleaming bright as leonine smiles parted wide. Some had not done away with their wings, almost as bright as bonfires on the floor. The pagans and Vodun worshipers formed circles around them, linked with others circles in their midst of Gnosis.

I maneuvered to the banks of seats not far from the stage.

First settled by the Helpers so we had a prime view along with Lisbeth and Deevi, I had returned to discover the rows packed end to end in Nephilim. Golden winged, bronze-skinned, and golden-eyed like their angelic parents, the brood of the fallen legions had rejoined with their lost sires and mothers. Deevi and the rest lost to me for a minute, I eased when Daniel rose up on the arms of his seat, scanning behind the shining horde until he saw me. He waved hard until I made moves in the proper direction.

Selaphiel had refilled and re-lit the golden censer on his racked keyboards. Its purple smoke spread across the floor of the rounded stage, falling down the steps like water. The flows shifted to a clear white. It gathered a cloud of steam that remained thick and bound, shrouding the band in a column that diffused the light of their wings. Gauzy and bright, the entire arena perfumed with myrrh, frankincense, and stank to the rafters.

Lucifer, Nathaniel, and Uriel stood side by side as they watched the audience, their guitars like shields. The rest toyed in their area, the Marys and Gabriel convening over a book of sheet music the Messenger held as they squatted between their adoptive mother and grandmother. Michael and Raphael cleaned their instruments, whispering to each other. Ramiel and Raguel waited on the top riser, neither speaking as they shut their eyes, deep in an abiding meditation.

I made it to my place beside Deevi. She quickly snatched my hand and jerked me close. Merry and Rosie had wedged in the row in front of us, trading their joint back and forth with Lisbeth, and a few seats down I saw the others lost among the many cousins I imagined I'd be surrounded with until I kicked. The thought of that, with a little one in her womb and all the responsibility in the world on the way, made the prospect of an end far less-appetizing than what once appealed to my self-loathing. I measured it as she clutched tight, our palms together, and waited like the rest.

My hope and brooding over the future ceased when Christ moved to his microphone. He had lifted out his own small red synthesizer, atop of which he rested a tambourine. Rubbing his eyes, his face, he exhaled hard.

Then the audience started to cheer. The roar built and built the longer he remained in silence.

Ramiel broke them into an uproar as Christ stuck his mic into the pocket of his brown trousers and struck his keys. He mirrored Selaphiel's electronic riff, riding its wave. Michael and Raphael's horns punctuated the transition. Out come the mic, with the Almighty begging Phil Collin's request to come to him.

Zeus remained on his hill and screwed wives that weren't his. Gilgamesh was a tyrant before he was a hero. I had met more than one Oni or Asura to know things did not move in terms of black and white on the other side of the world either.

Of the few, this vision of God was *trying*. Trying to be better. Trying to be right. Not out of spite, not out of requirement, not out of expectation. He tried because if we succeeded so did he. He could have left us after he arose, bitter and dejected, but instead he came here, to this moment, and did something more than he had to.

A selfish part of me wondered if he had done all this to save me. We all have that selfish want because we want to know God loves us as we are. We want to know we can love ourselves because if we can, perhaps we are knowing he loves himself too. Or herself. Or themselves. As he sang and marched the lowers circle past the cloud he had summoned, Christ proclaimed the next mission.

He proclaimed, screamed, about something that had happened on the way to heaven after his death and resurrection, tears filling his eyes. The Savior pointed to all of us. "I'm not leaving unless you come with me! I'm on your side! You are all that I need! Believe me! Believe me!"

The whole Council of El sang the last section without him, alongside their stepmother, grandmother, and the immortal Nathaniel. And we sang with them, mortal and blessed and damned and forgiven and freed, together as one body while the Godhead looked toward a brighter, clearer future.

"Ooooo yeah!" Christ shouted as Lucifer buried Stuermer's end solo deeper into our hearts and minds. He kept the mic raised, his new whip to take against the world's temples. "I'm not doing this for a dollar! I'm not doing this for a throne! I'm not doing this to certify heaven or to send others to hell! I'm here for you! Your children! The Garden is ready!"

There was something more he said for a few good minutes before the band wrapped, but by then Deevi and I had snuck out. Angels and demons substantiated new bodies around us as we escaped. He announced tour dates the world over starting in the West Bank and what remained of Gaza, but it was lost on us as we broke out the doors of Madison Square Garden, into open streets where more people celebrated the promise of a new kingdom.

The next dawn already brightening the sky in the east behind the skyscrapers, Deevi pulled me ahead. "But where are we going?"

"There's a diner not too far from here that's always open," I answered. "I think it's time we got on with tomorrow."

THE END

ACKNOWLEDGMENTS

Everything I do is for Margo and Ben.

I want to thank John Hartness for always believing in me. Erin Penn deserves huge credit in helping me put this manuscript together in a cogent fashion. I need to thank Samuel Montgomery-Blinn and Ziggy Nixon for their words and encouragement. I owe my parents a lot, most of all for always raising me in a safe, open household where inquiry was allowed. There are too many writers before me to thank, but let's go with Garth Ennis, Kevin Smith, and Clive Barker.

I also need to thank Reverand Wormley of St. Mark's Evangelical Lutheran Church in St. Louis, Missouri, who made me believe I had the Devil in me when I was seven because that's what they do to children. Bad move, padre.

I also need to thank the people who cannot be named for the sake of jobs and security, which include clergy, parishioners, and former members of the Holy Roman Catholic Church who were kind enough to offer words, debates, questions, and also encouragement. A lot of good people are fighting a good fight and feel alone in it because of the institution where they reside. Always remember that there are good people wherever you look for them, including in the places these stories take aim at¾like the Vatican. I also want to acknowledge Pope Francis, who moved heaven and earth to cleanse the many sins of his church before he went to be with God. I also need to thank Dr. James Tabor, Dr. Jeremy Schott, and Dr. Sean McCloud of the Religious Studies program at the University of North Carolina at Charlotte. I also need to make a special mention of David Hayward, aka The

Naked Pastor, who's art and worldview played a dramatic role in these novels.

Finally, I want to thank Jesus Christ and the founders of his movement. I read the Bible so many times in its many different variations (including the books that were left out) before and during the writing of these novels that I could not help but listen, and in listening I found profound safety, courage, and love. Please bless my child and all children.

ABOUT THE AUTHOR

Raised in the hills of North Carolina and Maryland, Jay Requard is a graduate of The University of North Carolina at Charlotte with a degree in History and Religious Studies. An award-winning author of Epic Fantasy, Sword & Sorcery, and Urban Fantasy, he is also the host of Pondering The Orb on YouTube. In his free time, he enjoys wandering, reading, and cooking for his wife, son, and a small star-cat named Mona Underfoot. They reside in New York City.

Find out more about Jay and his books at jayrequard.com.

ALSO BY JAY REQUARD

Blessed & Possessed Series (Urban Fantasy)

The Driver of Serpents

The Delver of Purgatory

A Wave of Lions (Epic Fantasy/Sword & Sorcery), which include the following titles:

The Curse of Shallow Bay

At the Mirror's Edge

The Queen in Silver

Atenia (Epic Fantasy)

Death & Dust: The Pale Sand Adventures (Dark Fantasy)

Spy/Counter/Killer (Sword & Sorcery), which include the following titles:

A Dangerous Brew

A Spirited Blend

A Spot Before Dead

War Pigs (Sword & Sorcery)

FRIENDS OF FALSTAFF

Thank You to all our Falstaff Books Patrons, who get extra digital content each month! To be featured here and see what other great rewards we offer, go to www.patreon.com/falstaffbooks.

PATRONS

Dino Hicks

John Hooks

John Kilgallon

Larissa Lichty

Travis & Casey Schilling

Staci-Leigh Santore

Sheryl R. Hayes

Scott Norris

Samuel Montgomery-Blinn

Junkle

Thank You for Supporting Independent Publishing!

We believe that you should be able
to read your books, your way.
That's why this Falstaff Books
print edition includes a digital copy
at no additional cost!

Just scan the QR code with your device,
follow the directions on Prolific Works,
and enjoy!
You can also join our newsletter when prompted,
and never miss an awesome Falstaff Release!